Will Cupid's Arrow Find Its Mark?

"My family is demented," Simon, Earl of Valentine, huffed and strode across the room before turning to his cousin. "Not one tight screw in the bunch. How would *you* like to be known as Lord Valentine the rest of your life? The king cursed the eldest sons of this family."

Matthew grinned. "Legend is the king was in love with the first lord's wife. Hence the name. Val, are you upset because Mama is here?"

Simon snorted and paced back across the room. "Of course not. I love your mother. If only she had a different name or a different life's objective."

"She loves her name."

"Yes, I know, and she takes it very seriously. Aunt Cupid is as queer as Dick's hatband." Simon grabbed the poker and stabbed at the fire. Logs crackled and snapped.

Matthew studied him. "Now, Val, Mama likes to play matchmaker, but she isn't addled."

Simon closed his eyes. "Just assure me she has no plans for me."

"You can never tell who Mama's next attempt will be," Matthew said.

Simon opened his eyes and glared. Pointing the poker at his cousin, he said, "Victim is more like it."

—From BE MINE by Deborah Matthews

BOOK YOUR PLACE ON OUR WEBSITE AND MAKE THE READING CONNECTION!

We've created a customized website just for our very special readers, where you can get the inside scoop on everything that's going on with Zebra, Pinnacle and Kensington books.

When you come online, you'll have the exciting opportunity to:

- View covers of upcoming books
- Read sample chapters
- Learn about our future publishing schedule (listed by publication month *and author*)
- Find out when your favorite authors will be visiting a city near you
- Search for and order backlist books from our online catalog
- Check out author bios and background information
- Send e-mail to your favorite authors
- Meet the Kensington staff online
- Join us in weekly chats with authors, readers and other guests
- Get writing guidelines
- AND MUCH MORE!

**Visit our website at
http://www.kensingtonbooks.com**

MY FUNNY VALENTINE

Peggy Daniels
Allison Knight
Deborah Matthews

ZEBRA BOOKS
Kensington Publishing Corp.
http://www.kensingtonbooks.com

ZEBRA BOOKS are published by

Kensington Publishing Corp.
850 Third Avenue
New York, NY 10022

First Printing: January 2002
10 9 8 7 6 5 4 3 2 1

Printed in the United States of America

CONTENTS

Can I Call You Sweetheart?   7
Winter Roses   91
Be Mine   201

CAN I CALL YOU SWEETHEART?

Peggy Daniels

One

New Mexico Territory, 1866

Across one more hard rock mesa, through one more dried grass valley, and Nick would be on Parish land. With the early January sun nearing the horizon and a cool wind in his face, he nudged his horse into a quicker pace, anxious to reach the home that he'd left three and a half years ago.

His older brother, Joe, had tried to talk him out of joining the war back East. His fiancée, Amber—sweet, passionate Amber—had tried to talk him out of leaving her. They'd both been unsuccessful. Nick had been stubborn, determined to go . . . and stupid. But he was almost home now, and he'd make it up to both of them.

Not that he expected making amends would be easy. Joe would be tough. Amber would be formidable. Nick smiled, remembering her temper, having born the brunt of it more than once. His hands tightened on the reins and his blood heated as he also remembered talking her out of a temper . . . more than once. He'd been a fool to leave home.

An even bigger fool to leave her. He'd realized that long before the war had ended. The war had raged on endlessly. Although the North had claimed victory, Nick had seen enough suffering, destruction, and dying men to know that there really hadn't been any winners.

He'd set out for home the very day he'd been discharged from the army. Not long now and he'd be back where he never should have left. He'd passed the old abandoned Webster silver mine an hour or so back and the town of Fleming was still visible behind him. A strong surge of homesickness had him giving his horse free rein.

Almost an hour later, right at sunset, Nick rode into the ranch yard. The setting sun cast the adobe and log house, barn, and bunkhouse in a golden glow. The buildings looked well tended and in good repair, but the yard was empty.

As he neared the house, he was greeted with ferocious barking, which gradually changed to enthusiastic woofing and finally friendly whining.

"Hello, Daisy girl." Nick slid off his horse and looped the reins around the hitching post. He bent down to scratch the happily wiggling yellow dog behind the ears and rubbed her belly. He dodged her lapping tongue with a chuckle. "I'm glad to see you, too, girl."

The front door opened and he heard footfalls on the porch. When he looked up, a smile on his face, he expected to see his brother Joe.

"Amber." He for sure hadn't been expecting to find her on his doorstep. Unlike the dog, she didn't look even a little bit happy to see him. *That* he had been expecting.

"Well, well, soldier boy's come home."

He met her cool green glare, then let his own hungry gaze slide over her. Her hair, glossy brown and streaked from the sun, was pulled back in the same thick braid she'd always worn. Dark lashes framed narrowed eyes. Her nose with the same tiny tilt at the tip was mildly sprinkled with freckles that would multiply come summer. She was beautiful, and none of the memories he'd hoarded over the years had done her justice.

There was a maturity about her now that he supposed was a natural progression of time. Her curves were fuller, her eyes brown, her cheeks charmingly flushed. He'd missed her every one of the days he'd been gone but hadn't realized how desperately until now. Without thinking, he reached for her, pulled her into his arms, and settled his mouth on hers.

Home. Finally, he was home.

Heat and memories flashed, fast and hot. She smelled like sunshine and grass and blue skies and wildflowers. Her lips were warm, and beneath his hands she was soft and feminine. He wanted more than anything to lay her down, slide into her warmth, and claim her all over again as his, but she wasn't returning the kiss. Just the opposite. She was struggling in his arms and pushing against his chest. He lifted his head, but he didn't release her.

"Damn you, Nick." Awkwardly, because he was still holding her close, she hauled back and slapped him across the face. *Hard.* "Let go of me."

"That's not what you used to say, honey." Tentatively, he shifted his jaw to make sure it still worked.

"Excuse me if my memory's rusty," she sneered. "It's been four years."

"Three and a half." He took a quick step back

when she looked poised to strike again. Damn, she'd always been pretty when she was mad. That definitely hadn't changed, but he wasn't completely dumb. He wasn't going to mention the fact to her right now. "Not that I'm not happy as cows in clover to see you, Amber, but I didn't exactly expect to find you waiting for me on my doorstep. What are you doing here?"

"What are *you* doing here, Nick? I thought the butt of your horse was the last we'd ever see of you."

He frowned. "I said I'd come home as soon as the war was over. It's over, and here I am."

"The war ended months ago." Her brows rose. "Unless the country's geography has changed recently, New Mexico isn't far from . . . from wherever you've spent the past *four* years."

"Kentucky, Tennessee, Virginia, points both north and south." He shrugged. "My unit didn't exactly stay in one spot for long, and believe me, I know exactly how long the war's been over. The whole army wasn't discharged all on the same day, though."

"Soon as I was scot-free, I headed home and"— he spread his arms, careful not to make a move in her direction and risk, just yet, another shot from her quick hand—"here I am."

"Sure enough. Here you are." She smiled but Nick couldn't find a hint of welcome in it. "Just like that. Ready to waltz back into our lives, obviously expecting to pick up right where you left off. Well, you can get right back on your horse and go to hell, Nick." Her smile disappeared. "You should have stayed gone."

"Nope." He'd known this wasn't going to be easy,

but he was seeing something in her eyes that said it might be even tougher than he'd anticipated. "The truth of the matter is that I never should have left. That's a fact, and I'm damned sorry I ever did."

"You're sorry?" Her brows rose and her green eyes flashed. There was no mistaking her fury, and he was directly in the line of fire. "Oh, well, great, that's fine, then," she continued. "You all but left me standing at the altar on Valentine's Day. You change both of our lives with *your* decision to go fight in the war. I heard not one word from you in all the time you were gone—"

"I wrote—"

"Evidently not to me and not to Joseph either, because neither of us received so much as one single letter—"

"I did write—"

"—from you. And now you have the audacity to show up out of the blue with a 'Honey, I'm home,' haul me into your arms like I don't hate your guts, which I do, and all you can say is 'I'm sorry'? Too little, too late, Nick. Ride out of here on the same trail you rode in on, soldier boy. You aren't welcome anymore." In a swirl of skirts, she headed for the house.

"Amber, wait." He lifted a hand but let it drop without touching her. Damn, this was a lot worse than he'd expected. "I know I hurt you leaving the way I did—"

She turned on him so fast, so angry, he took a hesitant step backward. "You have no idea what you did to me when you left!"

To his horror, tears welled in her eyes. In all the years they'd spent growing up together, never once had he seen her cry. Not at eight years old, when she'd hooked her thumb with a fishhook, not at thirteen, when she'd been thrown from a horse, not even at eighteen, when he'd told her he was leaving to join the war. The sight of her tears now tore at his heart worse than any words ever could.

"How could you do it, Nick?" She swiped at her eyes. "How could you just . . . leave?"

"I'm sorry." He rushed on when she opened her mouth. "I know that's pathetically inadequate, Amber, but I am sorry. If I could go back and change things, I would. I swear, I would."

"Swear all you want." She sniffed and blinked hard. "It's too late now."

"It doesn't have to be. I'm home."

"For how long?" She shook her head. "No, it doesn't matter. Do whatever you want, Nick. Stay or don't stay, I don't care, but stay the hell away from me."

She turned away again, but he wasn't ready to let her go, not ever again. He reached for her and was ready this time when she swung at him. This was the Amber he remembered, the Amber he knew best. He caught first her right hand and then her left as she aimed for his face.

The setting sun glinted off the gold band on her finger. He went stock-still. She froze in his grasp. He had trouble catching his breath, and the ground giving way beneath his boots couldn't have caused any greater lurch in his gut. His heart all but stopped, then started pounding again, fiercely against his ribs.

"What the hell. . . ." He pulled her hand, her left hand, up between them. *"What the hell is this?"*

* * *

Amber had dreamed of this moment a hundred times. A thousand times. But none of those times had prepared her for the reality of seeing Nick again.

He was as tall as she remembered, his shoulders as wide, his voice as deep. His eyes were the same compelling brown, although the lines at the corners were new. His lips were the same, as was the smile she'd seen upon them, lazy and wicked, when she'd first come out of the house. Her gaze had lingered there longer than was sensible as she'd recalled the brush of those lips against her own. A memory she couldn't, wouldn't dwell on now.

For that brief instant when she'd first seen him, with the events of the past years completely void from her mind, pure involuntary joy had swept through her. Her breath had caught and her heart had hummed. Her tummy had done that funny little shimmy only Nick could cause and she'd almost, *almost* flown into his arms. She'd caught herself only when reality had surfaced with a vengeance.

This was the same Nick who had dipped her pigtails in ink during their school days. The same Nick who had given her her first kiss behind the barn when she'd turned fifteen. The same Nick who had sworn he loved her, promised to marry her, then left her to go fight a war. The same Nick who had arrogantly demanded that she wait for him. She'd sworn she wouldn't. And she hadn't.

"What the hell is this, Amber?"

Despite the overwhelming impulse to turn and run, she forced herself to stand her ground. Deep down in her heart, in the tiny place that had never given up hope that he would return, she'd known that someday she would have to tell Nick what she'd done. The decision she'd made after he'd left. After he'd left her. The decision she would make again, reduced to the same choices.

She tilted her chin and looked him straight in the eye. "You may not have wanted to put a ring on my finger, Nick, but someone else did."

He dropped her hand like he'd touched poison. As casually as possible with her heart beating wildly in her chest, she smoothed back a lock of loose hair and brushed at her skirt.

"Who?" he demanded. A desperate, wild light came into his eyes as the significance of her being *here* finally began to sink in. He shook his head. "No. *No!"*

He glanced around, violence in his stance, his eyes, and his words. "Where is Joe?"

"He's . . . he isn't . . . h—he's not here," she stammered. "I tried to write to you but I didn't know where to send the letter. . . ."

"I don't care about any damned letter! Where the hell is my brother? In the house?"

"No." She reached for Nick, but he shook her off and took a step back, and another. He turned away, running toward the barn, but not before she saw the anguish in his eyes.

"Joseph," he hollered. "Damn you, Joe. Where the hell are you?"

"Nick, *wait."* She picked up her skirts and ran after him, across the yard, into the shadows of the barn.

Nick stormed past the stalls, startling the horses, calling his brother's name, tossing aside anything that got in his way, feed pails, pitchforks, and hay bales, cursing and calling out all the while.

He flung open the door to the tack room and slammed it shut again when he found it empty. He turned around as she reached him, reached for him with both hands, grabbing fistfuls of his shirt, feeling his muscles bunched with fury beneath her fingers.

"Stop it, Nick. Stop and look at me," she demanded. Tears filled her eyes, and this time she made no attempt to stop them from sliding down her cheeks. "He isn't here. Joe isn't here."

Nick froze. He looked down at her, his chest heaving, his own eyes brimming with tears and hostility and accusation.

"Where is he, then? Checking the cattle? In town? At your parents' place?"

He grabbed her shoulders and shook her, not hard enough to hurt her but not gently either. "Where the hell is my brother, Amber?"

"He's not here," she whispered. Knowing there was no easy way to tell him, she just said it. "He's dead."

First shock, then confusion filled his eyes. "He's . . . what? No. He can't be . . . dead?"

She nodded and tried to pull him into her arms, but he resisted, holding her away from him, his fingers biting into her skin through her blouse.

"You're lying. He isn't dead!"

She nodded.

"No . . . how can . . . he can't! *No. No!*"

"I'm sorry," she whispered as she watched understanding and acceptance fill Nick's eyes. "I am so, so sorry."

He let go of her then, turned, and walked a few steps away, his shoulders quaking. She wanted to go after him. She wanted to hold him, cry with him,

and share his grief, as no one had been able to
share hers. She'd been waiting almost a year to
share the anguish and horror of Joe's death with the
one other person in the world who had loved him
as much as she had. But still she waited, sobbing
silently.

"How?" Eventually, the single word, no more
than a choked whisper, came from Nick.

"Last spring . . . during the roundup . . . his
horse . . . a rattlesnake spooked it. We were looking for strays in the foothills near Bear Butte. The
horse reared and Joe fell."

"Was he bit?" Nick turned around, the tears on
his checks glistening in the moonlight.

"No. He hit his head on a rock. He died . . .
instantly." She took a step and reached out for Nick,
afraid he would push her away again, but he didn't.
Instead, he pulled her into his arms, holding her
tight against him.

With a sigh, she settled her cheek against his
chest. He stroked a hand through her hair and in
grief, they forgot everything that had come between them, everything that still stood between
them, and just held on to one another. They clung
and wept. Neither had words of comfort to offer
the other. Their only comfort came from holding
and being held and from knowing they both felt
the same ache, the same loss. For long minutes,
that was enough.

Eventually, though, Nick pulled away. Amber
wiped her cheeks with shaky fingers and stood, suddenly bereft without his arms, a feeling she thought
she'd gotten over years ago.

He cleared his throat and looked down at her. She
saw that he'd wiped away most of his own tears, yet

wetness lingered on his lashes. His face was grim and lines bracketed his mouth.

"Amber?"

She swallowed down the urge to step back into his arms. "Yes?"

"How the hell could you have married my brother?"

"Mama?"

Nick started as a tiny voice came out of the dimness at the entrance to the barn. Beside him, Amber startled, then rushed to scoop up the small body belonging to the voice.

"Joey, baby, what are you doing outside?"

Joey? Baby? No, a child, obviously. Just as obviously, Amber's child, because he'd called her Mama.

And his brother's child? The musket ball embedded deep into the flesh of Nick's thigh a few years ago during a battle near Chancellorsville hadn't hurt as much as the pain searing through him at the thought of Amber and Joe sharing a child.

Conceiving a child.

The shock of jealousy and betrayal nearly brought Nick to his knees.

"I woked up and couldn't find you, Mama."

"I'm sorry, baby. I was . . . I'm here." Nick saw her furtive glance toward him. "Let's get you back inside before your toes turn blue."

The child giggled. "Blue like Grandma Mary's eyes?"

"Yup, that's right, and wouldn't you look like a silly boy with blue toes?"

"Nope, blue toes would be fun. Sammy O'Grady don't have no blue toes."

"That's because Sammy O'Grady is tucked up tight in his toasty warm bed about now, right where you're supposed to be and where you're going quick as I can get you back inside the house."

"Can I have another story first?"

"Not a chance, little boy blue toes." She joked with her son, but Nick heard the strain in her voice.

The boy giggled. *"Pleeease?* Just one more? The one about the dog? Daisy likes that one, too." The little boy smiled. *Joe's smile.* Nick sucked in his breath, hot knives of betrayal cutting deep, straight into his heart.

"Not tonight, big guy." With her son in her arms, Amber turned back toward Nick. "I have to put him back in bed. Will you come inside?"

"No." He couldn't go into the house where he'd grown up, the *home* Amber had so obviously made with Joe. "I, ah, gotta . . ."

"Go?" Amber finished for him. "I'm not surprised. That's what you do best."

Was that disappointment he heard in her voice? Definitely disapproval. Not long ago, she'd told him to hit the trail and not look back and now she was angry that he was going? Damn, but he didn't understand this Amber at all. Confused, he stood his ground while she turned away, carrying the child.

"Who's he, Mama?" As Joey was carted off, back to bed, the little boy watched Nick over his mother's shoulder through Parish brown eyes and thick lashes. Even in the settling twilight, the family resemblance was impossible for Nick to miss. There was no doubt the child belonged to his brother.

Nick went stock still. *Was there?*

Amber hesitated only briefly at her son's question but kept walking. "He's your . . . daddy's brother."

Suspicion snaked through Nick, leaving a ripple of unease. Was it possible . . . ?

Without a word, closely watching the child, Nick was drawn across the yard. Amber left the door open and he hesitated only briefly before stepping inside.

He could see touches of her everywhere in the house. A tablecloth and a pretty vase covered the scarred wooden table in the kitchen area. New curtains, flowery curtains, covered the windows. Lacy things rested on the arms of the stuffed chairs and a knitted blanket covered the back of the sofa. Small rugs were strategically scattered over the gleaming floors, and the place was spotless. No cobwebs, dust, or clothing littered the rooms, just a few toys.

Nick's mama had kept the place immaculate, too, until she'd died a little more than half a dozen years ago. After that, while he and Joe had lived here alone, more times than not the place had been a mess. Hell, the place had *always* been a mess because Joe claimed he was nobody's maid and Nick didn't mind the clutter.

Edgy with nerves, confusion, and determination, Nick refused to think about the past and turned his focus on the child. In the light shed from the lamp burning on the mantel, Nick took a closer look at the little boy. He called himself a hundred kinds of fool, but he had to know the truth.

The child had wavy brown hair and a shy smile. The color and shape of his eyes and the slope—the stubbornness, most called it—of his jaw was pure Parish.

"I don't wanna go to bed." The jut of his chin came straight from his mother.

Nick stepped forward. "Can't blame him there, *Mama*," he mocked Amber. "It's not every day a boy gets to meet his long-lost uncle." He was amazed at how normal his voice sounded when his insides shook like unset jelly preserves.

"You was lost?" Joey's eyes rounded. "I was lost once, for a long, long time. Daisy found me." His voice quivered. "I didn't like it none. Mama neither." The boy glanced up at Amber. "She cried."

"He covered himself with straw and fell asleep in the corner of a horse stall one afternoon," Amber explained. "Joe and I were in a panic until we found him."

"Are you really my uncle? Sammy O'Grady hasn't got no uncle."

Nick got the feeling that little Joey and Sammy O'Grady had a healthy competition going. And right now, Joey was winning. "Blue toes and an uncle, both in one night. Bet you can't wait to tell Sammy O'Grady."

Joey smiled, another of Joe's smiles. Nick could only stare at the miniature version of his brother and remember how often neighbors had commented when he and Joe were young on how much they looked like twins instead of merely brothers.

How old was Joey? Nick hadn't spent much time around kids so he couldn't be sure but certainly no more than three, maybe not even. But almost three or three and then some? Those extra months could make all the difference.

Joey yawned and knuckled his sleepy eyes.

"Bedtime, sprout. Say good night to your Uncle Nick."

"Can he read me a story?" Joey wheedled.

"Nice try, but not a chance. Not tonight."

"Tomorrow night?" He was one persistent little guy, and very good at prolonging his bedtime, Nick thought. That might have amused him if his gut wasn't tied up with questions.

"We'll see," Amber hedged.

Joey yawned at Nick, resting his head on his mother's shoulder as she headed down the hallway toward the bedrooms. She turned right, into Nick's old room. Joey slept in *his* room.

Which meant Amber slept in Joe's.

Only Joe wasn't sleeping there with her anymore. Nick's initial flare of jealousy wilted into shameful satisfaction and gut-wrenching guilt. Jealous as he was of whatever relationship Joe and Amber had shared, he could never be happy that his brother was dead.

Amber stepped out of the bedroom, closing the door quietly behind her. She watched him from the length of the short hallway. Stalling for time before facing him because she knew he would have questions . . . and demand answers? Or was she merely wary of being alone with him because she'd so clearly moved on with her life and that life didn't include him anymore?

Nick ran a weary hand through his hair. This had been one hell of a homecoming. The woman he'd loved had married his brother. The brother he'd idolized was dead. And now there was a child.

His voice was low, gritty, and very determined. "Is that boy my brother's son, Amber? Or is he mine?"

Two

"He could have been your son, Nick." Amber looked him straight in the eye as she came down the short hallway, stopping directly in front of him. "There was a time when I thought he would be, but no. Joey is Joseph's son."

He studied her quietly for a moment. She was so damned beautiful, she made his teeth ache, but if she was lying to him, she'd become very good at it since he'd been gone. She'd never used to tell a lie worth a damn.

Disappointment struck deep. He'd be lying to himself if he denied wanting Joey to be his.

"If you're staying, there's an empty bed in the bunkhouse. I'm sure you understand that you can't stay in the house."

"The bunkhouse is fine." He was staying all right. "The yard was quiet when I rode in. Where is everyone?"

"In town. It's Saturday night." She moved toward the door, opened it, and waited with her hand on the knob. "We can catch up on ranch details in the morning. If you're still here."

He followed her to the door, ignoring her barb. When he reached her, he paused, letting his gaze settle on her mouth while he leaned down and brushed a soft kiss along her cheek. Her jaw tightened, but he had to give her credit for standing her ground. "Good night, Amber."

"Good night, soldier boy."

"See you in the morning."

"I'll believe that when I see it."

"If I'm here, you can make me flapjacks for breakfast."

"If you're here, you can make your own flapjacks, and make enough for Joey. He likes them, too."

"Does he?" Nick refused to read anything into the fact both he and the boy like flapjacks. And Joseph had hated them.

He stepped outside into the crisp night air, and Amber wasted no time in closing the door behind him. His horse was still tied to the hitching post so he gathered the reins and led the animal across the yard to the bunkhouse.

From the back of his saddle, he untied his bedroll and hoisted it onto his shoulder. Inside the bunkhouse, he found an empty bed and spread out his meager belongings. He hoped Amber had the rest of his stuff packed away somewhere because he was in need of new clothes; the ones on his back and the few extras he owned had seen much better days.

Outside again, he led the horse toward the barn. Halfway there, he changed his mind and swung up into the saddle. Tired as he was, he knew he wasn't going to be able to sleep yet. His homecoming was only partially complete. He still needed to see his brother.

Finding the family graveyard about a mile from the homestead was no problem. Even without the glow of the moon, he could have easily found his way through the sagebrush and dried tobosa grass to the small collection of tombstones. The area was well tended, the stones clean, and the small amount of grass well-kept; dried flowers adorned the graves. Did Amber spend a lot of time here, he wondered, mourning her dead husband?

After sliding out of the saddle, Nick loped the horse's reins around a piñon tree and knelt first at his parents' graves. His father, Bertram Merrick Parish, had died nearly a decade ago from an infection caused by an injury that had never healed. Claire Joanne Parish, Nick's mother, had died of fever a couple of years before he'd left for the war. They now rested side by side for eternity. He recited an almost forgotten prayer and straightened the bouquet of wildflowers, then stood and turned to the other grave with the newer headstone.

"Joseph Francis Parish." His brother. His friend. His rival. His enemy. "If you weren't already dead, brother," Nick whispered, "I would kill you now."

Nick's chest ached so bad he could barely draw breath. His eyes burned with tears and the cold turned his cheeks numb where the wind hit and dried. "You couldn't find a woman of your own, so you had to steal mine? Did we look enough alike in the dark that she didn't care who she had in her bed?"

The image of them together ate at him almost more than the fact that, based on little Joey's age, they hadn't waited more than a short handful of months after Nick had left to get married.

"I saw your son. He looks like you." Nick let out a shaky breath. "He looks like me, too, and he should have been mine, but neither one of you even gave me half a chance to come back. Were you always in love with her? Behind my back were you wishing she was yours . . . even before I went off to fight? Hell, I should have stayed here and fought you."

The thought of Amber being married to anyone was painful, but she'd married his own brother. His brother. And Joe wasn't even alive for Nick to beat the crap out of. How the hell did a man fight a ghost, a memory in a woman's mind?

His chest heaved and he almost sobbed, choking out the words. "I leave you alone for a couple of years and you not only steal my woman, you go and die on me. *Damn you, Joe.* How could you have been dumb enough to fall off a horse and hit your head and *die?* Hell, we've both fallen off almost as many horses as we've ridden and never got more than a mess of colorful bruises and a couple of broken bones between the two of us."

Nick sank to his knees, taking deep breaths and wiping at the useless tears blurring his eyes. "What am I going to do now, can you tell me that? What am I supposed to do? I came back to the two people I love most in this whole damn world and what do I find? You're dead, and she's your widow."

He sat back on his butt and ran his hands through his hair, dislodging his hat, then down his face. "What the hell are *we* supposed to do now?" he repeated, shivering with chill and fatigue, engulfed by weariness.

"The way I see things, I have only two choices—stay or go. God knows, the easier choice right this minute is getting back on my horse and being halfway to Las Cruces by sunrise. Amber is expecting me to go. She wouldn't be surprised.

"Or . . . I can stay." He laughed, a harsh, humorless sound in the empty night. "I can stay and marry your widow and raise your son as my own. Does that have you turning over in your grave? I damn well hope so, brother, because she was mine first."

Nick rose to his feet, swaying almost as if he were drunk. He wished he were drunk. Or dreaming. He wished the past few hours, hell, the last four years, were one big, bad dream. He wished he'd never gone off to fight in the war. He wished he'd married Amber on Valentine's Day when he'd had the chance. He wished it was his son tucked up tight in bed, waiting for a kiss from his daddy, from *him*.

He wished, more than any of the other wishes, that his brother was alive. Because no matter how much he hated the idea of Joe and Amber being married, Joe being dead was so much worse.

"Whatever else, I swear I'm not glad that you're dead," Nick whispered before turning away from the gravestones. "I swear, Joe, I'm not."

With stiff fingers, he untied his horse from the tree and stepped into the saddle. The horse moved restlessly beneath him as he sat for long moments, wondering which direction to head.

Whatever decision he made, he knew he'd have to live with for the rest of his life because if he left Amber again, he wouldn't get a third chance. If he left her now, she'd never take him back.

So, what the hell was he going to do?

* * *

If anyone had asked, Amber would have hotly denied waiting for Nick to return. But there was no one around to ask, except Joey, and he was as anxious as she for Nick's return.

She'd doused the lamps last night after he'd left the house and watched him go into and come back out of the bunkhouse. She'd almost believed him when he'd said he was back to stay and then he'd mounted his horse and rode out of the yard.

She'd known the minute he climbed into his saddle that he was leaving again and this time for good. She'd be a fool to believe otherwise and being a fool over Nicholas Parish once in her life was enough.

Not that she blamed him for leaving. His brother was dead, and she hadn't waited for him like he'd asked. No, she couldn't blame him, but she wouldn't feel sorry for him either. She would not.

Four years ago, she'd loved him with every breath she'd taken, every touch they'd shared, every promise they'd made. He'd broken those promises first. She would not feel guilty for doing what she'd done. Marrying Joe was the best decision she could have made . . . for herself and for Joey. Given the same choices, she would do exactly the same again.

"Mama, Mama," Joey hollered from his vigil by the window where he'd been waiting and watching for Nick since after breakfast. Daisy scrambled to her feet, tail wagging at the excited tone in her young master's voice. "He's comin', Mama, he's comin'!"

"Joseph Nicholas Parish, how many times have I told you not to yell when I'm standing in the same room?" Amber used the excuse of chastising her son to move up behind him at the window. "I can hear you just fine."

"Look it, Mama. He's back." Joey all but danced with excitement, but when she glanced out the window, her heart thudded heavy with disappointment.

"Look again, Joey. That's Grandma and Grandpa." How could her son mistake his grandparents for Nick? For heaven's sake, they were riding in a buggy.

"Oh." Joey's excitement waned visibly. "Do you think he's comin' back?"

"I don't know. I've told you that about a dozen times this morning." Amber drew her son into her arms for a hug to take the sting out of the words that came out more impatient than she'd intended. Joey wasn't the only one disappointed that Nick hadn't returned, and she didn't like the feeling one bit. "Let's go say hi to your grandparents."

"Okay." Joey tugged free of her arms and ran to open the door before her parents could knock. The same way her son couldn't talk in a normal tone of voice, he couldn't seem to walk without running either. She watched him with a smile. Joey was her life and no matter what the circumstances that had brought them to this point, she wouldn't want it any other way.

"Grandma! Grandpa! I got me an uncle!" Her parents looked surprised and not particularly happy to hear Joey's news.

"Nick's back?" Henry Wade asked over his grandson's head as Joey flung himself into his grandpa's arms.

Amber knew men didn't come any better than her father. He'd been married to her mother for almost thirty years. He'd never once raised a hand to his only children or his wife and he'd certainly never left her . . . well, just never left her. A rancher all of his life, her father was broad-shouldered, weather-skinned, and salt of the earth. His hair was graying, but he was the kind of man who knew his responsibilities and took them seriously.

"Sweet Mother of. . . ." Mary Wade crossed herself. "I was hoping that boy would have sense enough to stay gone."

"Then you don't remember Nick very well, Mama," Amber replied. "Sense, good or common, wasn't something he was strong on. Anyway, he was here last night. He's not here now."

Amber's mother, a strong woman with vivid blue eyes, slightly more gray hair than Amber's father, and a tender heart, had become Amber's best friend during the time Nick had been gone.

She'd held her daughter while she cried, agreed with her that Nick wasn't worth crying over, and helped dry her tears, expressed concern over her hasty marriage to Nick's brother, and stood beside her to help her make every difficult decision that had to be made.

Amber often wondered if she could have come this far without her mother's unconditional love. She was thankful she'd never had to find out.

"Where did Nick go?" her father asked.

"I don't know, Daddy. He showed up last night after I'd put Joey to bed. We talked for a bit and then he rode out again. I didn't really expect him to stay after . . . everything."

"Does he know about Joseph?" her mother asked.

Amber nodded. "I told him, and it was awful."

"That's understandable, honey. Those boys were closer than most brothers, especially since their mama died. And you and Joseph?" her mother asked. "Does Nick know that the two of you were married?"

Amber twisted the wide golden wedding band on her finger. "Yes, he knows."

"And how did he take that news?"

"About like you'd expect."

Her mother glanced thoughtfully at her grandson. "Henry, will you take Joey outside for a bit? Amber and I need some time alone."

"Sure enough. Come on, sprout. Let's go give the horses some hay while your mama and grandma have themselves some girl talk."

"Wait, I'll get his coat, Daddy. I know the sun is shining, but it's still cold outside."

When Joey was bundled up and ready to go, his grandpa took his hand and the two went outside together. "Can I drive the horseys, Grandpa?" Amber heard Joey ask as she shut the door behind them.

Her father spent a great deal of time with Joey. Sitting on his grandpa's lap in the buggy or sharing a saddle while they both held the reins were two of Joey's greatest pleasures. Of course, Henry Wade had full control at all times, kept the horses at a slow walk, and they never left the yard. Amber knew her father had agreed when she heard Joey's squeal of delight—through the closed door.

"Come on, honey." Her mother came up and put her arm around Amber's shoulders. "They'll be fine. Let's go brew ourselves a cup of tea and you can tell me about Nick."

Amber let herself be steered into the kitchen. She set out a plate of cookies she'd baked yesterday while her mother made the tea. When they were seated at the table, they both nibbled and sipped quietly for a few minutes.

Her mother reached over and took her hand, squeezing gently. "So, Nick wasn't happy to hear that you'd married his brother."

"He was angry," Amber confessed. "And hurt."

"I'm sure he was," her mother replied.

"Then he wanted to know where Joe was and I . . . I had to tell him he was dead."

"Oh, honey." Her mother gave her hand another reassuring squeeze. "That must have been hard for you both."

"Harder for Nick." Amber gave up pretending to eat the cookie in her hand and set it down on the plate in front of her. "Oh, Mama, he cried. I have never seen Nick cry, ever."

"I'm sorry for his loss, of course, but you've certainly shed enough tears over him. Over both Parish brothers. I can't say that I'm happy he's back." Her mother watched her in the way only a mother can watch a child, no matter how old the child, as if she knew every secret that child had ever tried to keep. "Are you glad he's back?"

"No. Yes. Oh, Mama, I don't want to be," Amber cried. "Seeing him again was a shock. I think I always knew somewhere down deep that he would come home again. I don't know if I hoped he would or hoped he wouldn't, but I think I always knew he'd be back. And until last night, I thought all of my feelings for him were dead. All of them. The anger, the resentment, the disappointment. The hatred. After he left, I did hate him."

"I know what you went through after he left." Her mother took a sip of tea. "What about the love? Did you think that was dead, too?"

"Especially the love."

"And is it?"

"I don't know. It has to be, doesn't it?" she demanded. "How can you still love someone after they hurt you so badly?"

"I don't know if it is possible, Amber. I don't know that it isn't, either. Only you can answer that."

Amber didn't want to answer that question because she didn't think she'd like the answer. Did she still love Nick? Maybe not, but she didn't hate him anymore either. Last night when she'd seen him standing outside, she'd been swamped with memories. Times she'd forced herself not to remember because they were both painful and bittersweet after he'd left.

She'd loved him once, very deeply, and she'd thought they would spend the rest of their lives together. Those kinds of dreams didn't die overnight or even over four years, no matter how badly she might have wanted them to, and she'd missed him.

Until she'd seen him again, she hadn't realized how much she had missed Nick. That was the one thought that had kept running through her mind last night when she'd been trying to sleep but had been waiting for the sound of his horse instead.

"What about Joey?" Her mother broke the silence that had settled between them. "Did you tell him that Joey is his son?"

"I lied." She couldn't hold her mother's reproachful gaze. "He flat out asked me if Joey was his son and I said no."

"Oh, Amber, honey . . ."

"I know, Mama, but I have to protect Joey," she defended. "Nick can't think he can walk back into our lives and pick up where he left off. What if I tell him Joey is his son? He'll want to tell Joey, and I can't risk my son falling in love with a father that we can't depend on. I can't risk Nick breaking my son's heart the same way he broke mine. He said he loved me and look where he left me. Alone and pregnant."

"You said he didn't know you were pregnant when he left."

"He didn't know. *I didn't know.* But we both knew it was possible."

"You were both irresponsible," her mother agreed, "but you and I have made our peace with that a long time ago. Nick has a right to the truth, Amber. Despite everything, he has a right to know his son."

"He gave up his rights when he left!" she cried, her eyes burning with unshed tears. "Joseph stood by me when I found out I was pregnant. He married me to give Joey a name. He was here when I cried, when I was sick. He was here when Joey was born, when Joey took his first steps and said his first words. *Joseph was Joey's father.*"

"Joseph was good to you, to both of you, but that's not the point right now." Her mother rose to get the tea kettle and refilled both of their cups. When she took her seat again, she said, "Nicholas is Joey's father. Joseph is dead, and Nick is back. Even if Joseph was still alive, Nick would have a right to know that Joey is his child. That's not the kind of secret you can keep, not forever."

"Maybe not forever, Mama, but for now I don't want Nick to know the truth." Amber took a fortifying sip of tea.

"Who are you really protecting, Amber?" Her mother hesitated. "Joey . . . or yourself?"

Amber ignored the question. "Maybe we're worrying for nothing. Nick left last night, and he hasn't come back. He said he would be here this morning, and he isn't. Maybe he left again, this time for good. After everything I told him, everything that has changed while he was gone, what reason does he have, really, to stay?"

"Don't kid yourself, honey." Her mother shook her head. "That boy loved you, and if he came home again, it was for you. It might take him a while to get over the idea of you being married to his brother, and if Joe was still alive, Nick probably wouldn't stay. But Joseph is dead. Nick will come back. When he does, Amber, you're going to have to decide what you're going to do."

"I've already made my decision, Mama." She reached for a cookie. "I can take care of myself now, and I'm doing what's best for Joey. Nick believes Joey is his brother's child. As far as I'm concerned, he doesn't ever have to learn the truth. If he even comes back. This time, he may be gone for good."

"He'll be back, Amber, mark my words. You're only fooling yourself if you believe he won't be."

"Uncle Nick! Uncle Nick!"

Joey was standing at the corral with Amber's father when Nick rode into the ranch yard for the second time in two days.

This time, Nick didn't have to wonder about the reception he'd get. Joseph was dead. Amber had moved on with her life and shared a child with his brother. The man he'd thought would one day be his father-in-law looked none too happy to see him, not that Nick could blame him.

Beside him was Joey, who had no idea what was happening around him, only that he had an uncle now and Sammy O'Grady didn't.

Nick had spent a long night in the saddle trying to decide whether to stay or go. Ultimately, he realized the decision had been made years ago, and he'd headed for the ranch. This was his home, despite the unwelcome changes, and he was back to stay.

He led the horse into the barn and tended to the animal before heading for the bunkhouse. As he'd expected, Joey jumped off the lower rung of the corral fence and came running when he saw Nick come out of the barn.

"Hiya, Uncle Nick." The boy obviously didn't have a shy bone in his skinny little body. He looked up at Nick with a curious expression on the face that reminded Nick enough of his brother to make his gut ache and his eyes burn. "Where you been?"

Nick hesitated. How much of death and dying did the little boy understand? If he told the kid he'd been at his father's grave, Nick wondered how he'd react. Uncertain, he hedged. "Riding."

"Can I go with you next time? You was up early. Mama said you was gone before she woke up." The kid barely took a breath between sentences.

Nick didn't want to think about Amber waking up sleep-tousled, pink-cheeked, and cuddly warm—not a smart idea with her daddy watching him closely from where he leaned on the top rung of the corral. Nick stiffened his backbone and let Joey pull him by the hand toward the boy's grandfather.

"Here's my Uncle Nick, Grandpa," Joey announced proudly.

"I've known Nick since he was about your size," Henry Wade told his grandson. The older man surprised Nick by holding out his hand.

His once future father-in-law hadn't aged much while Nick had been gone. His hair was a little thinner on top and a little grayer, he had a few more wrinkles on his face, but the man was still solidly built. Nick stepped closer to shake the proffered hand.

"I'm real sorry about Joe's passing," Henry offered. "That must have been one hell of a shock to come home to."

Nick nodded. "Among others."

As if sensing the grown-ups were going to talk awhile, Joey wandered farther along the length of the corral, dragging a stick in the dirt to where Daisy was lazing in a patch of sunshine. The boy roused the dog and they chased one another around the yard, Joey making pretty good horse noises, and Daisy with her tongue lolling in a happy grin. The two men watched the boy.

"That surprised me, too, Amber marrying Joe." Henry Wade continued the conversation. "But they seemed happy enough together."

Nick stiffened, but kept his gaze on Joey.

"You probably don't want to hear that, but they were both pretty angry and pretty shook up when you left the way you did."

"Maybe," Nick countered. "Maybe not. They sure didn't wait long to hook up with each other, did they?"

"Nope, it's a fact they didn't, but I guess it's only natural that they'd turn to one another. The three of you had always been close. Just because you left didn't mean their friendship had to end."

"Friendship." Nick snorted.

"If you're thinking it was more than that while you were still here, you'd be wrong." An edge entered the older man's voice. "You'd be doing both your brother and my daughter a disservice in the process. Something I'm sure you didn't intend."

"No, sir." An uneasy silence settled between them.

"So what brings you back after all these years, Nick?"

He shrugged. "The war's over and this is my home. Does it surprise you that I'm back?"

"Nope, but things change. How long you planning to stay?"

Nick glanced sideways at the older man. "Now you sound like your daughter, so I'll tell you what I told her. I made the mistake of leaving once, and I won't be making that mistake again. I'm back for good."

Henry nodded. "I kinda figured that."

Nick's gaze once again found Joey and a longer silence settled between the two men. Joey threw his stick for the dog, who instead of retrieving it and returning it to his master, plopped down in the winter grass and started to chew. Joey rushed the dog and the two of them played a comical game of tug-of-war over the stick.

"I want her back," Nick blurted out, wondering whom he'd surprised more with his sudden pronouncement, himself or Amber's father—although when he looked at Henry, the older man didn't seem all that surprised.

"I figured that, too." Henry's eyes narrowed as he watched Nick. "Even though she was married to someone else? And not just anyone else, but married to Joe?"

Nick glanced away. "Am I crazy?"

"Who's to say?" Henry shrugged. "Do you love her?"

"Never stopped." Until that moment, Nick hadn't realized it was true. Last night, he'd thought he hated both of them, her and Joe. He didn't. He couldn't. Despite what they'd done. They'd all made mistakes, himself included. Amber had as much to forgive as he did if they ever had a chance of starting over together.

Henry tipped back his hat, settling his elbows on the corral railing behind them. "Getting back in her good graces won't be easy."

"I don't expect it will be," Nick agreed.

"She can be stubborn."

"I remember."

"Nick . . . ?" Amber's father laid a hand on his shoulder.

He tensed. "Yeah?"

"Hurt her again and I'll have to kill you."

"Yeah." Nick's smile was grim. "Thanks for not doing it the first time."

"Everyone makes mistakes." Henry patted him once and dropped his hand. "You made a whopper when you left, but I think you've learned from it."

"Yes, sir."

"Good luck, son."

"I'll need it."

Amber's father nodded. "That you will."

Three

Nick hadn't lied to Henry Wade. Amber was going to be his again. He couldn't leave her alone any more than he could breathe without air. Once, she'd felt the same way. She would again; it was only a matter of time and patience. A great deal of patience, Nick thought wryly.

Once, before they'd been lovers, they'd been friends. He'd start by rekindling that friendship. One day at a time, one step at a time, he'd go slow until they were right back where they'd left off. That was his plan and as long as he could keep his possessiveness and jealousy under control, it was a good plan.

Of course, the thought of his brother making love to Amber still drove him crazy. Nick wanted to think he'd get used to the idea, but he didn't know how or how long that would take, if ever. Joey was a constant reminder, but he was a great kid and every time Nick saw the boy he couldn't help wishing Joey was his son.

Yesterday, after Nick's conversation with Amber's father, he had been invited for lunch and spent the rest of the afternoon with Amber, her parents, and Joey. Mrs. Wade had been initially cool toward him. Amber had kept her distance as much as was possible, but Nick made a point of drawing her into the conversation by reminding her of things from their past, school days, friends they'd shared, and asking about happenings in the area while he'd been gone.

The Wades had left late in the afternoon. Nick had lingered, ignoring Amber's subtle hints that he find something else to do, and she was too polite to actually come right out and ask him to go. She didn't seem comfortable leaving him and the boy alone together, so that worked in his favor, too.

This morning, at his suggestion, they had gone riding. He'd wanted to see the herd, check on the winter pastures, and, of course, spend time with Amber. Joey had begged to ride with Nick, and he'd enjoyed the boy's childish conversation and steady questions about the cattle, land, birds, and wildlife they saw.

Amber had even seemed to relax for the first time in his presence, and they shared a good morning. This afternoon, she was going to show him the ranch books.

He walked across the yard to the house from the barn where he'd been looking over the horses. As he neared the house, his nephew pulled open the door.

"Hi, Uncle Nick. Mama's in the kitchen. I'm supposed to be takin' a nap, but I'm too old for a stupid ol' nap. Sammy O'Grady still takes a nap, but he's younger than me by four months. He's still a baby, but not me. I told Mama so, but she said I could only stay up till you got here then I had to go lie down. I'm only gonna pretend to sleep, jist so she don't get crosser with me. She gets really cross when I don't do what she says. I don't like Mama bein' cross, but I don't like takin' no nap either." Joey stuck out a mutinous bottom lip, and Nick had all he could do not to laugh.

"To bed, young man." Amber came into the living room from the kitchen and swept Joey up into her arms. He squirmed to get loose, but she held tight. "Thirty minutes with the door closed. Not a peep out of you and you're sprung. Any shenanigans and I add ten minutes every time I have to remind you to be quiet. And tuck in that bottom lip, mister, before some big old roadrunner comes along and perches on it to do his business."

Joey giggled and cajoled, "I'm not sleepy, Mama, and Uncle Nick's here. He don't want me to take no dumb ol' nap, do you, Uncle Nick?"

"Nice try, smart guy, but Uncle Nick's not going to help you out this time. He knows better, don't you, Uncle Nick?"

"Yes, ma'am." Nick did his best to look contrite. "Sorry, kid, looks like nap time for you."

"You gonna be here when I'm sprung?" Joey demanded.

"I'll be around."

" 'Round where?"

"No more questions, Joseph Parish. Say good night to Uncle Nick."

" 'Night, Uncle Nick."

"Sleep tight, kid."

"How come I hafta say good night when it's still day and not night at all?"

"Good night, Joseph."

" 'Night, Mama. Can Uncle Nick tuck me in?"

"Next time." Mother, son, and dog disappeared into Joey's bedroom. Nick could hear Joey's continued attempts to persuade his mother to forgo the dreaded naptime. Amber emerged from the room and shut the door firmly behind her.

She rolled her eyes at Nick as she came back down the hall. "I really don't know how much longer I can convince him to stay in his room for even a half an hour, but, Lord, I need that time, fast as it flies by, to retain my sanity and get me through until his bedtime. Come on into the kitchen. I have the account ledgers spread out on the table."

"Will he sleep?"

"Like a log but not for long. I swear that boy can tell time, even in his sleep. Do you hear it?" She smiled at him, a pure smile, with no clouds from the past in her eyes. "Silence. Blessed, childless silence."

Nick chuckled. "He does like to talk."

"That boy chatters like a magpie."

"He's a great kid, Amber."

"He is. He's my life, and I love him more than I ever imagined it possible to love someone, but maybe just once a day, I wouldn't mind if he'd run out of questions."

"When he wakes up, he can tag along with me for the rest of the afternoon. I'm going to poke around in the barn. Make sure we have enough tack supplies and start a list for town."

The way she hesitated, he knew she was going to say no. He fought to keep his voice even despite his irritation. "He's safe with me, Amber. I'm not going to hurt the kid just because I'm jealous as hell that he's not mine."

"I don't think that." She frowned. "I know you would never hurt him." Still, she hesitated. He was about to tell her to forget it, when she seemed to come to some great decision. "If you're sure your ears can endure his chatter, I'll gratefully accept your offer. He's all yours."

He's all yours. Did she have any idea how much he wished that was true? He strove for a light-hearted tone despite the dull ache in his chest. "My ears will be fine. Now, let's get down to business before the chatterbox wakes up."

"Do you want to start with current accounts and work back or would you like to pick up from when you left?" She motioned him into a chair and sat down beside him.

She leaned closer and her familiar scent, wild-flowers and womanly soap, engulfed him. The instant rush of heat had him shifting restlessly. He struggled to remember what she'd just asked him. "Yeah, um . . . let's work backward."

With a greater effort than he'd thought himself capable of exerting, he focused on the ledgers in front of them instead of the woman beside him. Amber's handwriting was familiar and easy to read. She'd kept detailed records, and it didn't take long for Nick to see that the ranch was in good financial condition.

Settling into a somewhat awkward pattern at first that became easier as they talked, Nick asked questions and Amber answered. They were both quiet for a moment when the handwriting changed to Joseph's much less legible scrawl.

Neither commented on the change, however, and their heads were still together when Joey's door opened. Nick glanced at the mantel clock and saw that almost an hour had passed.

The little boy knuckled sleepy eyes, yawned, and tottered down the hall, a ragged stuffed dog dangling from one hand. He brightened when he saw Nick was still there. He crawled onto his mother's lap and aimed a sleepy smile at his uncle. "Hi."

"Hi." Nick smiled as the boy nestled against his mother's breast. He would not be jealous of a small boy, but damn he couldn't help remembering a time or two when she'd held him in just the same position, when sleep had been the last thing on either one of their minds. To divert his memories and the blood stirring his body, he motioned toward the stuffed dog. "Who's your friend?"

"Yellow Pup." Joey held out the stuffed toy for his inspection. "He's like Daisy, 'cept not real."

"Yellow Pup, huh?" Nick took the dog and made a show of checking it over. "That fits."

Joey took back the dog and handed it to his mother, sliding off her lap. "Gotta go use the privy."

"Hurry," she urged. "Need help?"

"No!" came Joey's indignant reply as he scurried across the kitchen, slamming the screen door on his way out.

Nick rose. "I'll go. When he's done, we'll head around to the barn. Thanks for showing me the books. You've done a great job keeping things going after . . . since . . . Joe's death." Her gaze wavered, and he could have kicked himself for reminding her of what she'd lost.

"Thanks." She rose, too. "Send Joey in when your ears have had enough."

He smiled. "Enjoy your afternoon."

"Oh, I will." She reached out, laying a hand on his arm before he turned away. "Thank you, Nick."

"You're welcome." He patted her hand, warning

himself to keep it light. Pulling her into his arms and kissing the daylights out of her wouldn't be a smart move and definitely not part of his plan. Yet.

Turning away, he quickly followed Joey out the back door before she could see the heat in his eyes and he did something really stupid.

He hoped to God this "friends" thing would get easier.

Amber wondered if Nick was trying to purposely confuse her or if he had no idea what he was doing. In the couple of weeks he'd been home, other than the first night, he'd treated her like a good friend or a favorite sister-in-law. Having him settle for a platonic relationship was about the last thing she'd expected.

That first night, he hadn't kissed her like he'd come home to renew just a friendship. Of course, that had been before he'd found out that she'd been married to Joseph, before he'd seen Joey. Maybe he'd changed his mind about wanting her back. Although she wasn't ready to trust him with her heart or with her son's heart, she wasn't happy either at how easily he'd settled for just friendship between them.

Nick had changed in other ways, too. Instead of the impulsive, always-on-the-go, impetuous thrill seeker he'd once been, he was much more settled. When a question or problem arose with the cattle, he took the time to discuss the situation with her or the ranch foreman before making a decision. The old Nick would have jumped in and done something rash without weighing the right or wrong of it first.

He seemed content to spend his days catching up

on chores around the barn and the bunkhouse, and he'd even made a few repairs for her in the house.

Other than church on Sunday, they'd been to town just once for supplies and then only briefly. Before the war, he'd enjoyed spending time in town playing cards and visiting friends. They'd frequently picnicked and socialized with other couples, as well. His only source of entertainment these days seemed to be Joey.

Nick was incredibly patient and kind with Joey. He never seemed to tire of answering his questions or showing him how to braid a rope, rub down a horse, or clean a stall. Nick took into account three-year-old Joey's attention span and ability level and kept the lessons simple. Seeing them together, and there'd been no way to keep them apart despite her early attempts, was both amusing and bittersweet.

She was nagged by the constant question of whether or not to tell Nick the truth about Joey's paternity. Some days, she thought Nick had every right to know, yet she never seemed to find exactly the right time or exactly the right words to tell him.

He had changed, yes, but since that first night almost three weeks ago, he hadn't said anything more about staying on the ranch for good. He hadn't mentioned leaving either but until she was certain of his plans, she couldn't risk Joey's happiness. Her son would be devastated if "Uncle Nick" left. She couldn't bear the thought of how he'd feel if she told him Nick was his daddy and then Nick left.

She didn't want to dwell, either, on how she'd feel if Nick left again. He had gotten into the habit, thanks to Joey's constant invitations, of sharing the evening meal with them and most of the time, lunch, as well. Several times, he'd lingered after she'd put Joey to bed. They'd talked about everything it seemed, except the past four years . . . and the future.

Amber roused herself from the porch swing, where she'd been lost in thought while the sun set behind the barn. She'd gotten spoiled with so much free time since Joey had started dogging Nick like a small shadow. Supper was simmering on the stove but she still needed to set the table.

Across the yard, the lamp went out in the barn. Amber heard Joey's voice and Nick's before they walked outside. Usually Joey was still dancing circles around Nick at the end of the day, but not tonight. The two of them had spent the afternoon "digging out fence holes," Joey had told her when he'd come rushing to the house not long after lunch. Nick had sent him for a jacket and permission to ride along. She couldn't wait to hear all about their "venture" during supper.

She rose from the swing, drawing their attention as she stood. "About time you two called it a night. I thought maybe you planned to eat with the horses."

Joey giggled, launching himself into her arms. "You're silly, Mama."

"Not as silly as you." She tickled him, enjoying his belly laughs. "Ready for supper?"

"Supper, supper, supper," he chanted.

"You'll join us?" she asked Nick. He nodded, and she turned toward the house, her son in her arms. Nick followed.

"Joey, help me clear your mess off the table."

Valentine's Day was still almost a month away, but she and Joey had been designing valentines for his grandparents and his best friend.

"Uncle Nick, I'm making valumtimes for Grandma Mary and Grandpa Henry and Sammy O'Grady. Wanna see?"

"Valumtimes?" Nick came up behind Joey and looked over his shoulder. He chuckled. "Valentines."

"Yup." He motioned Nick closer and whispered in his ear, "One for Mama, too."

Joey's idea of a whisper carried across the room to Amber, who was taking plates off the cupboard shelf, but she pretended not to hear. That way she could ignore Nick for a while, too, because memories of Valentine's Day weren't happy ones for the two of them. Not anymore.

"Nice work," Nick praised her son as he helped pick up scraps of paper, lace, and ribbon. "Did your mama ever tell you the story about our first Valentine's Day as sweethearts?"

"You and Mama was sweettarts?" Joey asked, wide-eyed, his glance darting between the two of them.

She nearly dropped the plates.

"We sure were. I was about nine or ten years old and your mama was a couple of years younger."

Amber realized which story Nick was about to tell and she set the plates down on the table with a relieved sigh. "Our schoolteacher, Mrs. Adams, came up with this truly brilliant idea to pair up children as valentines for the day."

Nick took cutlery from the drawer and placed a fork, spoon, and knife next to each plate. Joey tracked his every move. "She put all the names of the girls in one hat and the names of the boys in another. Then, she drew one boy's name and one girl's name, and they were paired up for the day."

"You and Mama was paired?"

Nick nodded.

"Some of the older kids had fun," Amber recalled, filling serving plates and bowls and handing them to Nick, who set them on the table where Joey now sat, eagle-eyed.

"But not your mama and me." Nick winked at Joey. "Do you like girls, Joey?"

"Yucky!"

"Exactly," Nick agreed. "I guarantee that will change when you're older, but I hadn't reached that point yet myself on that particular Valentine's Day. I'm afraid I wasn't very nice to your mama."

Nick had called her Amber "Waddle" instead of Wade, but she wasn't about to tell that to her three-and-a-half-year-old son. "He hid my chalk and pulled my braids."

"Did ya?"

Nick could maybe fool a three-year-old with the look of contrition on his face, but not her. "I'm not proud of that now, squirt, but, yeah, I sure did. And I did something even worse, too."

They said a quick prayer and she served the food.

"What'd ya do to Mama?" Joey asked around a mouth full of mashed potatoes.

"Joseph Parish, close your mouth while you're eating."

He chewed and swallowed. "Yes, ma'am."

"Your mama and I," Nick continued, "were forced to eat lunch together. I didn't like it, and your mama didn't like it either."

Joey glanced at his mother. She shook her head.

"And I—" Nick hesitated, glanced at her and back to Joey—"I don't think I should tell you any more. To this very day, I am very ashamed of my actions."

"Tell me, tell me!" Joey bounced in his chair.

"Do you promise to never, never, ever do what I'm about to tell you?"

"Promise."

Nick leaned forward. "I poured ink into her tea without her knowing it. When she drank it, her teeth turned black. They were black for days and days."

More like weeks and weeks and no matter how hard or how often she'd scrubbed, the ink hadn't budged. It had lingered between her teeth for weeks, and Nick had been horrible. At first he'd howled with laughter, and every day after until the stains faded, he'd snickered whenever he'd seen her.

"Truly?" Joey stopped eating.

"Truly."

His bottom lip puckered. "Meanie."

"Yes, I was very mean," Nick agreed, solemnly, "and not that an apology made things right but I did tell your mama I was very, very sorry."

"He was punished, too," Amber assured her son. "Mrs. Adams kept him after school every day for a month. And for one whole month, Nick rode over to my house before school and after school and did all of my chores."

"My mama and daddy were very angry with me. Grandma Mary and Grandpa Henry were mad at me, too."

"Me, too," Joey declared.

"Don't be mad at him, baby." Amber ruffled

her son's hair before picking up their plates and carrying them to the sink. "I think Uncle Nick learned his lesson."

Joey didn't look convinced.

"How about. . . ." She smiled at her son. "Just for being mean to Mommy when we were kids, we make Uncle Nick give you your bath tonight. How's that?"

A sly smile crossed her son's face. He was quick to forgive and having his new uncle give him a bath probably sounded like a lot of fun. Unlike naptime or bedtime, Joey loved bathtime. "Okay."

She finished clearing the table while Nick got out the tub and filled it with water that had been heating on the stove. While she checked the temperature, Joey shucked his clothes.

Nick lifted him into the tub. Joey showed Nick his favorite toys and they made boat sounds and amusing fish sounds while she put away the food and washed the dishes. Joey didn't even protest when Amber insisted on washing his hair. She let them splash together for a while longer while she got a clean nightshirt from Joey's room.

He was yawning when she returned, no doubt caused by the combination of no afternoon nap and the warm bathwater. He was all but sleeping by the time she got him dried off and bundled up, and Nick carried him down the hall to bed. Without a peep of protest, he laid his head on the pillow, tucked Yellow Pup against his chest beneath his chin, and was out before she could pull up the covers and place a gentle kiss on his brow.

She brushed back a damp lock of hair and whispered, "Good night, Joey. I love you, baby."

Nick, too, whispered good night to the sleeping boy, and they returned to the kitchen. She made coffee while he dumped the bathwater outside and put away the tub.

When the coffee was ready, Nick took his into the parlor, settling himself into the comfortable old sofa. Hesitating only briefly to weigh the wisdom of it, she joined him there. For long moments, they silently sipped their coffee and watched the fire slowly dying in the grate.

Beside her, Nick was restless and eventually he broke the silence. "Amber, I've been lying to you ever since I came back."

She almost choked on her coffee. "H—how have you been lying?"

"I've been pretending to be your friend. I'm not, I mean, I am, but I want to be more." He turned toward her, shaking his head, clearly confused. "How did we get here? What happened to *us?* How did things go so incredibly wrong?"

"You're kidding, right?" She, too, turned on the sofa and looked at him. He wasn't. She set down her coffee cup before she threw it at his head. "Okay, let's see. When I was seven or eight, Mrs. Adams paired us up as sweethearts for a day. You remember, the story you just told Joey? Clearly, that was a mistake because I ended up with black teeth."

He frowned. "Honey, I was only ten years old."

"Regardless"—she waved a hand in the air— "half a dozen years later, maybe a couple more, I turned fifteen and you decided I wasn't so bad anymore and you kissed me. One thing led to another and four years later, we announced our engagement. You with me so far?"

"Amber, that's not—"

"Good. Where was I?" She was angry now. "Standing at the altar, almost, waiting for you. Because of our history with Valentine's Day, we decided that would be the perfect day to get married. At least, that's what I thought. Apparently, you had been thinking about one last grand adventure before tying yourself down to me."

"I didn't think of getting married that way," he interrupted. "I just . . ."

"Wasn't ready? I got that." She'd been humiliated and hurt and remembered both emotions distinctly, but not angry, not then, not yet. "When war broke out back East that's all you could talk about. Do you think I didn't see your gaze on the horizon more often than not? While I'd been busy making wedding plans, you'd been making plans to join the army, only you didn't tell me until just two days, *two days,* damn you, before the wedding.

"I like to tell myself that you didn't have a clue how much your leaving hurt me, that you had no way of knowing how long the war would last. But, dammit, Nick, did you really think you could be gone for almost four years, then come back and pick up right where we left off? Did it truly never occur to you that I might move on with my life, that I might find someone else?"

"No, it didn't, and even if I had thought about it, I would never have expected—"

"Then you're even more arrogant than I remember."

She watched him frown. "I loved you, Amber. I thought you felt the same way."

"I loved you, Nick," she parroted. "I thought you felt the same way. Yet, you left me so close to the day of our wedding that I might as well have been standing at the altar. I had the dress, the flowers, the food for the reception."

"I'm sorry, more sorry than I can ever tell you." He dropped his head, ran both hands through his hair, and looked up. "I was incredibly selfish, but damn you, I asked you to wait for me."

"*Damn you, Nick.* I asked you to stay." She released an angry breath she hadn't realized she'd been holding. "Looks like neither one of us got what we wanted."

His hands dropped to his knees, his eyes narrowed. "Is that why you married my brother? To get back at me? For God's sake, Amber, *my own brother.* How could you have done that to me, to us?"

She'd done it because of Joey. Because she'd been scared, very scared and yes, finally, angry, too. Joe had somehow guessed she was pregnant, and he'd stood by her. "Believe whatever you want, Nick. You weren't here and we did what we had to do."

"What does that mean . . . what you had to do?"

She bit her lip at the slip, then shrugged as nonchalantly as possible. "Joe was here. You weren't. You made your choice. I made mine. It's done."

"You haven't mentioned love." He stared at her, his voice tight. "Did you love my brother?"

"Yes! He was here for me. He did the right thing. He did what you should have done. I loved him then, and I love him now. I will always love him!" Joe had been by her side when she was too terrified to know what to do or where to turn, for that she would always be grateful. She *would* always love him. Just not the way Nick meant.

She saw the fury in his eyes just before he grabbed her, his fingers digging into the flesh of her upper arms, dragging her against his chest. She struggled, but this time she wasn't strong enough to push him away or maybe he was just more determined. His gaze dropped to her mouth only seconds before he closed the distance between them and kissed her.

His was no gentle kiss. He was angry, but she was angry, too, and fought him. One strong arm slid around her waist while his hand cupped the back of her head, holding her tight against him. He plundered, parting her lips, thrusting his tongue into her mouth. Long forgotten, incredibly sweet sensations swamped her and she fought, barely managing to contain a moan. He lifted his mouth from hers but she could feel his breath warm upon her lips. She trembled.

"Tell me now, Amber," he whispered. "Tell me you love my brother now. Tell me you don't feel what's still between us."

"I don't—"

The hand in her hair tightened. "You're lying. I love you, dammit. I have always and will always love you." He kissed her again, as though by sheer determination he could force her to his will. "Tell me that you loved him more than you loved me."

She struggled fiercely, pushing against his chest, but he refused to release her. Tears stung her eyes. "I will always—"

"*No!* Can't you see . . . ? I'm half mad with jealousy. *Of my own brother.* My brother is dead, and still, a part of me hates him. I'm so damned jealous of him that I can barely breathe," Nick hissed, his jaw taut, his cheeks hollow, and his eyes burning. "The idea of you and him together . . .

making love . . . You are mine, Amber! Only mine!"

"No!" she sobbed. Still, she struggled.

"Yes! You were mine first. You will be mine again! I love you," he whispered, his lips hovering just above hers. The pulse in his throat throbbed wildly. "I love you, and before we're done here, you will tell me, Amber, you will tell me that you still love me!"

She tried to fight him but the feelings were too strong, too long denied, and she did love him. She'd always loved him. Even after he'd left her. She'd hated him, but she'd loved him, too.

"Damn you! I do love you!" she cried out, over and over, unable to deny herself or him any longer. "I love you! I have . . . I will always, always love you!"

Nick swept her up into his arms and carried her down the hall to his brother's bedroom, to his brother's bed. But he would not let himself think about that now. She'd admitted, finally, what he needed to hear.

He set her on her feet long enough to sweep back the blankets. Carefully, he lowered her to the soft, clean, fragrant sheets and followed her down. His touch gentled. His knuckles brushed along her cheek, down her jaw, and he was dazed by the softness of her skin. He loosened her hair from the single braid and spread it across her on the pillow. "Tell me you don't want this, Amber, and I'll stop."

"No . . ."

"No stop or no don't stop?" He nuzzled her neck.

"Tell me. I need the words. I won't force you, and I won't let you pretend I'm him either." He rose above her. "Open your eyes. Look at me, Amber. *Say my name. Say it.*"

"Nick . . ."

"Again." He found the buttons down the front of her gown and tugged them open, one by one, until her dress lay open revealing the delicate lace of her chemise. *"Again."*

"Nick."

"Again . . ." He kissed her eyes, her nose. Her mouth. Sweet kisses, slow, drugging, deep but not nearly deep enough.

"Nick, yes!"

Impatient now, he pulled the dress off her arms, down to her waist. She lifted her hips and he tore the dress free. He untied the petticoats from her waist and swept them away with her pantalets. He tugged the chemise over her head and she lay before him naked, gloriously, beautifully, completely naked.

With a few efficient motions, he was as naked as she.

"This is where I belong, Amber. In your bed, in your arms . . . inside your body." She cried out when he plunged deep. "I don't care if my brother has been here since me. I don't care that you were his wife . . . that you bore his child. You were mine first. You are mine again. *You will be mine forever.*"

"Yours . . ." she whispered. Her arms closed around him, holding tightly and her eyes slid closed.

"No, damn it. Open your eyes. Tell me he made you feel this." He touched, stroked, savored, and fire leapt between them. She shivered. "Did he, Amber? Did your nails rake his back in pleasure?"

Her eyes opened, mere slits, filled with desire. She panted, "No."

"Did you arch beneath him and cry out when he came into you?"

"I didn't—" Her eyelids slid closed again, shutting him out and he wouldn't allow that.

"You did, dammit, *with me,* you did! But did you with him? Open your eyes, Amber. Did you? *Did you?"*

"No!" He held her tight, his fingers tangled in her hair. Her eyes opened, their gazes clashed. "We never had this. We never had anything like this. *We never had anything.* I've had only you. Joseph was my husband, but he was never my lover!"

"What?" Nick demanded, incredulous.

"We never—"

He kissed her, raw desire sweeping away all but the most basic thoughts from his mind. She was his. *Only his.* She whimpered and he drove deep one last time.

Together, they shuddered.

Together, they shattered.

Together, they slept.

Four

Amber awoke slowly, drifting in a state somewhere between slumber and consciousness. Without opening her eyes, she stretched, arms above her head, toes pointed, and let out a small, contented moan.

Curling onto her side, she snuggled into the pillow, sated, a little sore and surprisingly drowsy because she could feel daylight behind her closed eyelids and knew it was late. She breathed deeply, inhaling lingering traces of Nick's scent from her skin and the twisted bedding.

A heated flush swept her body, head to heels, as memories gradually returned. She remembered arguing with him on the sofa, his bewilderment at their situation and her anger. She remembered the startling pleasure of his mouth on hers when he'd kissed her again, finally, after nearly a month.

After nearly four years.

She remembered his jealousy, her anger . . . and his determination. With a small shiver, she remembered his mouth on her skin, his fingers in her hair, his hands on her body. She remembered the heat, the passion, and the sheer joy of his touch.

The pure joy of touching him.

She remembered him telling her he loved her still, and she could remember telling him that she loved him. She remembered telling him she would love him always. She remembered telling him—

Ohmygod! Eyes wide, heart pounding, breathing way too fast, she bolted upright and scrambled out of bed, only then realizing that she was naked. She searched frantically for her nightgown and robe, found them in her armoire and hastily dressed.

She twisted open the doorknob. Across the hall, Joey's bedroom door was open, the room empty, and she all but flew down the hallway to the kitchen, skidding to a stop at the sight of Nick and her son sharing breakfast at the table.

Her son.

His son.

Their son.

He had to know that after what she'd revealed last night. One glance at his stiff shoulders, tight mouth, and accusing eyes confirmed the knowledge. Nick knew Joey was his son.

"Mornin', Mama," Joey spoke around a mouthful of breakfast. "Uncle Nick made flapjacks. A'most as good as yers. Yummy." He smiled, syrup dripping down his chin.

Uncle Nick. Amber watched Nick's jaw tighten. His gaze on her could have frozen a red-hot branding iron, yet she sagged in relief. Obviously, Nick hadn't said anything to Joey, but, oh, he was angry. More than angry, he was furious. Not a single trace of last night's demanding yet gentle lover remained.

She broke eye contact, but her chin came up. "Is there coffee?"

"On the stove. Help yourself."

She did. After she'd filled a cup, she took a fortifying sip, and then another, before joining them, sliding into a chair next to Joey.

She risked another glance across the table at Nick and saw that he watched his son as though Joey would disappear if he took his gaze off the boy for mere seconds. She could see the awe in his eyes, the wonder in his gaze, and none of the anger he'd directed toward her, only gentle amazement.

Now what? she wondered, finding it nearly impossible to sit there listening to Joey's usual endless chatter, watching Nick's complete adoration of his son, and not want to scream in frustration.

What would Nick expect from her? From Joey? She had no doubt, absolutely none, that he would demand to claim his son. The look in his eyes was too possessive. He would never settle for his previous status as uncle. She watched as he reached out trembling fingers, *trembling,* and touched his son's cheek, softly, reverently.

No, he would settle for nothing less than full and public possession and what would that do to Joey when Nick's gaze was once more drawn to the horizon and he decided again that he'd had enough ranch life for a while? Joey would be hurt. He would be devastated, and she would not let that happen to her son.

Her maternal instinct flared—as brightly, every bit as strongly as the possessiveness in Nick's eyes. He would not hurt her son. What Nick wanted did not matter. She wouldn't let it matter. Only Joey mattered, and she would protect him to her dying breath.

Joey plopped the last bite of flapjack into his mouth, chewed, swallowed and emptied his glass of milk. Before Nick could react, she rose and swept her son into her arms.

"Come on, baby, let's get that sticky syrup off your face and fingers and get you dressed."

Nick's chair scraped across the floor as he stood. "Wait a minute, Amber." His words were pure demand. "We need to talk."

"We do," she agreed, "and we will, but not right now." She darted a meaningful glance at Joey. No way did she want, in front of their child, to have the kind of conversation she knew they were going to have. "My father is riding over this afternoon. He'll spend some time with Joey, and we can talk then."

She'd expected him to refuse. Instead, he surprised her by nodding in tight-lipped agreement.

His gaze softened when he looked at Joey. "See ya later, squirt."

After one last longing glance at the little boy in her arms, Nick pulled open the back door and left. She released a drawn-out breath and her shoulders slumped.

Maybe her father wouldn't come today. Maybe she wouldn't have to have things out with Nick until after she'd figured out how to convince him not to tell Joey the truth. Maybe he would be content with the knowledge that Joey was his without demanding that Joey know, too. Maybe the cows would dance and the chickens would sing. *Fat chance.*

Joey wiggled in her arms. "Hurry, Mama. I gotta go with Uncle Nick."

"Not today, baby." No way was she allowing them to be alone together again. She wasn't letting her son out of her sight until after she and Nick had hashed things out between them. "Let's finish those valentines we started yesterday."

Making valentines obviously wasn't as exciting as being with Nick, but she was glad Joey didn't argue with her. "Okay."

She hugged him until he squirmed. "Squishin' me, Mama."

Reluctantly, she loosened her hold. When she let him down, he scampered out of the kitchen and down the hallway toward his room. Some things never changed. He still seemed incapable of walking anywhere.

"Come on, Mama!" he hollered as he ran.

Or talking in a normal tone of voice.

But things had changed. To what extent remained to be seen.

Nick waited. Impatient as hell, but he waited.

He didn't go to the house for lunch. He didn't think he could endure another meal watching his son across the table without blurting out the truth.

His son.

His beautiful, perfect, amazing son. He'd fallen in love with Joey before he'd found out the truth. He hadn't known it was possible, but he loved the boy now even more.

He set aside the saddle he was attempting to repair, unable to concentrate on even the simplest chore. Through the open tack room doorway, he listened for the sound of Henry Wade's arrival. If Amber's father didn't show up soon, Nick was going to confront Amber during Joey's naptime. He'd waited about as long as he could for an explanation.

He picked up the saddle again, desperate for a

distraction from his thoughts. Finally, he heard the unmistakable clip-clop of an approaching horse, then Joey's loud welcome and Henry's quieter reply.

About damn time.

He didn't wait for Amber to come to him but instead left the barn and crossed the yard to the house. She saw him coming and alarm filled her big brown eyes. Tough, he wasn't going to be put off any longer.

"Henry." He nodded a greeting to her father.

"Afternoon, Nick."

Nick reached Amber and took her arm before she could escape. "I need to borrow your daughter for a bit. You don't mind keeping an eye on Joey for a while, do you?"

Something in Nick's voice must have warned Henry, and unless her father was blind, he couldn't have missed the alarm in his daughter's eyes.

Henry glanced at her. "Amber?"

"It's okay, Daddy," she reassured him. "Nick and I have some things to talk about. I'll be fine."

Not convinced, he cast a suspicious glance between the two of them. "You're sure?"

Nick remained silent.

"I'm sure." She bent down to Joey. "Mind your grandpa, now. Nick and I will be in the barn."

"Me, too." He pouted.

"Not this time, baby." She tapped his protruding lower lip. "Show Grandpa the valentine you made for Sammy."

" 'Kay." He took his grandfather's hand, tugging him toward the house. "Wait 'il you see it, Grandpa. I done a good job. Mama said so."

With one last glance over his shoulder, Henry allowed himself to be towed into the house by his grandson.

Nick didn't release Amber's arm. He held tight as he led her across the yard, into the barn and back to the relative privacy of the tack room. With a hard kick, he slammed shut the door and swung her around to face him.

"You lied to me."

"Yes."

He waited for her to continue. Instead, she tilted her chin at him in that defiant way that he both admired and despised, and remained silent.

He swore. "Yes? That's all you can goddamn say to me?"

"I'd do it again, Nick." She stood her ground, never blinking. He didn't think she was trying to provoke him on purpose, but she was doing a fine job of it nonetheless. "Given the same circumstances, the same choices, I would do it again."

"Why? He's my son." He took a step forward. "He is my son, and you kept the truth from me intentionally."

"I believe we've already established that," she replied primly.

He could only stare. "When did you become such a bitch?"

He saw a flicker of something in her eyes, but just as quickly it was gone. "About four years ago."

Direct hit. He rubbed his chest. "Do you have any idea what I felt when I woke up this morning? When I looked at Joey and realized he was mine?" He tucked both hands into his pockets because he wanted to shake her so badly, and he couldn't trust himself not to reach for her. "You had no intention of telling me the truth, did you?"

"I don't . . . know."

He shook his head. "You can't keep him from me, Amber. I have a right to know my son and for him to know me. I have every right to claim him."

"You have no rights," she hissed. *"None, do you understand? You left me. You left me pregnant. Alone, scared nearly to death, and pregnant!"*

His gut twisted and he was too ashamed to hold her gaze. He knew she wouldn't care, but he said it anyway. "I'm sorry, honey, so damned sorry."

She snorted. "Like that makes a damn bit of difference now."

Yeah, he knew that. "Did you know you were pregnant when I left?" he asked softly, most of his anger spent.

"No." Her voice shook. Helpless, he watched tears fill her eyes. "But we both knew the possibility existed, Nick, and you left anyway. I was afraid to tell my parents. I didn't know what to do. I didn't know where to turn."

He'd been so damned selfish, only he'd been too blind to see it . . . until now. He hated himself for not being there for her. Thank God Joe had been. He owed his brother an apology and a hell of a lot of gratitude. "So you turned to Joe for help?"

"Not right away." She brushed at the tears. "He came to me. Somehow, he'd figured it out for himself. When Joe suggested we get married, I agreed, although not right away. At first, I waited for you. I thought you'd realize you'd made a mistake and be back in a couple of days.

"A couple of weeks passed, and I was terrified. I started asking myself all kinds of questions I couldn't answer. What if you got killed fighting in the war? What if you never came back?

"Then I got angry, furiously angry, at myself and at you. I didn't want our baby branded a bastard, and by then, I didn't have a lot of time left to consider the right or wrong of it. When Joe asked me again, I said yes."

She looked him straight in the eye—maybe to make him feel bad, maybe just to make sure he understood. "He was here, Nick, and you weren't. He did the right thing when he found out I was pregnant and we both realized you weren't coming home anytime soon."

"He stood by you when I didn't." Nick's shoulders slumped.

"Yes."

Nick could only imagine what she'd gone through, the torment she'd suffered, and the misery she'd endured because of him. "I never would have left if I'd known you were pregnant." Too little, too late, he knew, but he needed her to hear the words.

"You knew it was possible," she challenged. "You should have waited to find out. I won't apologize for keeping the truth from you, Nick. Joseph and I did what we thought was best for Joey at the time. As it turned out, we made the right decision. I made the right decision when you returned, too. You will not tell Joey that you're his father."

Burning anger replaced his shame, his guilt. "The hell I won't."

"The hell you will! I won't let you hurt him!"

"How can the truth hurt him?" Nick shook his head, confused. "I know he thinks Joe was his daddy, and I'm sure he loved my brother. But I know, too, and so do you, that he'll accept the idea of me as his father. He might be confused at first, but we can help him understand."

"No."

"He's my son. You can't keep him from me forever."

"Maybe. Maybe not. I won't let you hurt him either."

"You keep saying that. *Why?* I have no intention of hurting him."

"I don't give a damn about your intentions, Nick. My only concern is my son."

"Our son."

"Yes, our son, and he loves you already. I won't even begin to deny that, and he thinks you're his uncle. You will not ride back into our lives, tell him you're his father and then ride out again when it suits you. You won't do that to him. You won't do that to me."

Finally, he understood. She was scared and worried for Joey and protecting him with every maternal instinct she possessed, but she was afraid for herself, too. "I ran out on you once, Amber. I'm not running anymore."

He reached for her, but she took a scrambling step backward. He frowned. Okay, so she didn't want him to touch her yet. He could understand that, too, but he had to make her understand a few other things, as well.

"I love you. I wasn't lying last night when I told you that."

"Last night was a mistake."

"The hell it was."

"The hell it wasn't," she shot back. "I won't be used again."

"I wasn't using you." He took a step forward and she took a step back. "I love you, and you love me.

I heard you last night, Amber, so don't even try to deny it."

"So what? I love you. Big deal. I've loved you for years. I've loved you for forever, it seems, but I've managed to live without you for the past four years."

She took another step back, attempting to put space between them. As far as he was concerned, there had been too much space between them already, for far too long. Four years too long. That had been his fault and his mistake. No more. His pulse pounding hard, he willed himself to find the right words.

"I love you, Amber." His fingers threaded her hair, holding her motionless when she tried to turn away. His mouth hovered inches above hers and he could feel her breath, warm and sweet against his mouth. He resisted taking what he wanted. First, they would talk. "I love you, and I love Joey, and I want the life we should have had."

She opened her mouth.

"Hush," he said, brushing his lips against hers. "You've had your say. It's my turn now and you're going to listen."

She scowled, and he resisted kissing her again only by the skin of his teeth. "Being Joey's uncle is not enough. I want more. I want it all. I want more days like the past few weeks. I want to spend time with our son, that precious, wondrous little boy that our love created. I want to teach him how to braid a rope and snap his fingers and ride a horse." He saw the doubt in her eyes and continued, determined to convince her.

"I know you don't like it, but I want to give him baths and tuck him into bed every night. I want to read him stories and watch him fall asleep. I want him to know he's my son. And, Amber, I want those things as much as I want air to breathe, and as desperately as I want those things, I want you, too."

He almost smiled at the way her eyes widened. He couldn't resist settling a small, tender kiss on her stunned mouth. "I want the right to go to bed with you each night. I want to sleep in your arms and wake up in your arms." He kissed her again, this time letting her feel his greed, his need. "I would never hurt him, Amber, and I will never hurt you again, ever. I swear."

"No!" She twisted against his hold.

"Yes." He lowered his mouth and kissed her again. And again. He invaded, stroked, and seduced, battling for his son, for her, and for their lives together, with the touch of his lips, the sweep of his body, and the pounding of his heart.

"I want to marry you, Amber. I want us to have more children, and this time, I'll be here to watch you grow round. I'll be here to feel the baby kick, I'll be here to rub your back when it aches and I'll be by your side to help you bring our children into the world. You won't be alone, Amber, not like with Joey. I'm sorry."

He punctuated his apologies with tender kisses. "I'm sorry. So damned sorry."

"I believe you, Nick," she whispered. "I do. . . ."

His forehead fell to hers in sheer, absolute relief. Finally.

"But I won't marry you."

His head snapped back. "Why not?"

She pressed against his shoulders. "Because I can never be sure that you won't leave me again."

They were back to that. "And what if you're

CAN I CALL YOU SWEETHEART?

pregnant again?" he challenged. "Have you considered that possibility?"

She paled. Her mouth opened but no words came out. He saw her struggle with the potential consequences of what they'd done.

"No, I can see that you haven't." He smiled a small, smug smile. "We are getting married. That choice, that decision was made between us last night in bed." He kissed the wildly beating pulse at the base of her neck. "Maybe no words were spoken but the promise was made all the same. We have a son, Amber. We have last night. Give us today and tomorrow, and every tomorrow after that."

"I can't," she whispered, swallowing against the tears he hated seeing in her eyes. "I just . . . can't."

"How can I convince you?" He was getting nowhere with her, but they had so much at stake and he refused to give up. "There must be some way. I'll do anything. Name it."

"I don't know." She looked as unhappy and confused as he felt. "I wish I could believe you. For Joey's sake and, yes, for my own, I wish to God I could believe you."

"You can."

"I can't! I've had almost four years to build up my defenses against you. Four years to dwell on the hurt and pain you caused me. I can't get over that in a few weeks."

"How long then? How long will it take? A month, six months? *Never?*"

"I don't know!"

He couldn't fight that and released her in surrender. But not defeat. "Then we'll wait and see. I'll give you time, but, Amber, if you're pregnant again, you will marry me. Right away, no more waiting."

"And Joey?" she asked, not agreeing, but this time not flat out refusing either. "Will you promise me that you won't say anything to him?"

He rubbed a hand across his face. "I won't tell him."

"Do you promise?"

God, she really didn't trust him. "Yes, I promise. For now. I won't promise to never tell him, though, you can't ask that of me. He is my son. I want him to know the truth."

She nodded.

He couldn't think of anything else to say, knowing somehow he would have to show her instead. He'd have to be patient until she realized she could trust him . . . or until she realized she was pregnant. He didn't know if he wanted her that way, but if it was the only way, so be it. Only time would tell.

Her father stayed for supper, and Nick surprised her by joining them, too, although Amber hadn't expected him. Her father spent as much time casting curious glances between her and Nick as he did eating.

Her daddy was an observant man, and the fact that Nick wouldn't look at her and the two of them didn't exchange one single word might have raised some suspicion, too. Only Joey's steady chatter saved the meal from total disaster.

Almost as soon as they were done eating, her father kissed her cheek, gave her an extra tight hug, and rode out of the yard. He had just enough time to make the leisurely half hour ride home before sundown.

She did up the dishes alone in the kitchen while Joey and Nick talked and giggled and played in the parlor. She stalled as long as possible before turning down the lamp and leaving the sanctuary of the kitchen. She found them on the floor together, their dark heads bent over Joey's "treasure" box.

Spread out in front of them were some of her son's most prized possessions: half a dozen multi-colored marbles, a few pretty or unusual stones, and a drawing of what was supposed to be Daisy. Nick was currently admiring an ordinary bird's feather Joey had found last summer.

Watching the two of them together, she let out a shaky breath and wrapped her arms tight around her middle. They were so much alike, and she'd denied seeing it for so long. They had the same curl to the ends of their hair. They both needed haircuts, she observed with a smile, but that had nothing to do with heredity. Their eyes were the same color, the same shape. They had the same stubborn jaw and they both lay on the floor propped up on their elbows with their ankles crossed exactly the same way.

Joey was a tiny replica of his father. Only Joseph's close resemblance to Nick had prevented Nick and anyone else who looked close enough and counted the months of her pregnancy from guessing the truth.

She stood unnoticed behind them, listening to Joey explain something to Nick, making wide exaggerated motions with hands like his father's. When he was finished, he giggled, Nick laughed, and she thought her heart might simply burst watching the two of them together.

Was she wrong to keep them apart? Was she wrong to deny Joey his father? The ache was fierce when she thought about all the time they'd missed . . . because of Nick, and she couldn't quite get passed that fact.

If he hadn't left, they would have been married by the time she realized she was pregnant. He would have been with her when Joey was born. He would have seen his son's first steps and heard his first words. He'd missed a lot. As a family, they'd missed a lot.

Because of Nick.

He'd made the decision they'd all had to live with.

She wanted the three of them to be a family. She loved him; that hadn't changed. She knew he loved Joey. She believed that he still loved her, that he'd always loved her, and that was part of the problem. He'd loved her before and he'd left anyway.

She wanted to trust him. The simple truth was . . . she didn't, and until she did, she refused to risk her son's heart and his happiness. Because how could she be sure Nick wouldn't leave again?

Five

Nick had been patient for two weeks. For an impatient man, that was a damned long time. As far as he could tell, he'd made no progress in convincing Amber to trust him and his patience had about run dry.

Through the parlor window, he watched the afternoon sky, nearly dark as night and heavy with clouds. A storm was brewing and it matched his mood.

He heard a sound behind him and turned. Amber stood just inside the parlor. Her fingers pleated the skirt of a mustard yellow day dress. Her hair, for once was loose and flowed almost to her waist. He wanted to pull her into his arms, bury his face in her hair and convince her to marry him. Only he didn't know how.

He cleared his throat. "Is Joey asleep?"

"Finally. You know how much he fights naptime." She crossed to the mantel and lit a lamp. "I thought you'd gone."

"You wished I'd gone, you mean."

"You said you had things to do in the barn."

He noticed she didn't deny wanting him gone. "I wanted to talk to you first."

"Nick, we have nothing—"

"I'm trying to be patient here, Amber." He stepped away from the window. "I've gone along with things your way for the past two weeks, hell, the past month and a half. We haven't told Joey I'm his father because you don't want to. I'm trying to understand why you don't think it's a good idea, but the boy has gotten to know me. I don't think the news would traumatize him."

"It's not that—"

"Then what? You still can't trust me?" Outside the window, the clouds gave way and the rain fell, not in gentle drops but in a great torrent. "I've done everything you've asked. I've been patient until I've wanted to howl with frustration and nothing's changed. I don't think you'll ever be ready to tell Joey I'm his father."

"That's not true!"

"Isn't it?" he challenged. "I've been home for almost two months. Would it matter if it was two years?"

"Yes—"

"I don't want to wait another two years, Amber, to claim you and to claim my son. When I left you, I was young and stupid and incredibly selfish expecting you to wait for me. How can I make you see that I've changed? I have learned from the worst mistake I've ever made in my life. There is no lure, no temptation or adventure that could entice me to leave you and Joey now or ever again." He shook his head. "Maybe I'm wrong. Maybe it's not a matter of trust at all. I hurt you terribly when I left, and not that I blame you, but maybe you're punishing me for it."

"I am not—"

"What do you call it then?" he demanded. "I can see Joey, I can play with him, I can share meals with him, I can bathe him and put him to bed, but I can't tell him that I'm his father." He stepped closer and she moved away, putting the length of the sofa between them. "You said you love me, yet you're careful not to be in the same room with me without Joey. I want to talk and you refuse. We've been alone exactly once since the night we made love and that was so you could tell me you aren't pregnant.

"I'm still sleeping in the bunkhouse, and we haven't made love again because you don't want to risk another pregnancy. I can understand that, Amber, I can. Yet when I ask you to marry me, you say no. What is that if not punishment?"

Her cheeks were pale but her eyes flashed. "I'll tell you what it is if you'll let me finish a complete sentence without interrupting."

He opened his mouth and closed it, clenched his teeth, and waited. For long moments, the sound of the storm outside was the only sound in the room. She didn't say anything, and finally he urged, "Well?"

"I . . . I'm not punishing you." She sat on the sofa and looked up at him. He watched, horrified, as tears filled her eyes. She sniffed. "M—maybe I am. I don't know anymore. I only know it still hurts so much that you could so simply . . . leave me. I've tried to understand, but I just can't forget how I felt when I watched you ride away to join the war instead of marrying me. You broke my heart. I cried, I raged, I ached, and I waited." She brushed at the tears. "I can't go through that again, Nick. I just can't."

He sat heavily on the sofa beside her, hanging his

hands between his knees. Quietly, he said, "I've done a lot of things in my life, Amber, that I'm not proud of. I never should have put ink in your tea when we were kids. I never should have called you Amber Waddle. I never should have pulled your braids or stolen your chalk, and I sure never should have punched Billy Sullivan when he asked you to dance at the Valentine's Day celebration when you were sixteen."

She sniffled. "I'd forgotten about that."

He rubbed the heel of his hand between his eyes. "Joe tried to stop me. He held me back when I would have punched the kid again. I was so damned jealous." Silence settled between them. Outside, the wind raged and rain pelted the windows. "Do you remember the first time I kissed you?"

She turned toward him, her eyes bright with unshed tears, some already shed still clinging to her lashes. "A girl never forgets her first kiss. Somehow we ended up behind my barn the night of my fifteenth birthday."

He gave her a small smile. "Honey, I know exactly how we ended up behind your barn. I'd been nudging you in that direction all evening."

"Really? I almost slapped your face," she admitted.

"I was the perfect gentlemen. I stopped when you asked me to." At the time, he remembered, that had been damned difficult.

"I was young."

"Yeah," he agreed, "but so damned sweet and so tempting that I almost lost my head." Memories heated his blood and thickened his words. "You almost lost more than that."

"I almost wanted to," she said, shocking him.

He turned to stare at her.

"Which is why I almost slapped your face instead." She laughed, a small, quiet laugh, but an amused sound nonetheless.

Some of the pressure in his chest eased while another kind of tension built. His voice still husky, he asked, "Do you remember the first time we made love?"

"That time. . . ." Her voice was as husky as his. "You wanted to stop."

"Yeah. . . ." He swallowed hard, remembering. "And you didn't."

She smiled the kind of smile only a woman knew how to smile, full of feminine secrets and allure. "I'd been nudging you in that direction since that first kiss when I was fifteen."

He stared, tried to talk, and couldn't. He tried to clear his throat and had trouble with that, too. "You should have told me. We wouldn't have waited another three years."

"I didn't know how, but I knew what I wanted Nick, and it was you. Maybe I pushed too hard. Maybe if I hadn't, you wouldn't have felt obligated to ask me to marry you."

"Hell, I didn't ask you to marry me because I felt obligated. I mean, I did feel that way, after we'd made love, but I *wanted* to marry you, Amber." He needed her to understand that. "Asking you was my choice, not something you forced me to do or something I did just because we'd become lovers."

He could no longer sit, so he stood and paced. "I know we didn't do things in the right order. I know we should have gotten married and then made love and then had a child. I was selfish and never considered the consequences. I can't be sorry for the result of those consequences, though, Amber. Joey wasn't a mistake. The only mistake was me not realizing and acknowledging that there might be consequences."

"There weren't at first, and I was as much to blame as you, Nick, if not more. Isn't it the man's responsibility to seduce and the woman's to say no?"

"Hell no!" He stopped in front of her. "A man doesn't beguile a woman's defenses with sweet talk and temptation and then expect that woman to still have sense enough to stop."

"You never did that . . . seduced me until I couldn't say no."

"Well, I sure tried. I'd try again, given half the chance." He went down on his heels in front of her. "I can't change any of those things, Amber, but I can try to make them up to you. *All of them.* Let me spend the rest of our lives showing you how sorry I am that I ever picked on you, bullied you, hurt you or made you cry."

"Nick—"

"No." He took her hands, lacing their fingers together. "Listen to me. Give me the chance to make you smile and laugh, to make you happy instead of sad, to cherish you and show you every day for the rest of our lives how much I love you. We don't have to tell Joey that I'm his father if you still need to keep that secret but, please, Amber, marry me. *Marry me.*"

"I can't." Her eyes filled with tears, and he watched, helpless, as he made her cry again. But she didn't hesitate, didn't pause even for a moment to consider his proposal and that hurt almost as much as her refusal. "This time, Nick, I'm the one who's sorry, but I can't marry you."

Amber realized, in less than twenty-five minutes, that she'd made a mistake. A huge, horrible mistake. During the remainder of Joey's nap, she went over every word Nick had said, every plea he'd made, and every reply she'd used to cut him down.

She cried and raged and gradually realized she was a fool. When her tears stopped, she remembered the look on Nick's face when he'd left the house, the anguish, the disappointment, and the grief in his eyes, and she cried all over again.

She let go and cried, hard, wracking sobs, for all the mistakes he'd made and all the pain he'd caused her when he'd left and for all the mistakes and all the pain she'd caused him since he'd been home.

Her throat ached and her eyes burned, but she was calm by the time Joey woke up from his nap and shuffled down the hall in his stocking feet. With Daisy beside him and Yellow Pup hanging by one paw from his little hand, he demanded to know where Nick had gone.

Instead of worrying about how she might someday have to explain to Joey that Nick had left for good, she knew that Nick was right about everything he'd said. She had been punishing him for leaving her. She hadn't even realized what she'd been doing until he'd forced her to see the truth.

She had flaunted his son in front of him, knowing he wouldn't go against his word and tell Joey the truth. And by punishing Nick, she'd been punishing Joey, too.

Joey should know Nick was his father. He'd lost

one father already. Circumstances had given him back his biological one. Who was she to keep the two of them apart? Joey loved Nick. Nick loved Joey. She had to believe that would be enough.

She swept Joey into her arms, holding him tight. Would Nick ever forgive her? Oh, God, she prayed, please don't let him be as stupid and stubborn as I've been.

"Squishin' me, Mama," Joey complained, and she immediately set him loose. He swayed a little and knuckled both his eyes. "Want Uncle Nick."

"Me, too, baby. Me, too." She kissed her son's sleep-flushed cheek. "He's out in the bunkhouse and I'll go get him in a minute, but I have to talk to you first. Will you come and sit on the sofa with me for just a few minutes?"

"Gotta pee."

"Of course you do." She laughed. "Let's go, and then we're going to talk."

"Then Uncle Nick?"

"Then I'll get Uncle Nick."

"Hurry, Mama."

Oh yes, she'd hurry.

She took care of her son's most urgent needs. Talked with him over a snack of honey bread and milk and left him in the house with Daisy while she ran across the yard through the rain to the bunkhouse.

Only a couple of other men were there when she pushed open the door. She must have looked fanatically determined, because they made their excuses and slipped out past her in no time, leaving her alone with Nick, who refused to look at her.

He had his bedroll open and was methodically packing his belongings. "Leave me alone, Amber. I got it, finally."

"You're leaving?" Fear, stark and absolute, knotted inside her.

"Don't get your hopes up." His voice was hard. "I won't be gone long, just a week or so, checking fences, looking for strays, that kind of thing. I'll stay in the line shack along the ranch's northern boundary."

"But the storm . . . you can't go out in this."

"I've been out in worse."

"W—will you do me a favor first?"

"What?" He looked up from packing clothes into his bedroll, watching her warily, and she didn't blame him.

"Will you say good-bye to Joey before you leave? He's awake from his nap and asking for you." She tried to smile through her panic. "Loudly."

"Joey does everything loudly." Nick rolled up the bedroll and tied it closed "I wasn't going to leave without saying good-bye to him."

She nodded.

"I'll be over in a few minutes," he told her. "I'm almost done here."

"Hurry, okay?"

Their gazes locked and his jaw tightened. "The sooner I say goodbye to Joey, the sooner I'm gone? Are you that anxious to get rid of me, Amber?"

"No," she whispered, again realizing how badly she'd hurt him. "Just hurry."

She left the door of the bunkhouse open when she left and ran back across the yard to the house. Joey was waiting when she stepped into the house.

"Where's . . . ?"

"He's coming, baby." She removed her jacket and shook off the rain, wiped a hand over her face, and tidied her hair, which was nearly plastered to her scalp. By the time she'd hung up the wet garment, Nick appeared in the open doorway.

He stepped inside. Rain dripped from his hat to his shoulders, which were covered by a slicker, and immediately created a small puddle on the floor beneath his boots.

He knelt in front of Joey. "Did you have a good nap?"

Amber watched, her heart pounding hard, while her son studied his father with wide-eyed curiosity. For long moments, he was uncharacteristically still and quiet.

"You're not my uncle. You're my daddy." Joey held Yellow Pup tight against his tiny chest and cocked his head to one side. "Mama said I'm your little boy."

Nick went completely still. His lips parted but no sound came out. Clearly astounded and speechless, he gazed up at her.

She gave him a tremulous smile. "Can I take your coat? Will you stay?"

"What . . . ? Yeah." His gaze went back to Joey. He stood and removed his wet slicker and hat without taking his eyes off his son. Amber took them and hung them next to hers.

Nick was still standing stock-still and Joey was quiet, too. She scooped him up into her arms and carried him to the sofa. Almost mesmerized, Nick followed and sat beside them.

Joey watched Nick through lowered lashes from the safety of her arms. "Mama said, if I want, I can call you daddy."

Nick closed his eyes. When they opened, she could see tears welling there. His voice rusty, he asked, "Do you want to call me daddy?"

"I guess so." Joey said, shyly. "How come you're cryin'?"

"Am I?" Nick rubbed the backs of his hands across his face. "Guess I am."

"Do you have a booboo? I can kiss it all better."

Before Nick could react, Joey had scrambled off her lap and onto his father's. The little boy threw his arms around his father's neck, then leaned back, and planted a loud kiss on Nick's damp cheek.

"All better, Daddy?"

Nick's eyes closed and his arms tightened around his son. His voice choked, he replied, "All better, Joey."

Tears blurred her vision as she watched the two of them locked together.

"Squishin' me, Daddy!" Joey giggled, wiggling to be free. Nick released him and once on the floor, Joey launched himself onto Daisy, who had settled on the floor near their feet. The dog woofed and rose to chase Joey, who was whooping and laughing and running circles around the sofa.

Amber smiled through her tears. Joey was back to normal.

She turned to Nick, and his arms came around her. He buried his face in her neck. She stroked a hand through his hair and held on tight.

"Thank you," he whispered.

"You're welcome." She drew back, cupping his face, stroking his cheek. "I should have told him weeks ago."

"He knows now." He turned his face to kiss the inside of her palm. "That's all that matters."

"He doesn't really understand. Not right now," she warned and then soothed, "but he will when he's older."

"I know, but at least now he'll call me daddy instead of Uncle Nick. I hated hearing that from him after I knew the truth."

"I was wrong to keep him from you—"

"Shh, that's over."

He cupped the nape of her neck, brought her forward, and kissed her with such wonderful tenderness that she almost forgot what she needed to say, but she owed him something. She pushed back, pressing a hand against his chest.

"I need to say this, please, Nick. I need you to hear it."

"All right." He leaned back but didn't release her. One strong, callused hand continued to stroke her cheek, her jaw, her shoulder, up and down her arm.

She took a deep breath, knowing this wouldn't be easy to say or for him to hear, but they needed to clear things between them before they could move on. "I love you, Nick. I didn't want to and until you came back, I'd thought maybe I was over you. I was wrong. After you came home, I told myself if I had any pride, I wouldn't let myself still be in love with you. I thought I should hate you, and when I didn't, I hated myself instead."

His hand found hers and squeezed. "Amber—"

"Please, just listen." He nodded and she continued. "I've always loved you, even when I cursed you and cried over you, I still loved you. I'd rather take a chance on our love and risk being wrong again than regret for the rest of my life never taking the chance at all."

"You aren't wrong, honey, and I won't make you sorry this time."

She believed him. With all her heart, she believed him. "I know you won't."

"You're stuck with me, you and Joey. For better because we've been through the worse, if you'll have me."

"Is that a proposal?"

"Damn straight it is. I'd get down on one knee, but the last time I did you said no." He smiled, confident, daring, and impossible to resist. "What do you say this time?"

"Yes." She threw her arms around his neck. "Yes, yes, *yes!*"

"Yes, yes, yes!" Joey singsonged while Daisy barked. They picked him up, included him in the hug, and danced around the room while chaos reined until Joey wiggled to get down. "Squishin' me! Squishin' me!"

They were married one week later on Valentine's Day—four years after their original wedding date.

By spring, Amber was pregnant again. This time, Nick was with her through the morning sickness, swollen ankles and backaches. He was there to hold her hand and encourage her throughout the birth.

Joey was thrilled to learn he was going to have a baby brother or sister. Still at the age where he thought all girls except his mama and grandma were yucky, he told anyone who would listen that he wanted a brother.

By Christmas, he got his wish. The following year, his parents presented him with another brother and on Valentine's Day a couple of years later, they gave him his first sister. By then, he was seven years old and although he still thought most girls were yucky, he decided his sister wasn't so bad.

Amber never once regretted her decision to take

another chance on loving Nick, and his gaze never again strayed to the horizon. He'd found the best part of the whole world right there on that small ranch in southwestern Nevada . . . the woman he'd always loved and the children their love created.

WINTER ROSES

Allison Knight

One

February 14, 1841,
Northampton, England

He was bored out of his mind.

Gavin Sinclair, Baron Dunleigh, wondered why he had come here as he watched a bevy of beautiful women whirl around the ballroom in their colorful gowns. He gazed at the guests milling around the lace-covered pillars festooned with red and white roses. All that was missing from the decorations were the ivy leaves advertising the occasion as a prelude to a proposal of marriage.

Gavin groaned. The last thing he wanted on his mind, and on the minds of half the single men in attendance he'd wager, was wedlock. Still, from the number of people attending this event, Lady Sutton's Valentine's Day ball would be declared a smashing success even if no betrothals resulted.

Gavin glanced toward the front arch embellished with smiling cupids, golden arrows, and festive hearts. Restless, he sipped a glass of inferior champagne, and wondered how soon it would be before he could take his leave.

He patted the pocket of his jacket. At least he didn't have to worry about his younger brother. Kenneth's message had arrived before Gavin left for the ball. The note assured Gavin that although Kenneth had some unfinished business, he would sail on the *Valiant Lady* in ten days, freeing Gavin from a necessary trip to their Caribbean property. About time Kenneth began to take an active part in their business enterprises despite his arguments.

"My lord," a voice interrupted his thoughts.

Gavin spun toward the speaker. Lawrence Oxley, a good friend of Kenneth's, stood before him, a worried look marring his effeminate features.

"What is it, Lawrence?" The young man seemed upset. Gavin waited for him to speak, hoping against hope that Kenneth was not involved in another fracas.

"Sir, I'm sorry to bother you, but . . ." He glanced at the crowd and murmured, "Someplace not so—so crowded?"

Gavin led him to a small alcove off the main hall.

"Better?" Gavin asked.

The young man nodded and gulped—hard.

"I'm sorry but I can't keep this to myself a minute longer. Kenneth will want to kill me, but I do believe you ought to know."

Gavin scowled. Kenneth! He'd been correct in assuming his younger brother was in trouble, yet again.

"Well, man, what is it that you think I should know?"

Once again Lawrence cleared his throat. "He's getting married. Going to Gretna Green."

An elopement! Gavin glowered at Lawrence. "When?"

"Tonight, my lord!"

Gavin felt his upper lip curl in disgust. He pulled his pocket watch from his vest and glanced at it. "I could have used more time to stop this affair."

"Sorry, my lord. It took some time to find you."

"I take it that you know whom he intends to wed and where." Gavin tossed his sarcastic words out. Kenneth had been nothing if not trouble from the moment Gavin took over his care after the death of their parents. Their recent verbal battles were legion.

Lawrence swallowed again, his Adam's apple bobbing against his collar. "Where but not whom. Oh, I've seen the girl but I don't know her name. She had her come-out last year. You had to have met her."

"I was at my Caribbean plantation last summer so I missed the Season. Don't you know anything about the girl?"

Lawrence seemed to be studying the floor for answers. Again, he cleared his throat. "I know she was sponsored by Lady Sophia Palmer."

Gavin groaned and slapped his hand against his forehead. "Sophia Palmer. My Gawd, that woman is a menace, an eccentric of the first water. She's anything but a lady. Have you no other information?"

"Her father was in the military," Lawrence murmured, as if that information might have some value.

"All right." Gavin realized Lawrence could tell him nothing further. "At least tell me where my brother is meeting this person."

Long after dark, Meredith Ward paced the first floor of the empty cottage. It was deathly quiet with everyone gone. She should have asked Bessy to stay the night, instead she'd sent the exhausted maid to her own home.

Merry lifted the lantern and started up the steps, thinking about the frantic activities of the week. On Monday her father had left for the Continent. Her stepmother's property needed attention. They'd spent nearly a week, mending, cleaning, and packing the clothing he needed for the trip.

Then Aunt Sophia had arrived yesterday, and announced that she wanted Charlotte to go with her to a northern estate, a party, one that would last a week. Once more, mending, cleaning, and packing garments had consumed all the rest of that day and today as well. It had been four o'clock before the carriage pulled away from the cottage.

Of course, Merry hadn't been invited and she winced, remembering the apologetic murmurs of both Aunt Sophia and Charlotte. Aunt Sophia had sighed. Merry, she said, had never had a Season, so her wardrobe was dismally unfashionable. Besides, Merry had to remain at the cottage in case her father sent word of some kind. There was no way Merry could accompany them.

Charlotte had hugged Merry with tears in her eyes. "I wish you could go. But Aunt Sophia's right. You would be so uncomfortable you'd be miserable."

Merry shrugged. Charlotte knew her so well. Although five years older than Charlotte, Merry knew her eighteen-year-old stepsister was prettier and enjoyed balls and parties more than she did. Merry really didn't mind that at the time there hadn't been enough money for her to have a Season. She was shy and had a difficult time mingling with people.

She and London would not have mixed well together.

Fortunately, Charlotte had had a Season. Aunt Sophia had sponsored her. Merry had been content to stay at home and care for her father.

She knew she wasn't the beauty her sister was, nor did she have the sparkling personality Charlotte possessed. Still, once in a while the thought of enjoying an evening, or even a weekend party, teased her imagination. Just one time it might have been fun.

Merry raised the lamp and opened the door to the room she shared with Charlotte. She set the lantern on the table beside the bed and gazed at the discarded gowns still draped over the dresser, bed, and chair. Silently, Merry began to pick up the garments and put them away.

When she had finished, she glanced around the room, pleased with the results. Merry couldn't stand confusion. A piece of paper caught her attention. She reached down and snatched the envelope. She lifted it toward the lantern. It was still sealed and bore no name on the cover.

She turned the paper over and over in her hands. When had it been delivered? Had it been meant for Charlotte or for her? Should she open it, or leave it until Charlotte returned?

Merry tapped the paper against her finger, wondering what she should do. Finally, she broke the seal, lifted the flap, and pulled a piece of paper lace from its enclosure. A valentine! She sighed with relief, not certain what she'd expected.

An oval picture of red and white roses encircled with ivy rested against a square of paper lace. Red and white roses? Entwined with ivy? Marriage?

Merry didn't bother with the sentiment printed over the roses because a note fell away from the lace. She grabbed the paper from the floor and leaned closer to the lamp. With increasing dismay she read the bold words spread over the paper.

"At midnight on the fourteenth. Meet me in front of St. Matthew's. I have a special license. Kenneth."

Merry stared at the words.

Special license? At St. Matthew's? The fourteenth?

Oh, no.

Kenneth planned to elope with her sister this very night! It couldn't be. Merry couldn't allow this. What would her father say? He had left the care of Charlotte in Merry's hands. She closed her eyes. She could hear his entreaty, *Now, don't let that sister of yours get into any trouble. You're older and much more sensible. You take care of her.*

Merry shuddered. An elopement! The family would be disgraced. Of course, Merry ought to have expected something like this. All during Charlotte's Season, and for weeks after, she had talked of nothing else but the handsome young man with the awful brother.

Gavin Sinclair, Baron Dunleigh, was, according to Charlotte, a monster. He had only just returned to England and was already ordering every moment of Kenneth's life. Merry vaguely remembered Charlotte saying something about Kenneth being required to travel to some island off the coast of the United States at the behest of his brother. Merry couldn't believe Charlotte thought marriage to Kenneth would change his big brother's attitude. It would only make it worse, much worse.

Merry chewed on her lower lip, trying to decide

what she should do. She hesitated, wondering if Charlotte had been expecting this letter. If she had, why hadn't she opened it? She grimaced; all she could do was thank the good Lord that Aunt Sophia had arrived and somehow this had been overlooked.

Merry knew she had to stop this foolishness. She had to discourage this young man before any harm could be done.

Thank God Charlotte was not at home. And thank the good Lord her father was out of the country. She had time to straighten out this mess. When Charlotte returned from her weekend with Aunt Sophia, Merry planned to make it clear to her sister that the days of her acting irresponsibly were over.

Placing the lantern on her bedside table, she slipped on her hose and reached for her boots. Shedding her gown, she stepped into her dark gray riding habit. It was less than an hour's ride to St. Matthew's. Telling Kenneth Sinclair that her sister was no longer available would take no time at all, then she could return home. She also intended to give him a good piece of her mind. Imagine asking a girl barely turned eighteen to leave the safety of her home and travel an hour just to meet him! The unmitigated gall of the man.

For a moment she considered her own safety; however, her family's honor was worth almost any sacrifice. Besides, she was dressed in dark clothing. Her cloak was black and the horse was named appropriately. Blackie had one hoof that bore a trace of white. No one would even notice her.

The valentine and the note seemed to glow in the light of the lantern. Merry stuffed them into her reticule and looped it around her wrist. She grabbed her cloak and rushed down the stairs. She let herself out the back door and hurried toward the stable.

A cold night wind slapped her in the face and she drew her cloak around her. It was highly unlikely that she would meet anyone on a frosty night like this. She had little to worry about.

A quarter moon shed little light as it climbed into the sky. Soon she would be back in her warm bed, her sister's suitor sent on his way.

St. Matthew's at midnight! And with a special license. Just who did Kenneth Sinclair think he was? A copy of the rogue of a brother he was wont to criticize?

The carriage swung from side to side and the flames in the lamps swayed with the motion of the vehicle. Gavin tried to relax. It was useless.

"I can't believe Kenneth would try something like this," he muttered into the empty space around him. Gavin didn't care if the woman's father was a military man. Whoever she was, she couldn't be the kind of woman he wanted for his brother.

Besides, Kenneth wasn't mature enough to consider marriage. However, now that the boy had passed his twenty-second year, Kenneth believed he should be able to do whatever he wanted, without any regard for what Gavin knew was best; he refused to pay any attention to what Gavin said.

Gavin sighed and wondered if he could find passage on a ship leaving England in the next day or two. He had to get his brother out of the country. And fast!

Suddenly the coachman yelled and the carriage

rocked. Something had struck the side followed by an inhuman scream.

"What the . . ." Gavin lurched forward.

He reached for the door as the coachman shouted for the horses to halt. Before they completely stopped, Gavin sprang from the conveyance.

"What was it?" he asked the coachman as the man tied the strings to the brake.

"Horse and rider, my lord. Ran right into us. Horse reared, hit the carriage, and the rider fell off. Back there." He pointed toward the rear of the coach.

"Bloody hell." Gavin snarled. He grabbed a lantern and started running back down the road. The thrashing and screams of an injured animal told Gavin more than he wanted to hear.

The coachman ran behind him. "Here, my lord. Sounds like you'll need this."

Gavin grunted and paused to accept the pistol the man held out. Suddenly ten years fell away as if they had never existed and the worst day of his life flashed before Gavin's eyes. His parents and his sister had been in a coach when it had hit a half-buried rock. The carriage had rolled, one of the horses had broken a leg, his father and sister had been thrown from the vehicle, and his mother had been crushed under the flaying horse.

They had been traveling through the wilds of Scotland, not a soul in sight, on the way to Gwen's wedding. It had been a joyous trip, Gwen going to Scotland to speak her vows with the man of her dreams. Gavin had joined his parents the night before to be on hand when his sister married. He'd elected to ride rather than tie his mount to the rear of the coach or he would have suffered the same fate.

The sounds of the injured creature drew Gavin from his thoughts. He raised the carriage lamp above his head and gazed into the gloom. Nothing yet, although the cries were louder.

A chill cut through Gavin. If the animal was this badly injured, what about the rider? Again, thoughts of that day ten years ago engulfed him. He had been able to do nothing for his mother, but he had assured his injured father and his sister he would find help and return immediately. It had been hours before he found any locals and trying to get those suspicious Scots to return with him to the scene of the accident had almost devastated him.

Finally, an old woman who could barely walk, offered assistance. But it was too late. His father had already passed on, and his sister died in his arms.

He shuddered with the memories. Well, this stranger didn't have to worry. Gavin would offer all the aid needed to get the man on his feet, no matter what it took.

He saw the horse first, a dark mount with one white stocking. The animal bellowed in agony. It was obvious one leg was broken and Gavin did the only thing he could. He quickly put it out of its misery.

Then he looked around for the rider. But there was something about that horse that caught him. He gazed at the dead animal.

Bloody hell! A sidesaddle. A woman? No, it couldn't be. He raised the lantern, frantic now. What if she was unconscious?

The coachman was beside him, panting heavily.

"M'lord, I heard the shot. Figured you might need some help."

"Stay with my carriage. I'll call if I need you. We may need to go for assistance."

The coachman nodded and trotted back toward the carriage. The one lamp left in the vehicle offered a muted glow in the black night. Swearing, Gavin raised the lantern and gazed into the darkness. She had to be around here someplace.

Gavin shouted, "Whoever you are, can you hear me?"

He tramped back and forth through the undergrowth, rationalizing that if she'd been thrown, she would not be in the road. He was about to call the coachman back to help in the search when he saw dark clothing heaped next to a log.

He rushed forward, struggling with warring emotions. If she was still alive, he would make certain she survived, but he had to wonder what a woman was doing riding through the countryside at this time of night.

Carefully, he rolled her over. She groaned and he nearly shouted with joy. She wasn't dead.

But she was unconscious. With shaking hands he placed the lantern against the base of the log and gazed at her face. He brushed the hair away and gently ran his hands down her neck, over her arms and legs and knew he should attempt to determine if there might be other injuries. Carefully, he patted her ribs, her hips, her thighs.

Her reticule hung from her wrist and he opened the bag, hoping to determine who she was and where she lived.

He examined the contents. A paper lace valentine, a note, a handkerchief, and six shillings were all it

contained. Holding the valentine to the lamp, he
read the bold scrawl across the bottom and shock
reverberated through him.

Kenneth's signature graced the oval of roses and
ivy. He opened the note and read Kenneth's message. A calculating smile lifted the corners of his
mouth. He needn't worry about finding Kenneth
passage on another ship. No, all he had to do was
hold this woman until Kenneth sailed.

She groaned again, and Gavin stuffed the valentine and note back in the reticule. She was coming
around.

"Where do you hurt?" Gavin asked.

She looked startled, then she tried to sit up.

Gavin placed a hand against her shoulder. "Don't
try to move," he said. She was pretty, but certainly
not the beauty Gavin knew his brother to have pursued.

She grabbed at his hand. "What time is it? How
long have I been here?"

"Only a short time. It's not yet ten-thirty." Gavin
tried to restrain his smile of satisfaction. Oh, yes,
this was Kenneth's bride.

"Please, help me up. I must be on my way.
Please."

Gavin was struck by the pleading tone in her
voice, but he wasn't about to tell her she wasn't
going anywhere she wanted to go. Not just yet.

"I'm afraid you have to depend on me tonight.
Your horse had to be put down."

"Oh, no," she whimpered. She took a deep breath
and added, "Please, sir, help me. I must get to St.
Matthew's before midnight."

"I think not."

Merry tried to shift herself into a sitting position

but her pounding head prevented it. She stared at the man. His face was in shadows and she could barely make out his features. Who was he?

Before she could ask, he turned to her. "Tell me who you are, and what you are doing out at this time of night. It is not safe for a woman to be traveling around the countryside in the dark."

"My name is Merry. I have to get to St. Matthew's before midnight."

"And is your aunt Sophia Palmer of London?"

Merry nodded and reached up to hold her head. The slight movement had liberated the pain in her head and she suddenly had the most horrid headache. For an instant she wondered how he had connected her to Aunt Sophia; however, her head was hammering so hard she couldn't think straight.

"Sir, who are you?" she whispered.

He grinned at her. "My name is Gavin Sinclair, Baron Dunleigh. I believe you know my brother."

She sighed with relief. What a coincidence! "Yes, I know your brother. Thank the good Lord you are here. You must help me. Your broth—"

"Oh, I believe you could say that I am helping you. Now, you must tell me where you live. I'll send a note telling them of your injuries," he stated.

"No, no," Merry blurted. "There is no one there. Please, we must get to St. Matthew's."

"Your destination has been changed. You may have injuries of which you are not aware. Until I've had my doctor examine you, you must consider yourself my guest."

Merry wailed with frustration. "But, sir, your brother is about to marry—" she tried to explain.

"No, he is not," he interrupted. Then he smiled. It was a grim smile and not at all reassuring.

Merry heaved a sigh of relief. The baron must have heard about the planned elopement and put a stop to it. She wanted to thank him, but a thousand tiny drums beating inside her head were making her dizzy. She struggled to sit up but he restrained her.

"I'll be back. Don't move," he ordered.

There was no way she could move, not without her head exploding. Why, she couldn't even respond. Trying to speak was now producing an unbearable pain. The whole world seemed to be spinning around her. She closed her eyes and prayed for sleep.

Moments later, against the throb of pain, she heard the jangle of reins and the rumble of carriage wheels. She heard voices and then she was lifted in his arms. His bouncing movements had her groaning in agony. Would her head never stop hurting? He must have sensed her discomfort, for he eased her gently onto the seat of the carriage.

"We're going to my home now," he told her as he took the seat opposite her. "We'll worry about your home at a later time."

Merry struggled against the dull thud behind her eyes and prayed for unconsciousness. She didn't have to worry about Charlotte disgracing the family. Kenneth's brother had stopped them.

The carriage began to move and Merry gratefully sank into a sea of black nothingness.

Two

Several times during the carriage ride, Merry regained her senses only to be plunged back into unconsciousness when the carriage hit a particularly bad bump. Each time she came to, she tried to raise into a sitting position, but dizziness had her sagging back onto the leather seat. Fortunately, Gavin asked nothing of her for she knew she couldn't have managed a sensible answer.

When the carriage finally stopped, Merry wondered if she would be able to enter the house under her own power. She wasn't given a chance to find out. Gavin had her in his arms before she'd managed to open her eyes.

She gave serious thought to demanding that he take her to her own home. However, she knew she was in no shape to argue with him just now. Perhaps in an hour or two, when the world stopped spinning and her head quit pounding. Then she would ask that he provide transportation to get to her cottage.

A fleeting thought about Blackie brought tears to the back of her eyes. She had been in such a hurry to get to the church, she hadn't noticed the carriage until it was too late. And now the horse was dead.

Poor Blackie. He hadn't been the fastest or the most handsome of steeds but he had been with the family for almost ten years now.

She groaned silently. How on earth was she going to explain Blackie's death to her father? She'd have to admit it was her fault, that she'd gone out at night. And then she would also have to tell her father about Charlotte's attempted elopement.

Before Merry could gather more thoughts, the baron eased her onto a feather mattress. She sighed with relief. Now, if she could remain quiet for a time, surely she would soon be herself.

She lay still wondering what would happen if she asked for water, when a soft feminine voice forced her to open her eyes. She blinked several times, trying to bring the blurred faces together.

"Close your eyes, dear. Don't strain yerself."

Merry followed the woman's instructions even though she wanted to ask who the woman was. What little Merry could tell, the woman was older. The mother of Lord Dunleigh and his brother?

The voice answered the unasked question. "I'm Lord Dunleigh's housekeeper. I'm going to get you undressed before the doctor comes."

Merry's eyes flew open and she groaned as the bed that was beneath her spun around. Even the ceiling refused to stay still.

"I don't want to see a doctor," she whispered.

"Well, my dear"—the woman leaned down and whispered back—"you don't have a choice. His lordship has already called for the man. Now, you just lie there, and I'll do all the work. Then after the doctor has checked on you, I'll see about some rose water for your head."

Gentle hands eased the garments from Merry's

body. "Your riding habit is ripped. We'll have to see about getting this repaired. Oh dear. There are all kinds of scrapes on your arms and legs."

When the shift was lifted from Merry's skin, the woman's gasp forced Merry to open her eyes again.

"I'll wager you are going to have some bad bruises," the woman muttered. "The doctor will want to tend to them. Now, I have one of his lordship's shirts for you."

Merry felt soft cotton caress her skin.

"Your name?" Merry asked.

"Oh, my dear, I'm Mrs. Perry, the housekeeper. I've been with his lordship for as long as he's had the title, ten years now."

Merry tried to smile but the effort hurt her head.

"Now," Mrs. Perry said, "I'll just tuck you in and tell Lord Dunleigh that you are ready to see the doctor. Uh, dear"—she paused—"would you want me to stay with you when the doctor comes?"

"Could you?" Merry asked, her voice thick with fear.

"I'll be happy to do that," she responded.

The doctor was gray-haired and just a bit gruff, but Merry tried to answer his questions. Mrs. Perry's presence helped. The doctor treated her cuts and scrapes and announced that, except for the headache, he could find no serious injuries. Then he patted her shoulder and told her she would recover. He left, probably to tell his lordship of his findings.

Mrs. Perry tiptoed from the bedroom with the whispered order, "You get some rest now."

Merry sighed and snuggled under the warm duvet. In an hour or two, she'd be ready to inform Lord Dunleigh that she'd like to go home. Of course, she'd have to thank him profusely for caring for her and for stopping the elopement that had caused all the trouble. She closed her eyes and drifted off to sleep.

Something pulled her from her dreams and Merry dragged herself into a sitting position. A dull ache behind her eyes brought her awake and she gazed about her. Sunlight, bright and crisp, shone through the windows. Oh, no! She'd slept through the whole night.

A deep male voice had her slipping back under the covers, fear coursing through her. She turned her head toward the voice, certain she knew its owner.

Stunned, her gaze froze. Gavin Sinclair, Baron Dunleigh, quite took her breath away. Never had she seen such a handsome man. He was tall, much taller than the few men she had met, perhaps a good three inches above her father's six feet.

He was watching her with the darkest blue eyes Merry had ever seen. Brown arched brows were raised in question and a mat of dark curls covered his head. His voice rumbled through her, causing the oddest sensation. She felt first hot, then cold, as goose bumps crept over her skin.

"How are you feeling this morning?" he asked.

She winced as she moved her head.

"It still hurts a bit, but my headache's not a real problem. I do have a large knot that's sore to the touch. I'm feeling well enough considering the tumble I took."

She shut her mouth in dismay. She was blabbering. She never chattered like that, certainly not around strangers, and Dunleigh was definitely a stranger. Had the bump on her head scrambled her brains? Or was the appearance of this man somehow affecting her head? But that was ridiculous.

She had never met a man who'd made this strong
an impression on her before. Surely Dunleigh was
no different from other men.

"I'm glad to hear that, although I imagine you'll
be sore for several days." He nodded and started for
the door. "I'll send Mrs. Perry up with a tray and
if you feel like it, I'll have water heated for a bath."

Merry cleared her throat. "Really, you don't need
to go to any trouble. I would like to go home now."

He gave her the oddest look and shook his head.
"I think not. Bed rest is what you need, at least for
today."

Merry started to shake her head, but the pain
she'd experienced when she awoke had become a lot
more intense. She rested her head on the pillow and
lay perfectly still, willing the ache away. No, she
had to go home. Maybe after she had a bit to eat
she would feel more like herself. One thing she did
know. She didn't like the sensations Gavin Sinclair
caused in her and she needed to get away from
him—the sooner the better.

Eating didn't help much and the rest of the day
floated past, with Mrs. Perry and Dunleigh himself
stopping by to see how she was faring. Merry slept
much of the time away. She blamed the work involved in preparing for her sister's week away and
the worry over Charlotte's attempted elopement as
much as the accident the night before for her fatigue.

Nevertheless by the time the sun had started to
set, she was more than ready to go home. She
wanted to go home, needed to. She shouldn't be
here. For some reason she didn't understand, Dunleigh frightened her. She decided that when next he
came to her room she would offer her thanks then

request transportation to take her to the cottage. It was truly fortunate that she'd told Bessy to stay home and rest for a day or two. For the present, Merry's absence would probably go unnoticed.

She could only hope that Gavin Sinclair had told his young brother to leave Charlotte alone. She didn't need Kenneth arriving at a deserted cottage. She would have to question his lordship about what he had told the younger man before Merry left.

In his study on the first floor, Gavin watched the sun disappear behind a wall of oak trees that marked the end of the drive. His hands clasped behind his back, he paced the room he used for business when he was at Dunleigh Manor. At least the woman was not seriously injured.

He'd been startled when he'd discovered that Merry was his brother's ladylove. For one thing, Gavin had assumed that his brother had pledged himself to a much younger woman. This Merry appeared to be older than Kenneth. And she just had her first Season?

"Strange," he muttered. Girls having their first Season were usually much younger that twenty-three or -four.

Another thing that had startled Gavin was the woman herself. She wasn't beautiful. Pretty, pleasant to look at, but not the kind of beauty his brother usually fancied. No, this Merry was attractive, but she was tall for a woman. He would have to describe her as statuesque, curvaceous, but much more conservative than the women Kenneth liked to partner. In fact, Mrs. Perry had commented that her riding attire which had to be repaired was long out of style, and had been worn around the edges. No money in that family, for a fact.

It didn't matter, for she was upstairs in one of his rooms and not wrapped around Kenneth. Obviously, this whole liaison had more to do with money and position than anything else, at least on her part. And Sophia Palmer had introduced her to society. He groaned and paused before the fireplace. He gazed at the flames, trying to remember what he'd heard about Sophia Palmer.

He'd met her once several years ago, when Louis Palmer was still alive. She had been eccentric even then, leaving her aging barrister husband at home alone while she played at the gaming tables of London. She flitted from one establishment to another, always attired in atrocious costumes, trying to disguise herself, but everyone in the place knew who she was. And as disgusting as it had been, the woman rarely lost at cards.

He'd heard more than one tale about her expertise, had even heard rumors the woman was not that skilled at cards, but rather that she was an accomplished cheat. He rubbed his chin as he started to pace again. Could the family be full of cheats? That might explain why this Merry had made a play for Kenneth. He struck his forehead with the palm of his hand. Of course. She was after money—Sinclair money.

So, what was he going to do with the woman he'd brought home with him last night? He couldn't let her leave. She would probably waste no time in contacting Kenneth and making other plans. Gavin didn't want that. No, he had to keep the two of them apart until Kenneth sailed for Barbados. The journey there and back would take at least five months, perhaps six. In that amount of time, this Merry would have found some other nabob to wed.

Still, this situation presented a problem. How was he going to keep her here? He wasn't about to lie to her. Oh, it was all right to indicate that, for at least today and probably tomorrow as well, she needed to recuperate, but that excuse would only last through tomorrow, if that long.

He would tell her the truth. He'd explain that he didn't approve of Kenneth marrying her, and he would ask her to stay at the estate until his brother had sailed. He grinned. Without transport, she'd stay right where she was.

With his decision made, Gavin left the study and made his way to his dining room. Suddenly, the tension of the last twenty-four hours dissipated. He realized how hungry he was.

"Mrs. Perry," he called, "tell Cook I'm ready to eat now."

He wasn't coming to check on her and that thought frightened her. She'd told him she wanted to go home. As a gentleman, he had to know she couldn't stay here. Come tomorrow, she'd insist that Mrs. Perry take her to see Dunleigh. She'd thank him for his hospitality, and ask if he could spare a conveyance to see her to the cottage. If he refused, she would have to make her own arrangements. Surely there was a village close by where she could hire someone to see her home.

She snuggled under the duvet and closed her eyes. She also had to figure out a way to tell her father about Blackie, without admitting her part in his death or her sister's outrageous plans.

A sharp knock on the bedroom door brought Merry out of a deep sleep. She glanced at the window, disgusted to see sunlight pouring into the chamber. Another day! She was still in his lordship's home. Stumbling out of bed, she grabbed the dressing robe Mrs. Perry had provided.

"Yes," she called. "One moment please."

A young woman stood in the doorway with a tray in her hands. "His lordship asked if I would bring you a cup of chocolate and a bun."

"Mrs. Perry?" Merry asked.

"Her sister's been taken ill and his lordship told her to go. I'm Sally. I help out here occasionally."

"Oh dear," Merry mumbled. So much for asking Mrs. Perry to take her to his lordship. "Thank you for the chocolate. Did Mrs. Perry say anything about my clothing being repaired?"

Sally looked puzzled for a moment. "No, can't say as she did. What happened to yer clothes?"

"An accident. Baron Dunleigh brought me here to recuperate, but I'll need my habit or something else to wear home."

Sally nodded her head. "I'll see what I can do. Now I have to serve his lordship's breakfast." The maid set the tray on the small table beside the bed, gave Merry a peculiar smile, and hurried out of the room.

Strange, Merry thought. She had always been given the impression that the peerage had servants falling over each other. She couldn't be certain, but from what little Mrs. Perry had said, she thought there was at least a cook and the housekeeper here. Despite the slight ache in her head, she tried to remember some of the things Charlotte had said about Lord Dunleigh. She distinctly remembered Charlotte saying she'd never met Gavin Sinclair because he was overseeing property in the Caribbean during her Season. Perhaps he hadn't taken the time to hire servants since he had returned.

Servants or no, Merry had to talk to him.

But no lady would go traipsing about a bachelor's home. Sally would have to carry the message that Merry needed to see Lord Dunleigh at the earliest moment possible. And she needed some decent clothing immediately.

By midmorning, anger, along with a healthy dose of fear, began to eat away at Merry. Sally had not yet returned. She had nothing to wear other than Baron Dunleigh's nightshirt and the robe Mrs. Perry had brought while her clothes were being repaired. Gavin Sinclair had not appeared. How on earth could she leave this house dressed as she was?

It was almost time for lunch before Sally reappeared.

"Sally, I need something to wear," Merry said.

"I'll have to ask his lordship." Sally gave her another strange leer.

"Oh, don't bother," Merry nearly shouted, her head starting to pound again. *Just bring me my riding outfit.*

Sally glared at her and tromped out of the room.

A short time later, another knock sounded on the door. Merry threw open the door, ready to demand that Sally take her to Lord Dunleigh, dressed inappropriately or not. Instead, she stared up into the dark blue eyes of Gavin Sinclair.

"Sally has been dismissed. I'll have to see to your needs for a short time."

Merry stared at him. Had he no other servants? Was she all alone with this man in this house? Something strange and wild fluttered in the region of her heart.

She felt faint at the thought. No lady occupied the dwelling of a single gentleman without destroying her reputation. Her fear escalated into horror. Gavin Sinclair, Baron Dunleigh, had ruined her!

He raised his arm toward her and Merry cringed.

"These belonged to my sister," he offered quietly. "They are not in fashion, but they will have to do for the present."

Merry swallowed against the concern that threatened to close her throat, realizing that he carried an armload of gowns.

"Thank you," she managed.

"Lunch will be served in half an hour. Can you be ready in that amount of time?"

Merry nodded her head. She couldn't say a word. Her throat had closed in alarm. She would eat lunch and then she would take her leave. No matter what, she would go home.

He started toward the stairs, then stopped.

"Turn left at the end of the staircase. The dining room is the second door on the right," he instructed.

She nodded and closed the door softly. She changed as quickly as she could, still sore from her late-night accident. Careful of the swollen knot on her head, she ran her fingers through her hair. She should braid the strands, but her head was still much too sore.

Despite the problem with her hair, in less than half an hour, she was dressed. The gown she chose was inches too short, and a bit snug through the bodice, but it would do. At least she was clothed for her departure. And depart she would.

She made her way down the stairs and turned left as he had directed. She found the dining room with

no difficulty and stepped inside as he entered
through another doorway.

Once more the most intense sensation took hold
of her. She struggled to contain the shiver that raced
through her. It had to be fear. Of course, she was
terrified of the man.

"Please, sit down," he said, his voice rubbing her
overwrought nerves.

The table was laid for two and Merry wondered
who else was in the house. There had to be a cook,
for she couldn't imagine him setting a table as well
as cooking a meal.

"Cook will serve in just a minute," he said and
Merry decided he read her mind. She stared down
at the table. Should she tell him now that she
needed some kind of transportation home, or should
she wait until they had finished eating?

Now she decided and opened her mouth to make
her request. At precisely that moment, the door
swung open and a woman of considerable age
marched into the room, carrying a tureen. The sa-
vory scent of spicy soup stirred the air. That smell
answered Merry's question for her. First, she would
eat.

Despite the difficult situation and her concern to
leave, Merry thoroughly enjoyed the meal. Cook
was a talented chef and Merry expressed her pleasure over each dish when Cook appeared with the
next offering. The older woman looked unhappy,
and Merry wondered if the cook had any help at
all in the kitchen. She was about to offer her own
services when Gavin Sinclair again seemed to read
her mind.

"Cook will have help in an hour. I hired two
older women from the village this morning."

He rose and said quietly, "Now, I would like to speak to you for a few moments."

Merry nodded. She needed to talk to him as well. She guessed that the topic would be the same. She was ready to leave and he wanted her to go.

She started to express her gratitude for his care but he asked that she wait until they had gained his study. His study? To say a few thank yous and a goodbye. Then she grimaced. Of course, he was going to tell her what he had told his brother. Perhaps he knew Cook was a gossip and didn't want information about Kenneth spread through the region.

She followed him through the door and took the chair he indicated.

"I want to thank you, sir," she began, "for caring for me. I really appreciate what you've done, but I must take my leave now. However, with Blackie dead, I'm going to need some kind of transportation."

"I'm sorry about your horse, and I didn't mind providing the care you needed. But I'm afraid you are not going anywhere."

She stared at him. Surely she hadn't heard him correctly. "Your lordship, what did you say? I think I must have misunderstood."

"You didn't misunderstand. I said you were not going anywhere."

"But, I—I must."

"No, I'm afraid not."

Merry jumped to her feet, a chill passing through her. "I must go home." She couldn't stay here with him, in an empty house with no chaperone. She didn't know this man, had no idea of what he was capable. She wouldn't be safe.

"You'll be staying for the next nine days." He stood as well.

"Nine days. No, I must go now." She was shouting, but she couldn't help it. She was suddenly scared to death.

"I can't let you leave."

"Why?" she whispered, terrified of his answer. What kind of a monster was Kenneth Sinclair's brother?

"You must know that I can never let my brother marry without my permission."

Merry bristled a bit. These arrogant aristocrats. She didn't care if Kenneth Sinclair married her sister, but only after a proper courtship period and at a decent church service. Definitely not a sordid elopement.

"I don't care about that," she began.

"I didn't think you would," he said, his voice hardening.

"Still, a late-night assignation is not the best way for a marriage to begin," Merry offered, wondering why he seemed angry. "Besides, Kenneth has not asked Father."

"Nor will he." Gavin Sinclair growled.

"Look, my lord, you may not approve, but Kenneth is old enough to do what he believes is right."

"But he's not going to marry you."

Merry stood there, her mouth open. His words roared through her. She was so shocked she could not respond. "M—m—me?" Merry stuttered.

"No, he's not asking your father and he's not saying any vows with you."

"No, no," Merry sputtered, "you don't understand."

"My permission has been denied." He turned

away from her and Merry grabbed at his arm. He had it all wrong.

"He's not wedding me. He's planning to wed my sister."

"Ha!" he shouted back. "Don't give me that. I know exactly what this is all about. I know for a fact that you were on your way to St. Matthew's to meet Kenneth."

She nodded her head as he spoke. "Yes, I was on my way to St. Matthew's. But—"

He didn't give her a chance to explain.

He reached into a drawer of the desk and withdrew a piece of paper.

"I found this in your reticule after you fell from your horse. I'd already been told about the elopement. In fact, I was on my way to stop it when you raced your mount into my carriage." He smiled and Merry wanted to scream. He still had it all wrong.

She took a deep breath. She had to make him understand. "I was on my way to stop my sister from disgracing my family too. Kenneth planned to marry Charlotte, not me."

"Nonsense," he snapped. "A convenient lie. Fortunately, Kenneth is leaving in eight days' time. He's sailing for Barbados and will be gone for six months. The day after he sails, you may go home."

"But I'm not the one he wants to marry," Merry whispered. She couldn't stay here with this man for the next nine days. That was out of the question.

"It matters not. I love my brother dearly, but he doesn't know much about women. I'm not going to let him make a mistake that will destroy his life."

Destroy his life? What about hers?

Three

Merry stomped out of the study. She was so angry she was shaking. What fear she had disappeared in a flurry of rage. How dare he tell her she wasn't leaving! And he was such a fool. She wouldn't consider marrying Kenneth. Why, she was three years older than he, nor was she the sort men pursued—petite and pretty.

Well, Dunleigh wasn't going to stop her. No, he was not. She was going home, and she was going now.

She marched into the dining room. She'd noticed a second door, one Cook had used which Merry knew led to the kitchen. Kitchens were usually at the back of the house. Stables were also at the back of the property. She intended to find the stables and take one of his horses.

In the kitchen, she found herself in an enormous and spotless chamber. The room was empty and Merry sighed with relief. She found a cloak, which looked much like her own, hanging on a peg. She wrapped it around her shoulders and walked out the door.

She found the stable exactly where she thought it would be. Letting herself into the building, she waited for her eyes to adjust to the dim light before she gazed around. Six horses occupied the stalls, but no one came forward. Whoever had driven the coach the night of her injury was not there. Nor was there a stable boy.

She'd have to take care of the horse herself. That was fine. She didn't have to have a saddle. She could ride without one. She'd done it often enough when she was learning to ride.

Merry grabbed one of the bridles and started toward one of the horses. She talked quietly as she approached a small chestnut mare. As she stepped up to the horse, a husky voice stopped her.

"I wouldn't if I were you."

She spun around and stared at the somber face of Lord Dunleigh.

"I'm leaving."

He leaned against the wall. "You don't want to do that."

She cringed as she assessed the amusement glistening from those dark blue eyes. Any moment, she expected to hear him laugh. She bristled.

"Oh, yes I do," she snapped. "Now, I need to borrow this horse. I'll see it returned to you tomorrow."

"I'm going to ask you nicely, Merry." His quiet voice rolled over her like a gentle wave. "Won't you stay here with me until Kenneth sails?"

She glared at him. "No!"

His hand shot out and grabbed her wrist before she blinked. He replaced the bridle on the appropriate peg. "Now, let's go back to the house." He looked undaunted, but she was just as determined.

She struggled against his hold. "I'm leaving. Let go of me."

"Sorry," he murmured. "Now, don't fight me. I don't want to hurt you."

She ground her teeth together and tried to ignore his steadfast gaze. He was not going to let her go, not willingly.

"I want to go home. If you won't let me leave, then you will hurt me."

He smiled at her, and her heart beat faster.

"Come back to the house," he said. "We can discuss this at another time."

She glowered at him, praying he wouldn't see her fear. At his touch her arm had felt like someone had lit a fire in her veins. And that smile. It caused the strangest sensations to rush through her. But it mattered not at all, for he started toward the door of the stable. Would he drag her back if she refused to go? Probably. And add more bruises to her already abused skin.

She twisted her arm and her hand to no avail. She realized he acted with a sense of purpose she wasn't going to be able to disturb. She was going to go back to the house. She had no choice.

And if that wasn't bad enough, she could think of no logical explanation for the heat his touch generated. She shivered. Was this man some kind of devil? For certain, now, she would have to leave this place.

But what would she do if he wouldn't let her go? She had to find a way to get away. She could wait until later, after sunset, then slip out of the house. If she was careful, darkness would cover her movements. Now she knew where the stables were and where she could find what she needed, so she'd wait. She'd leave tonight. He wasn't going to keep her here against her will, not the way he affected her.

Once they were inside the house he stopped in the hallway. "Would you care for a game of cards?" That smile was back.

"I don't play cards," she mumbled.

"And you know Sophia Palmer?" He chuckled. "I'd have thought she'd taught you some of her tricks. Well then, do you play chess?"

She nodded.

"Would you like a game or two? It will help pass the time." He pointed toward the side of the house opposite the dining room. "I have an extensive library. I'm certain there must be something there that will interest you. I give you leave to read any of my books."

She frowned. "You don't have to entertain me. After all, if you refuse to let me leave, then I'm nothing more than your prisoner."

"Now, Merry," he said, his voice exuding charm, "you are not a prisoner. Not unless you deny you are my guest."

She snorted. "Ha! You won't believe me when I tell you I am not my sister. I repeat, I have no desire to wed your brother, and if I don't get home, Charlotte and Kenneth will find a way to make new plans. You had best let me go."

"You're going nowhere," he said quietly. She couldn't help but notice the sternness underlining those words. "Now, let's play a game or two of chess before tea. I'm a formidable player and I have a feeling you might be very good yourself."

Merry sighed. She might as well accept his invitation. At least it would pass the time until tonight.

"All right. Let's play."

She followed him into a room across from the staircase. She gasped as she slipped through the door. Extensive library? She had never seen so many books in one place in her life. She thought of the small number of volumes on which she'd spent her coins over the years. Yet here were hundreds of tomes, three walls full of literature. Oh, what she wouldn't give to spend weeks in this room.

No! She didn't mean that. There was no alternative; she had to quit this place tonight. But for now there was a game of chess to play. She noticed a chessboard set on a small table placed between two chairs and before a mullioned window that looked out over a garden. She let her gaze drift around the rest of the library. To someone like Merry, who could become buried in a world of books, this room was as close to heaven as she thought she could get. She sighed.

"You like to read?" He broke into her thoughts.

"Yes, I do enjoy a good book."

He smiled at her, and her breath caught in her chest. That smile! He was a beautiful man. And that smile touched her heart. Breathing became difficult and she couldn't deny the moisture on the palms of her hands.

Oh, no! What was the matter with her? She couldn't let him do this to her.

She took a step back, and he reached out to touch her arm, forcing her to a stop. His fingers felt like a firebrand, searing her skin. She stared at him, instinctively knowing something significant had passed between them. His dark blue eyes scorched her soul. Her mouth suddenly became dry and she licked her lips. She had to get away from this man immediately.

"The game?" he asked. His voice slid through her, warming her insides, and she shook her head to clear her jumbled thoughts.

The game. What game?

He pointed toward the chessboard and she remembered. "Yes, let's play," she muttered. Anything to keep her mind occupied on something other than Dunleigh. She moved to the table and sat before the black figures.

He took the chair opposite. He looked surprised at her selection. "Sure you want the black? Most women who play select white."

"Black is fine," she said.

The game began. She forced herself to concentrate. She refused to look at him across the table as she moved her pieces.

He won the first game.

Merry reviewed his moves and realized she could beat him. A sense of satisfaction surged through her. Ah, yes, this time she would win, at the game of chess and tonight, when she left this place.

They played throughout the afternoon. Gavin won the first, Merry the next. Gavin changed his strategy and it took Merry two more games before she beat him again. A sharp knock interrupted their play.

"Teatime, my lord." A tall, stocky woman carrying a tea service walked into the room.

"On the table, Mildred," Gavin instructed. "My companion will pour." He looked in Merry's direction.

Gavin was surprised to notice that Merry was frowning. He grimaced himself. Over the last several hours he realized something that shocked him.

The time had passed swiftly. Merry was delightful company, and she was a very intelligent woman. Definitely not the kind to attract his superficial brother.

He remembered her reaction in the office when he had called her bluff. It had taken her some time to deny that she was the woman intent on wedding his brother. Obviously, she had to think up some kind of tale to make him believe she was not the bride-to-be. But why? She was a delight.

He was missing something here. What reason could she possibly have to justify her wedding a younger man, a man who would be bored with her in no time at all? It had to be about money. Nothing else made sense.

He considered his original assessment of the physical charms of this woman. Pretty, but not beautiful. He smiled at his own folly. There was something about her, something so wholesome and natural, that when she drew near, it took his breath away. There was the innocent demeanor that glowed from her eyes, the lack of concern she had about her figure, the intelligence shining through her eyes.

He found himself drawn to her. For the first time in many months, a woman didn't bore him after talking to her for several minutes. No, there seemed to be a quality about her that made her appear genuine. He shook his head. No wonder Kenneth was interested.

Well, she was too much woman for his frivolous brother. She would make Kenneth's life miserable. And his brother would make hers miserable as well.

What he was doing was better for both Kenneth and Merry. Gavin studied her as she looked longingly around the room. Yes, those two would be miserable together. He was doing the right thing.

"Select any of the books," Gavin offered. "I'm certain before the end of your stay you will have the opportunity to read several more. We'll dine at eight."

She smiled at him before she looked away. Intuitively, he knew that smile was false, forced. However, just before she turned he'd caught an intense longing, as if he had placed a delicious dessert in front of her and then grabbed it away. He frowned. Instinct warned him that she planned to run—again. And soon. He stared at her, trying to read her mind, to learn when she would attempt to run.

Probably after dark. Tonight? It made sense. He would be prepared. She wasn't leaving here until Kenneth had sailed.

She'd try to take one of his horses, he was sure of that. Waiting in the stable for her would be the best option for him. It wouldn't be the first time he'd spent the night in a stable. And if tonight was not the night, then he would keep watch tomorrow night, and the next, because she was going to try to escape. It was as clear as if she had announced her plan aloud.

Tea finished, Merry glanced at the books lining the walls and then at his lordship. Once more those strange sensations twisted through her. Taking a deep breath, she excused herself. This wouldn't do at all. She had to get away from here and away from Dunleigh.

Upstairs in her room, she sorted through the gowns, searching for something suitable for dinner.

One garment appeared to be adequate and yet sturdy enough for the journey to the cottage. But it was far too short. She'd have to release the hem of the garment to cover her legs, for she'd probably have to ride astride. Once she got to the stables, time would not permit a search for a sidesaddle. She would have to do without one.

Dinner, his lordship had said, was at eight. She glanced at the small clock on the mantel. There was more than enough time for some reading before she had to dress. But she hadn't accepted his offer of a book, and she doubted she could find her way back to the library to get one now.

What was wrong with her? She was leaving this place and the sooner the better. If she collected a book, she would lose all sense of time. It had happened to her too many times before. She couldn't afford to have any distractions this night.

She stood at the window and surveyed the property. Lord Dunleigh was not quite the monster her sister had described. He'd insisted that he entertain her this afternoon. Had his concern been for her, or because he was afraid she would try to escape again? She'd never know.

Nor could she understand the emotions that whirled through her when he was close. She recalled his touch in the library and her breath caught. What kind of magic did he possess that his touch could feel like fire on her skin? She'd never known anything like that before, and she wasn't certain she wanted the experience again. But what had caused it and had he felt it as well?

She grabbed the heavy twill gown from the bed and began to remove stitches. It was almost the dinner hour before she finished. She splashed water on her face and carefully washed around her cuts and scrapes. Then she donned the gown, ran her fingers through her hair, wishing for a decent brush and hairpins. Well, there was nothing for it. She would leave the room in borrowed clothes, her hair finger-combed and undone.

A few minutes to eight, she left her room. Soon, she reminded herself, she'd be gone.

Despite the delicious food, she couldn't relax. Tension simmered through her and she prayed his lordship would not notice her nervousness even though she did little more than push her food around her plate.

Finally, when she knew she could not endure another moment, Dunleigh pronounced the meal finished. He moved behind her to pull her chair from the table, but Merry was too quick. Silently sighing with relief, she jumped up and stepped back. Her left foot caught in the threads of the twill dress and she lost her balance.

She would have fallen if he had not caught her. Again, his hands around her waist seared her skin under her gown and she turned around in his arms. She wondered if her face registered the same surprised look she saw on his.

Before she had a chance to offer her thanks and pull herself from his arms, he drew her closer. She watched in fascination, as slowly his head moved toward hers.

With the touch of his lips she gasped with delight. Warm pleasure, like sweet honey, spread through her and she leaned toward him. As if she had signaled some kind of acceptance, he gathered her closer and his lips met hers again. And again. The strength of his body, the heat from his lips,

even the intensity of his kiss produced the most unusual sensation Merry had ever felt.

She loved this.

She shifted in his arms, trying to get closer to
him, to become a part of him. All thought stopped
and she clung to him, allowing him to fire her desire, hold her tighter, press her closer to his rigid
body. The kiss went on and on and she kissed him
back with everything in her soul.

Breathless, she pulled away. She gazed into those
dark blue eyes now shimmering with want.

Thought returned.

Oh Lord! What had she allowed? And what had
she done? She'd kissed him back, allowed him to
hold her as if she were a brazen woman, a wanton.
She felt a different kind of heat collecting on her
cheeks.

Shame, embarrassment, humiliation!

She took a step back, kicking at her skirts. After
all, the dress had to share in her loss of dignity.

He cleared his throat and she stared at him.

"That never should have happened," he murmured.

She couldn't have agreed more, but she couldn't
speak. If nothing else had transpired, these kisses
made her departure essential. She couldn't stay here,
unchaperoned, for another day.

She gritted her teeth and glared at him. "I'm going to my room now."

To her surprise, her voice sounded normal, just
like her ordinary speaking voice. She spun around,
unwilling to let him see any more of her reactions.

"Merry," he whispered, "you responded to me.
You couldn't have kissed me the way you did if my
brother meant anything to you. A marriage between

the two of you would be a disaster, a terrible mistake. You have to see that now."

She shrugged. So that was the reason for the kisses, she thought, as disappointment almost overwhelmed her. Over her shoulder, she said, "My *sister* wants to marry your *brother.*"

She glanced at his face. He didn't believe her. Well, so be it. She was leaving and if he chose to pursue the situation with his brother, he would soon find out what a fool he'd made of himself. She had more than enough problems on her hands now. How was she ever going to forget those kisses?

Gavin watched her retreat. He shouldn't have kissed her. He hadn't intended to. But there was something about the astonishment on her face when he caught her and the feel of her in his arms that had common sense fleeing. And she had responded. Bloody hell! What was he supposed to have done then? She felt so good, her body leaning into his, her lips clinging to his, the heat from her mouth curling through him. He could no more have stopped kissing her than he could prevent himself from reacting to her nearness.

He needed to calm his body with a dip in some ice cold water but there was no lake on his property. Instead, he stomped off to his study. A snifter of brandy would have to do the calming, and then he had to wait in the stables for her to make her move.

He was certain she would try to escape this very night. If she hadn't decided on the day, those kisses they had shared would have made up her mind. He downed the brandy and shivered as the heat burned its way to his stomach. He had to find a decent place to wait before she made an attempt to leave.

Gavin hurried toward the stable, staying in the shadows as much as possible. He slipped through the half-open door and looked around. A lantern would have been a great help, but he didn't want any kind of signal alerting her to his presence.

He felt his way along the wall, until he found the ladder leading to the loft. At the top of the ladder, he could wait comfortably on the fresh hay.

There wasn't much of a moon, so surely she would bring some kind of light with her to find the bridle, and saddle a horse. Then he would put a stop to her attempt. She wasn't going to marry his brother.

He thought about the kisses they had shared. She felt nothing for Kenneth. She couldn't have kissed him that way if she had. She was into money—Sinclair money, and she wasn't going to trick Kenneth into marriage to get her hands on the funds Gavin had accumulated for him. No way! He intended to put a stop to any marriage.

He climbed the ladder and stepped onto the deck of the loft. He glanced around. Now that his eyes had become adjusted to the limited light, he could make out many of the details of the stable. A grim smile crossed his face. If she tried to leave tonight, she would not succeed. He settled down to wait.

Merry heard the sound of several doors slamming over the next hour. She'd managed to retain her cloak when his lordship had dragged her back from the stable after their confrontation that afternoon. Although the twill dress was dark, the blackness of her own cloak offered her more security. She wouldn't stand out in the dull light of a quarter-moon.

She sat stiff and immovable on the chair in the bedroom, staring out of the darkened window. Tension kept her wide awake. She was leaving this place tonight. Gavin Sinclair, Baron Dunleigh, would not stop her. She was going home.

She prayed that she'd get home before some emergency brought Aunt Sophia and Charlotte back from the weeklong party. When they did return, she intended to talk to Charlotte and explain about Lord Dunleigh's objections to a union between Charlotte and Kenneth Sinclair. Perhaps she could even change her sister's mind.

In any event, she would stop that wedding. She wouldn't wish Gavin Sinclair on anyone as a brother-in-law. He would devour Charlotte like the lecher he was. There would be nothing left of her vulnerable, delicate sister if Gavin Sinclair got to her.

As the minutes ticked past, Merry kept remembering the kisses she and his lordship had shared. She tried to brush them from her mind. She had to concentrate on what she had to do.

It was after midnight when Merry slipped from the room. She stole down the stairs, pausing often to listen for any indication someone was about.

Praying silently, she slipped through the kitchen and struggled with the door to the outside. The door squeaked. She jerked to a stop, her breath caught in her throat.

She stood frozen, afraid to move.

But nothing happened. She pulled at the door, and slid through the opening. Trying to stay in the shadows, she crept to the stable. She paused before the partially open door and listened. Nothing!

So far, so good, she thought as she crept around the stable door. She waited for her eyes to adjust to the gloom and then took a swift glance around. Nothing had changed since her visit that afternoon.

She grabbed a bridle and started for the mare's stall. Even if the small animal was not the swiftest horse in the world, she looked sturdy enough to make the journey back to the cottage.

Engrossed in her task, she paid little attention to anything around her. Suddenly, a hand shot out. She screamed with fright.

"I think not," Gavin Sinclair breathed in her ear. "I asked you to stay, to be my guest. It seems you are not interested in my hospitality."

She trembled, shaking so badly she couldn't respond. In the dim light he looked furious. She wanted to tell him he couldn't make her stay, that this was kidnapping, that her father would demand satisfaction, but she couldn't say a word.

He turned her around, never letting go of the hand he held.

"We are going back to the house, now," he said, the words laced with anger. Merry wanted desperately to see his face, but he stood in the shadows and she could not make out his expression. "You are going to bed," he continued. "Your late-night adventures have come to an end."

He dragged her through the door. They traveled through the kitchen, up the stairs, and toward her bedchamber. Reality finally replaced the terror that had made any struggles impossible.

She twisted, trying to free her hand.

"No!" he commanded. His harsh voice roared

through her and for one more instant she froze. No! she silently screamed. She was leaving—tonight. She went limp and he grabbed at her. She jerked free and flew down the stairs before he realized he'd been tricked.

She didn't get far. He caught her at the bottom of the stairs. Before she could demand her freedom, he swung her into his arms. Once more, he bounded up the stairs, as if he were carrying a feather pillow. She felt the anger pulsing through him. Again, she froze. He wouldn't hurt her, would he?

To her chagrin, he dropped her on her bed and then walked away. She heard the door close behind him and in the silence that followed, she heard the tumblers fall. He had locked her in.

Four

Merry leapt from the bed and stumbled to the door. She tried the knob. It turned but the door did not open. She banged on the door.

"Let me out," she shouted.

Dunleigh's angry voice from the other side snarled, "Don't wake Cook. She'll refuse to fix anything to eat tomorrow if she doesn't get her rest. She's not the youngest person on staff."

"I don't believe you," she shouted back. "You just don't want her to know how despicable you are."

"That's enough," he said quietly. She heard his footsteps move away from the door and she slammed her hand against the wood. How dare he lock her in!

She marched back to the bed and threw herself on the mattress. She couldn't believe that he would do something like this. He had locked her in her room, treating her like a wayward child. All she wanted to do was go home, and he was denying her that right. Oh, she was going to have a lot to say to her sister, and she'd tell her father as well. Dunleigh could not be allowed to get away with something like this.

She yawned, suddenly aware of the hour. She was exhausted, as much from nervous apprehension as from real fatigue. After all, she hadn't done anything today except stomp around the house and stable and play chess, certainly not her usual endeavors. She sighed. There was nothing more she could do tonight. Tomorrow. She would figure something out tomorrow.

Morning came and Merry sprang from the bed to try the door.

It opened!

She sighed with relief. She heard noises from below. The master of the house had stirred. He was probably eating his breakfast.

Breakfast. At the thought of the word, she realized how very hungry she was. After all, she had eaten almost nothing the night before at dinner. The last bit of substantial food she'd consumed had been the tea she had shared with his lordship. What she wouldn't give for a bit of toast and a pot of chocolate right now.

She washed her face and hands and patted the remaining cuts and scrapes dry. They were almost healed. She grabbed the gown she had donned the day before and ran her fingers through her hair. Perhaps she would ask his lordship for a decent brush and some pins.

She made her way down the stairs and turned toward the dining room. First things first. Food!

He sat at the head of the table, engrossed in a newspaper as she entered the room. "Good morning," she muttered, only because it was the polite thing to do.

"Aye, yes, good morning," he returned. "It looks to be a beautiful day. I thought I might show you around the property. A bit of exercise will do us both good."

"I don't have walking shoes," she snapped.

"No need to worry about the shoes. We'll ride. I do take it you ride well?"

She nodded and eyed the food spread out on the sideboard.

"Well, hurry up and eat and I'll see about having the horses saddled."

She cleared her throat. "I don't want to ride with you, sir. And besides, my riding habit has not been repaired," she said.

He smiled, and once again Merry felt weak, unsure her legs would support her weight. Good Lord. What kind of charm did this man possess that rendered her nearly senseless just with a smile?

"I've had one of the women I employ repair the riding habit you had on the night of the accident. I'll have her bring it to your room. If you change your mind about riding, I'll be in the stable. You know where it is." He grinned at her, almost as if he dared her to make a comment.

He rose from his place at the table and disappeared through the door Merry knew led to the kitchen. She grabbed a plate and filled it. A woman Merry had never seen before came in from the kitchen.

"I've fresh coffee, m'lady."

"Thank you," Merry said, not bothering to cor-

rect her form of address. She glanced at the
woman, wondering what the servant thought of
Merry's presence in his lordship's house. She
groaned, imagining the gossip that would be
spread before she got away from this place. All
the more reason to make plans. And this time,
when she left, she had to make good her escape,
get back to the cottage.

Perhaps the ride around his property was the
answer. She should not have been so quick to dis-
count viewing the estate. But he had said she
could change her mind. And that was exactly what
she was going to do.

She ate quickly, drinking her coffee fast enough
to burn her tongue, and rushed back to her room.
Her riding habit lay on the bed. She slipped off
the twill gown and pulled at her chemise. Once
more she noticed the yellow, green, and bluish
marks left by the bruises she had received during
her accident. She sighed, hoping they would be
gone before Sophia and Charlotte returned.

She shoved the skirt of her habit over her hips.
Would he leave without her? She tied the strings,
and grabbed the bodice and jacket. She doubted
she had ever dressed so quickly. A quick glance
at her hair made her shudder. It would have to
fly in her face.

On the dressing table she passed on the way to
the door, she noticed a brush and next to it a
small pile of hairpins. She paused, alarmed to
think that he was such a ladies' man that he knew
flying strands of hair would annoy a rider no end.
Still she should be grateful. Dunleigh was trying
to make her enforced stay less troubling. Unless

one of the women had brought the pins and brush?

Yes, that must have been who had supplied what she needed for a chignon. She ran the bristles through the strands and fingered the bump from the accident. It was still sore, and it was a reminder of what had happened to her and why. She couldn't forget, not for a moment, that she had to get home before Charlotte and Aunt Sophia returned. She had a wedding to stop.

She pulled her hair into a bun and secured it before she made her way down the stairs and out to the stables. He was leading a beautiful black mount, saddled and ready to ride.

"I see you've decided to join me." He smiled, and she exhaled, trying to lessen the effect he had.

Gaining control, she announced, "I see no reason to cut off my nose to spite my face. I love to ride and this will be new territory." She gazed at the horse. She had hoped to have the small gray mare for a mount.

"Here"—he handed her the reins—"let me get the mare."

She sighed with pleasure. She was going to ride the smaller animal. Then she'd have an excellent chance to see just what the horse could do.

A few minutes later they were on their way. Lord Dunleigh led the way through the fields behind the house into a stand of trees.

He drew to a stop waiting for her. "Dunleigh Manor sits on the west side of the property that stretches for several miles. The village is north of the property. But don't get any ideas. It's eight miles away. And, not an easy walk, especially in your riding boots."

She said nothing. Instead she urged the small horse forward. Even being out in the weak sunlight was better than being confined to the house. He caught up with her quickly enough and they rode together until they came to a small stream.

"We'll water the horses here, before we start back."

She sat the mare until he dismounted and came around to help her down. He reached up and his hands around her waist produced a shiver.

"Cold?"

She shook her head. She wasn't about to tell him that just his touch caused all kinds of unusual reactions in her. No, she could never relate such information. She stepped away, and tried to regain her composure, something that disappeared whenever he touched her.

She walked to the stream and bent down to fill her hands with the icy water. She splashed her face and shook her hands in the cold liquid. The mare nudged her and Merry laughed.

"You want a drink too," she said and rubbed the velvet nose of the animal.

She stood and glanced in the direction of his lordship. Merry's breath caught in her throat. She had no experience but she recognized raw desire. Dunleigh wanted her, and that thought sent a thrill to her soul.

She took a step back. She didn't understand what was happening to her. She didn't even like him, and yet he excited her in a way she could never have imagined, could never explain. She grabbed at the mare's reins.

"I'm ready to go back," she said.

"All right," he said, walking toward her. "And this afternoon, since you play such a good game of chess, I thought a game or two before tea . . ."

His voice trailed off as she shook her head.

"No, I don't think so. I want to take advantage of your collection of books. I'm certain I can find something to read." Silently she reprimanded herself. She'd better plan now to avoid his lordship for as long as she was confined to his home. And she needed to come up with a foolproof plan of escape.

After lunch, Merry found several books in the library that appealed to her. She gathered them close. "I'm taking these to my room. I'll read there."

"Oh, there's no need for that. I've work to do in my office, so you might as well enjoy the good light in this room."

She stared at him, trying to read his mind. Was he attempting to manipulate her? He was right about the light. This was a perfect room for reading. And if he was going to be working in another part of the house, she could avoid him in here as easily as she could by going to her room.

She nodded and took one of the barrel-backed chairs before the window overlooking the garden. She waited for him to leave and then she opened the book. Over the next hour, she tried to read, but the words on the page blurred. She kept seeing the face of the man in whose home she was confined. Finally, Merry slammed the book shut and sat staring out the window into the garden.

She scolded herself. She had to get him out of her mind.

On the opposite side of the house, Gavin sat staring at the ledger. He needed to check what the steward had done before he could figure out how many fields he wanted planted this year, how many more sheep he could expect in this year's herds. Then there were the births and one death he wanted to recognize, as well as all the other things that had taken place from the time he had left for the Islands until now. But the close-penned lines of his steward became fuzzy, vague, indistinct.

Merry's face danced through his head and he groaned. He was not a callow youth. He had a great deal of self-control, or at least he'd always believed he did, but Merry consumed his attention.

"Bloody hell!" he muttered. His brother wanted her and yet here, he, Gavin Sinclair, had his body reacting to just the thought of her.

He shifted in his chair and stood. Ignoring the papers on his desk, he strode to the door. Perhaps if he spent all of his time with her he could get her out of his system, learn something about her that would wipe out the desire he felt.

He marched down the hallway and into the kitchen, startling Cook and the two women he'd hired from the village.

"My guest and I will have tea in the library." He waited for Cook to acknowledge his order, then strode to the room where he knew Merry was reading.

Merry shifted in her chair. Although she had

picked up two other books, it was no use. She couldn't concentrate. Reading held no appeal for her this afternoon. She laid the book she held aside and stood. Perhaps a walk in the garden would ease some of the tension she felt. She started for the door.

Before she got to it, the door swung toward her and the object of her thoughts entered the room. She gazed at him and opened her mouth to explain that she was on her way to the garden.

"Tea is on its way," he announced before she said a word.

"Oh, I was going for a walk."

"Merry"—he stepped toward her—"it's cold out. And I'd rather you didn't leave the house. You might be tempted not to return. Now, come, sit down. Tea will be here at any moment."

Merry returned to her chair and took her seat. She stared at him, aware of the slight smile on his lips. His dark blue eyes gazed into hers and once again her heart doubled its beat. Her palms grew damp and she had problems drawing air into her starved lungs. Why? Why did this man affect her this way? If she couldn't avoid him, she would have to learn to tolerate the feelings he engendered until she escaped.

A knock on the door announced tea and she silently finished her quick lecture. She poured and Gavin began to talk about the political situation in England. At home with her father, she had often been involved in discussions about some of the things happening in their country. Her father always wanted to argue the benefits of this action or that, and she had managed to absorb as much information as was available.

Now she was quick to offer her opinion to Gavin. And he listened!

The afternoon faded into night and just before eight Gavin asked if she wanted to change for dinner. She stared at him and realized the lamps had been lit and the sky, visible from the garden window, was dark. They had talked away the time, and she hadn't even noticed.

After dinner, he pulled out her chair and his pleasant demeanor faded. He grabbed her arm, turning her toward him. She jerked against his touch, but he didn't release her.

"You know I can't let you leave." The stern look he gave her made her shiver.

"What do you mean?"

He sighed, obviously not happy with what he had to say, "I'll have to lock your bedchamber door again tonight."

"Why?" she asked, stunned.

"Because"—his expression was grim—"given half a chance you'll bolt and we both know it."

He looked determined, and somehow she knew arguing with him was useless. She shrugged. She would have to find another way to leave this place.

That day set the pattern for the next three days. When she awoke in the morning her door was unlocked. After breakfast, Gavin invited her to ride and then he went to his study to work on estate business, he said. Merry went to the library. After a lunch they now ate together, he joined her in the library.

Gavin shared the newspaper with her, or she read while Gavin continued work at the library desk. If time permitted, they played several games of chess and Merry chuckled to herself. She was getting skilled at beating him, no matter what strategy he employed.

After tea, she retired to her room to dress for dinner. She spent most of her time while she prepared for the meal by scolding herself for her behavior. She was being held against her will; she was nothing but a prisoner and here she was enjoying her imprisonment. Still, she was breathless when she descended the stairs to join Gavin for dinner.

After the evening meal, she went to her room and prepared for bed. Once she retired, she heard his lordship's footsteps pausing before her door. He wished her good night and waited for her response, then turned the key in the lock.

On the fourth night, they went through the ritual of saying good night, but instead of going to bed, she paced the floor of her bedroom, intent on seeing just when he unlocked her door. If he released the bolt after he thought she had gone to sleep, she might be able to get away.

Hours passed and Merry decided that he must unlock the door early in the morning. And that would do her no good. She crawled into her bed, furious at the thought that her loss of sleep had gained her nothing.

Merry arose very late the next morning. His lordship had already left for his morning ride and the food on the sideboard had disappeared. She started for the door to the kitchen. Maybe she could talk Cook into fixing her something.

The two women hired after she arrived stood in the hallway, their backs to Merry. She paused, unwilling to call attention to herself.

The taller of the two women was giggling like a young schoolgirl. "I tell you, Sally is furious. Imagine, she thought she'd have his lordship to herself. Then she found out he'd brought his own woman. And telling Mrs. Perry the girl had been injured in a riding accident." Both women laughed, and Merry stood rigid. They were talking about her.

She stepped back, unwilling to be seen. However, she left the door open a bit. It was never good to listen to gossip, especially about one's self, but she couldn't turn away.

"He's never brought a woman here before, according to Cook," the second woman commented.

"This one must be special," the first woman said, and leaned toward the second, whispering something. They both started laughing and Merry felt her face grow very warm. She stepped away from the door and rushed toward the stairs and her bedroom. Her appetite had disappeared.

She collided with his lordship at the bottom of the staircase.

He grabbed her to prevent her from falling. For an instant she hung in his arms, her body warming with the reaction she now recognized as his effect on her. She glanced into his face. His eyes gleamed with desire and her whole body responded. Her arms reached up to his shoulders as he lowered his head

She knew he was going to kiss her, but she couldn't step away. She wanted the kiss, wanted it with everything in her. She leaned into him, closing the distance between them.

His lips brushed hers, once, again, then again. She sighed with pleasure as his lips took hers.

This time his tongue slipped over her lower lip and she gasped. He took advantage of her open mouth and delved deep with his tongue. She almost fainted from the intense sensations fanning through her. He tasted her and suddenly the need to reciprocate grew until it could not be denied.

She touched his tongue with her own, and he crushed her closer. He held her tight as if he knew she could not have supported herself if he released her. And she did not want him to let her go, not ever.

Her only thought was to return his kiss, to let him know she loved how their mouths intertwined. Her fingers threaded through the dark silk strands of hair as his warm breath seared her mouth.

Heat, like hot flames, coursed through her veins and she dragged small drafts of air into her starved lungs. Her breasts tingled and her woman's place pulsed with a new sensation. She wanted to be absorbed by him, become connected to him completely, become a part of him.

He lifted his head and a bitter ache lanced through Merry. She didn't want the kisses to end. She tried to coax his head toward hers but he muttered, "This must stop. Now!"

The words drew her up short. What was she doing? She stood frozen in place, stunned when she realized she had let this man kiss her, bestow an intimate kiss on her. Her face burned, this time with shame. She had let him kiss her in a way no man had kissed her before. And look at the way she had reacted. That disturbed her even more than his kisses. She had wanted him to kiss her and keep kissing her. She didn't want him to stop.

Even more embarrassed than she had been after the first kiss, she stepped back, straining against his hold. He released her immediately and she wanted to sob her frustration. How could she have allowed him such freedom?

She jerked out of his arms and glanced at his face. Something inside her crumbled. He didn't look the least bit upset or unnerved by what had taken place, as if he often bestowed those kinds of kisses on any willing woman.

She smothered a groan. "Don't do that again," she ordered.

"You kissed me back, Merry," he whispered, his tone sounding harsh.

She wanted to reply with a scathing retort, but her mind still reeled from what she had allowed. She rushed up the stairs. She needed time alone, time to think, time to plan an escape. For escape she must and immediately. Not only to stop Charlotte from doing something to disgrace the family, but also getting away from his lordship at the bottom of the stairs. If she wasn't careful, Merry decided, she herself would commit the ultimate disgrace.

In her room, she paced the floor, fighting for a composure that seemed to elude her with every step she took. Panic clawed through her and the word *escape* pounded through her head. She had to find a way to leave this place and Dunleigh. And it had to be now.

Gavin stomped off to his study. How could he have let his lust gain the upper hand? All right, she had kissed him back, but she seemed an innocent, as if the kiss he bestowed was different from every other kiss she had ever received. Besides, he reminded himself, this was the woman his brother wanted to marry.

Bloody hell! Kenneth was not going to wed her. Gavin had already decided that. And keeping her here with him was the best way to prevent a union between them. Of course, that didn't excuse his own behavior. He'd have to find a way to stay away from her. No more games of chess, no more lengthy discussions about topics of interest to him, subjects she seemed capable of understanding.

That had to be the reason for his being so taken with her. She was exceptionally bright, and she seemed to understand his viewpoint. He'd never spent any time with a woman who was able to argue so knowledgeably.

He paced before his desk, his expression somber. She was a real temptation though and he had to guard against getting himself entangled with her. Lawrence had said she was the daughter of a retired military officer. Sophia Palmer had introduced her to society, so she had to be of the peerage. It wouldn't do at all for him to compromise her, not unless he wanted to marry her himself.

He'd have to stay away from her, but somehow keep tabs on her whereabouts so that she didn't leave before Kenneth sailed. That was the only thing he had to worry about. Stay away from her until he could take her home, after Kenneth sailed.

He forced himself to sit down and begin his work. Somehow, he had to force her from his mind.

Of course, he'd still eat his meals with her. To avoid her completely would probably give her the false impression that he was no longer interested in whether she left his house. Meals were acceptable, but that was it. And no more standing outside her bedroom door, battling his lust.

She'd be surprised to hear that bolted door was as much for her as for him. If he was honest with himself, he had to admit that something about that locked door provided a mental deterrent. Oh, yes. He locked her door as much to protect her from his lust as to keep her confined to the house.

Five

During the next hour, as Merry paced, she contemplated a dozen escape schemes, but for every idea that surfaced at least three reasons arose that made that particular plan unworkable.

"There has to be a way," she murmured, as she crossed the carpet yet again. "I have to find a way."

Eventually, a knock interrupted her musings.

"My lady."

Merry recognized the voice of one of the women from the kitchen.

"Yes," Merry called through the closed door.

"His lordship says lunch is being served. He would like you to join him."

Merry stared at the door. What to do? Oh Lord, what should she do? Should she swallow her embarrassment and join him, let him believe she was resigned to staying until Kenneth sailed? Or should she demand a tray in her room and raise his suspicions?

Join him, a small voice inside her head responded. *You know you want to.*

She shivered against the sudden sensations that

shot through her. What if he tried to take her into his arms? What if he tried to kiss her again?

She squared her shoulders. She wasn't going to let him get close enough to do something like that. She was going to be strong and cold, cold like ice. Then he would leave her alone.

"I'll be right there," she called through the door. Quickly she combed her hair and reworked the bun at the back of her head. She splashed water on her face, hoping to cool the heat still being generated by her shame. Swallowing her pride, she opened the door and made her way to the dining room.

Dunleigh was waiting for her and she knew she was blushing as he stared at her.

"I must apologize," he murmured. Merry stared into those deep blue eyes and decided he was sincere. "I promised that would not happen again," he added.

"I should have stopped you," Merry replied. In all fairness, she had to accept some of the blame. "Can we forget what occurred?" she asked, wondering as the words tumbled out of her mouth if she could forget those kisses.

"Of course. It is best forgotten," he commented.

Merry slid onto her chair. For some reason the fact that he agreed, and so quickly, hurt. She lowered her eyelids. She didn't want to have to look into the deep blue eyes that stirred something in her soul.

Having skipped breakfast, Merry did the meal justice despite the fact that they ate in silence. For once she refused to look at him. She had nothing to say to the man at the head of the table and she wanted him to say nothing to her. Her wish was granted.

When the cheese and fruit course was presented, he rose from the table. He glanced at her and then toward the window, a frown creasing his brow.

"Enjoy the last course. I have things I must do outside. The sky looks very heavy, as if it will storm. I expect we are in for some miserable weather."

A storm? Merry started at his words. Had her prayers finally been answered? Was this the distraction she needed? He'd never expect her to leave in a storm. She fought the smile trying to spread over her face. Yes, she wanted to shout. Tonight! If they had a storm tonight, she would leave this place, and his lordship. So, why did she suddenly feel like crying?

Now she started praying in earnest. If he locked her in again, she would never get away. However, if he thought there was no danger of her leaving, he might not bother with securing her door. She watched as he strode from the room, as if he wanted to get as far away from her as fast as he could.

Well, let him go, for if the weather cooperated, she would escape this very night. Carefully, she slipped an apple from the bowl. She rose from the table, the fruit in her hand. She'd save this for tonight. It would serve her well when she tried to saddle the small mare.

She left the dining room and hurried to the library. How long had she been here with him? She counted the days and groaned. Aunt Sophia and

Charlotte had undoubtedly returned to the cottage two days ago. Oh, good Lord, another reason why she had to get home tonight. Knowing Aunt Sophia, she'd have sent for their father as soon as she realized Merry wasn't at home. Thank goodness her bruises and scrapes were nearly healed.

However, if her escape was to be successful, Merry needed something that would give his lordship the impression that she had willingly accepted her situation. She couldn't afford for him to be suspicious. Nor could she allow him any reason to bolt her bedroom door. She glanced around the room at the books and groaned.

Then the idea hit.

Reading!

She could take a book to the bedchamber she occupied. He'd notice it gone. Of course, she wasn't stealing the volume because he would find it after she left. And she'd leave one in the library with a marker in the middle. That should indicate that she planned to stay at least until she finished the tome.

Smiling, she selected two volumes, one a history of Rome, another a book on animal husbandry. She grinned as she remembered the heated discussion they had had over how to improve the quality of wool from his sheep. She opened the one on history to the middle, placed a piece of ribbon on the page, closed the book, and laid it on the table next to the chair she often used. The other book she carried up to her room.

Once more, she paced the floor, stopping occasionally to peer at the sky. Baron Dunleigh had spoken the truth when he said the sky looked heavy. She could see nothing but dark gray clouds massing to the west. It would surely be a stormy night. And in the darkness she would be able to escape.

She refused to analyze the desolate feelings that tried hard to push to the fore. Nor would she think about all the pleasant times they had shared together. Still, she couldn't help but remember the many times she had beaten him at chess, or how easily he talked to her about estate problems, the economics of island plantations, what would happen to the monarchy with Queen Victoria on the throne. And she fought hard not to remember his kisses and how she felt when his lips touched hers.

She shivered as she glared at the dark clouds. She could feel the cold from the approaching storm seep into her room. But she had to leave. She had to. If she stayed . . .

She refused to allow herself to continue that thought. She had to go—tonight, no matter how cold, or how miserable the weather.

Dinner was as quiet as luncheon had been. Merry said little and he said nothing. He seemed to have withdrawn into a world of his own. However, to her dismay, the threatened storm had not yet developed. Unless it turned stormy, she was convinced he would lock her bedroom door.

Again, before dessert, Lord Dunleigh excused himself and Merry grabbed another apple from the dish on the table and made her way to her bedchamber. She stood at the window and staring at the dark sky she prayed for rain, cold, wet rain and lightning with thunder. Thunder would block any sound she might make in her escape.

Her pleas for a storm must have found a listener, for splatters against her window announced the arrival of the rain. The drops became heavier as the dark clouds moved over the estate. Thunder rumbled in the distance. Merry was tempted to drop to her knees in thanksgiving. Surely, his lordship would not lock her in on a night like this.

As the rain pelted the house, Merry heard his tread on the stairs. She held her breath. Now she would know. He paused before her chamber, as he usually did, and she held her breath.

"Good night," he said.

"Yes, good night," she responded. However, she heard no key in the lock, no tumblers turn.

She wanted to shout with joy. He wasn't going to secure her door. She could leave. She brushed at the tears that had no explanation. *Silly woman,* she scolded. *This is what must be.* She had no right to cry because she could finally escape.

She sat down to wait. If the storm continued as it looked like it might, she could afford to wait until the household had retired for the evening. She definitely couldn't leave until she was certain his lordship had gone to sleep.

One hour passed and Merry found the delay a sheer torment. Still, she let more minutes elapse. Finally, standing in front of the door, she listened carefully. She eased it open a fraction and peered through the gap. She had to make certain no one wandered through the hall. But silence ruled. The only sound she heard was the drumming of the rain.

Carefully, she grabbed the cloak she had left in her room, stuffed the apples in her reticule, and once again stood at the door. She glanced longingly at the small lamp on her table, but she would have to brave the darkness without any kind of aid.

She slipped through the opening and down the stairs. She felt her way to the dining room, through the door to the kitchen. Fortunately, Cook had banked the fire and the soft gleam from the glowing embers helped Merry find the back door. She eased her way through the kitchen and out into the rain.

The bitter cold had her pulling her cloak close. The trip to the stable was miserable. Icy rain pummeled her, stinging her face, and soaking her cloak. She fumbled for the doors to the stable until a burst of lightning guided her to the latch.

Inside, she released the closure of her cloak and shook as much water from the garment as she could. Hoping for another flash of lightning, she left the door open. Fate seemed to be with her, for a forked display lit the interior and she found the bridle.

Another flare of light illuminated her way to the mare. In no time she had the bridle on the small horse, who stood quietly munching on the apple as Merry worked. She decided against trying to find a saddle and donned her cloak. Then she led the mare from her stall.

A bale of hay provided a means to mount. Merry grabbed the reins and guided the mare to

Take A Trip Into A Timeless World of Passion and Adventure with ensington Choice Historical Romances! —Absolutely FREE!

Let your spirits fly away and enjoy the passion and adventure of another time. Kensington Choice Historical Romances are the finest novels of their kind, written by today's best selling romance authors. Each Kensington Choice Historical Romance transports you to distant lands in a bygone age. Experience the adventure and share the delight as proud men and spirited women discover the wonder and passion of true love.

4 BOOKS WORTH UP TO $23.96— *Absolutely FREE!*

Take 4 FREE Books!

We created our convenient Home Subscription Service so you'll be sure to have the hottest new romances delivered each month right to your doorstep — usually before they are available in book stores. Just to show you how convenient Zebra Home Subscription Service is, we would like to send you 4 Kensington Choice Historical Romance as a FREE gift. You receive a gift worth up to $23.96 — absolutely FREE. There's no extra charge for shipping a handling. There's no obligation to buy anything - ever!

Save Up To 30% On Home Delivery!

Accept your FREE gift and each month we'll deliver 4 bra new titles as soon as they are published. They'll be your to examine FREE for 10 days. Then if you decide to keep the books, you'll pay the preferred subscriber's price. Tha all 4 books for a savings of up to 30% off the cover price! Just add the cost of shipping and handling. Remember, y are under no obligation to buy any of these books at any time! If you are not delighted with them, simply return th and owe nothing. But if you enjoy Kensington Choice Historical Romances as much as we think you will, pay th special preferred subscriber rate and save over $7.00 off bookstore price!

We have 4 FREE BOOKS for you as your introduction to KENSINGTON CHOICE!

To get your FREE BOOKS,
worth up to $24.96, mail the card below
or call TOLL-FREE 1-800-770-1963
Visit our website at www.kensingtonbooks.com.

Take 4 Kensington Choice Historical Romances FREE!

YES! Please send me my 4 FREE KENSINGTON CHOICE HISTORICAL ROMANCES (without obligation to purchase other books). Unless you hear from me after I receive my 4 FREE BOOKS, you may send me 4 new novels - as soon as they are published - to preview each month FREE for 10 days. If I am not satisfied, I may return them and owe nothing. Otherwise, I will pay the money-saving preferred subscriber's price plus shipping and handling. That's a savings of over $7.00 each month. I may return any shipment within 10 days and owe nothing, and I may cancel any time I wish. In any case the 4 FREE books will be mine to keep.

Name _____

Address _____ Apt No _____

City _____ State _____ Zip _____

Telephone ( ) _____ Signature _____

(If under 18, parent or guardian must sign)

KN012A

Terms, offer, and prices subject to change. Orders subject to acceptance by Kensington Choice Book Club. Offer valid in the U.S. only.

the stable door. The animal balked, but with soft words and a great many caresses, the mare finally moved out into the rain.

Merry threw caution to the wind and urged the animal into a gallop. She was going home.

Gavin stood at the window watching nature's fireworks as the storm he had predicted arrived in all its glory. A peal of thunder rattled the windows and he wondered if Merry had been awakened. As a gentleman, if storms frightened her, he ought to see to her comfort. For several minutes he argued with himself. But, he rationalized, she was a guest in his home. If she was afraid of storms, he should at least offer assurance that the storm wouldn't harm her.

Of course, given how she tempted his self-control, he wouldn't touch her. He could offer a bit of brandy, or at least let her know he was concerned about her.

He pulled on a pair of pants, slipped on a dressing gown, and left his room. He ambled down the hall, telling himself he was only going to offer her reassurance, nothing more. But when he paused before her door, he realized it stood partially open. Frowning, he shoved it open, banging it against the bedroom wall, and stepped into the room. It was empty.

He raced down the stairs and rushed to the library. Perhaps the storm had bothered her enough to drive her to the one room she seemed to like above all others. However, the library was empty as well. No light gleamed from any room on this level. He checked the kitchen. No one in the kitchen. He rushed back to his room and finished dressing.

Surely, she wouldn't have tried to run, not on a night like this. He had thought her intelligent, but to attempt to ride in this kind of storm was not only foolish, it was downright dangerous.

He raced for the stables, and shouted a few curses when he found the door open.

She *had* made a run for it. Was marriage to Kenneth so important to her that she would be willing to risk her life? Or was it the money, the Sinclair money she was after?

As quickly as he could, he saddled his horse. He led the animal from the stables, mounted, and raced down the road. The mare Merry had chosen was skittish in storms and bolted at the first crack of thunder. There was every chance Merry had been thrown before she left Dunleigh land.

As if to confirm his fears, during the next flare of light he caught sight of a riderless horse streaking toward home and the stables.

"Bloody hell," he shouted into the wind and rain. She had survived one fall a week ago, but could she survive another? And could he even find her in this weather?

He ignored the mare as she dashed past him to the warmth of the stables. The animal would be all right for a short time, he decided. The important thing now was to find Merry. He offered a quick prayer that she had not been injured again.

He traveled along the road toward the gates of the estate. The frequent lightning flashes provided considerable light as he searched the trail, but shouting her name was useless with the thunder obliterating all sound but its own roar.

She was sitting at the side of the road a few feet from the gates to Dunleigh. A bolt of lightning provided a glimpse of her face. She was furious. He sighed with relief. If she was that angry, she couldn't be badly hurt. Suddenly, he wanted to laugh. He halted his horse, dismounted, and stepped next to her.

"Going somewhere?" he asked, trying to keep the grin from annoying her more.

"I'm going home," she shouted above the mighty rumble of thunder.

Gavin grimaced before he said, "I'll take you there myself in a few more days." Still, she hadn't stood. Had she been hurt? he wondered.

"Can you stand?" he asked, surprised at the concern he heard in his own voice.

"I haven't tried," she snapped, and Gavin chuckled. Her anger had not abated one bit.

"Well, we have to get out of this rain, and I must see to the mare. I suppose I should have told you she doesn't like storms, especially the thunder." He frowned, thinking about what could have happened to her. "I didn't think you would try to run away during a deluge."

Merry pulled herself to her feet and stared at the mud on the edges of her cloak. She had no intention of looking at him, nor was she going to stand there and pass the time. The only thing for her to do was to go back to the house and try once more to convince her jailer that she was not the one planning to marry Kenneth Sinclair.

"Let me give you a hand up," Gavin said, holding out his hand. Merry ignored it.

"Merry, walking back to the house will take the better part of an hour. Riding will take only a few minutes. If you insist on walking, you will only get that much wetter." His voice held a bit of censure and a great deal of impatience.

She also heard the concern and glanced in his direction. What lightning flashes there were now seemed far away, and the thunder nothing more than a distant growl. If she'd only waited a little longer the mare probably wouldn't have bolted. She sighed with frustration.

It was still raining, and she shivered as the cold drops ran down her neck. She was wet and very cold and she wanted to go home.

"All right," she muttered, and accepting his help, she swung her leg over the saddle. He hoisted himself up behind her and coaxed the horse into motion.

They traveled in silence. And Merry was glad. She had nothing to say and she willed her companion to refrain from any comments as well.

Chilled to the bone, she shivered against him, still he remained silent. She'd been furious when the little mare had dumped her, but something told her his lordship would find her. That should have made her even more angry but she wasn't nearly as upset as she should have been.

She needed to go home. She couldn't chance another encounter with him, not again, and yet here she was on his horse, going back to his house. And she wasn't unhappy about the situation.

What is wrong with you? a small voice scolded. She refused to consider an answer. *Think about getting warm,* she told herself.

In truth, she was freezing. Her teeth started to chatter and she huddled into her soaked cloak. Nothing seemed to help warm her. Without a word, he eased her back into his warmth but she didn't have the strength to pull away. Her hands and feet were numb with cold and she couldn't stop trembling.

A dark shadow took shape and Merry recognized the outline of the house. His lordship stopped at the back entrance, and she felt him grasp her around the waist. He lifted her from the horse but when her feet touched the ground, needles of pain shot through them and up her legs. She lost her balance and sat on the wet ground.

He shouted at her, his voice shattering the quiet of the night.

"What's wrong? Where do you hurt? Why can't you stand?"

She glanced at him. "My feet. Needles," was all she could manage.

He dismounted and knelt beside her. In the dim light she could read his concern. He slipped one arm under her knees, the other around her shoulders, and stood.

She opened her mouth to object, but the sharp stabs in her feet told her that standing or walking would be impossible.

She let him carry her into the kitchen. He put her in a chair before the banked fireplace.

"I'll be back in a few minutes. I must care for the horses. Will you be all right until I return?"

His voice touched a cord in her body. He was really worried about her. A lump formed in her throat and she couldn't speak. She nodded before she stretched her frozen feet toward the hearth.

She was still cold. She sat before the fire, too tired to stand and remove her cloak, in too much pain to bend over and remove her boots, too cold to stop the shivering. She sat, her teeth chattering, her mind a blank. She was cold, so cold she knew she would never be warm again.

Suddenly, he was behind her. She felt him, though she didn't turn to verify his presence. He touched her shoulder and she sagged in the chair.

"We have to get you warmed up, out of these wet things." He stood before her. "I'll carry you to your room if you don't think you can walk."

"Carry me," she surrendered. She couldn't walk, but it took too much effort to tell him that. He lifted her into his arms and carried her through the house, up the stairs, and into her bedroom. She rested her head on his shoulder, snuggling next to his heat, trying to burrow into him so that she could get warm. Still, she shuddered, her teeth chattering with each step he took.

"You've got to get out of those wet things," he murmured as he set her on the bed.

"C—can't," she mumbled. "Hands too cold." She lifted her arms, then let them fall to her side as she started to shake violently.

Gavin shuddered himself as he stared at her. Her hair dripped against her neck, her wool cloak held the moisture pressed to her body, soaking her through and through. She had to get out of her clothes. But what would he do if she couldn't?

"Merry, I'll get a shirt for you to put on, but you have to remove those wet things." He grabbed a linen and handed it to her.

"For your hair," he said before he turned toward the door, glancing back. She just sat there, making no attempt to take the towel or remove even her soaked cloak.

"Merry," he said, his voice commanding, "undress."

She sat there shivering, occasionally shaking furiously. He wondered if she heard him.

He hurried to his room, shivering in his own wet garments. He stripped his wet clothing off as he went. He grabbed dry clothes, threw them on, then grabbed one of his linen shirts. He padded barefoot back down the hall and tapped on her bedroom door.

When no answer came, he pushed the door open. She sat exactly as he had left her, still wearing all those wet clothes, her hair still dripping. He didn't want to admit it, but he'd have to undress her himself. For some reason, she was too cold, or lacked the strength to do it herself.

Of course, he could wake up Cook, but it would take her forever to dress and he doubted she could climb the stairs. The two women he'd hired from the village went home each night. It would take him even longer to summon one of them. He sighed. Of course Mrs. Perry had yet to return from helping her sister.

To keep Merry from catching her death, he would have to remove her things and get her into something warm. He gritted his teeth and told himself he must remember this was an emergency.

She very well might die if he didn't care for her. That was it. He had to remember that her life depended on him helping rid her of her soaking, cold garments.

He stood before her, "Merry, I—I." He cleared his throat and began again. "We must get you out of these clothes. Can you hear me?"

He reached over, and with his fingers he lifted her chin. Her cold flesh alarmed him. He sensed time was of the essence. She had to get warm and fast. He grabbed the cloak from her and threw it aside. He stooped down and pulled the boots from her feet, which felt like ice. She pulled her feet out of his hands and shook fiercely. He stood and reached for her bodice.

For an instant, her eyes lost their glazed look and she lifted her hands to stay his own. But the effort cost her. She dropped her hands and closed her eyes. He ripped the bodice and stripped it from her as quickly as he could before he threw it to the floor.

"Merry," he whispered, "I have to remove your skirt. It's wet and must come off." He eased her into a prone position, took his pocketknife and cut the ties. He yanked the skirt over her hips and tossed it to the floor. Her petticoats came next, then her hose. He took notice of some of her bruises, and shivered. Thank the Lord she'd suffered no more cuts or scrapes this evening.

Then she was wearing nothing but her shift. It was as wet as her other garments. Taking a deep breath, he slipped it off.

And froze.

She was the most beautiful woman he had ever

seen. She had full curves, lush, the kind men only dream about. Her tiny waist emphasized her full breasts, her lavish hips, her long, shapely legs that seemed to go on forever. He drank in the sight of her, forgetting he was supposed to warm her so she wouldn't grow ill.

She started another wild episode of violent shudders, and he cursed himself. He slipped the shirt he'd brought over her curves and reached for the towel he'd attempted to hand to her. Quickly, he pulled the pins still clinging to her bun from her hair and wiped the moisture from the strands.

He whispered, "I'm going to get some brandy." He added silently, *for both of us*.

He pulled the duvet up to cover her, tucked it around her and bolted toward the door, his whole body on fire. Desire lanced his soul. Bloody hell, what he wouldn't give to lie down next to her, to trace all those perfect curves.

He rushed down the stairs. She needed something to warm her, and he needed something to wipe the image of her flawless body from his mind.

Six

Gavin raced up the stairs, the decanter and two snifters in his hands. He didn't bother knocking on the door, but charged into the room. Merry's face was flushed and he sighed with relief. She was improving.

He placed the glasses and decanter on the table, poured himself a dollop of brandy, and swallowed it. The liquid burned a path to his stomach and warmth enveloped him. He moved toward the bed, and noticed that Merry was still shaking. He placed a hand on her cheek, stunned that her flushed face was anything but warm.

She mumbled, "C—cold."

He glanced around the room. There was no fireplace in this guest room. He needed to increase the temperature. A warm bath might help, but in this room a bath would probably be her death.

His room. He had a fireplace in his bedchamber. Wrapping her in the duvet he carried her into his own room and laid her on his bed. Then he turned his attention to the embers in his fireplace.

In no time, he had a blaze going. He hurried back to the chamber Merry had occupied and grabbed the brandy decanter and both snifters. Back in his room, he poured a bit more for himself and some for Merry. However, when he placed the glass against her lips, she turned her head.

"Merry, this will warm you," he said.

"Water," she murmured.

He turned to his pitcher, which contained water, and poured a small quantity into another glass. Lifting her in his arms, he held the glass to her lips and she took a sip. He eased her back onto the linens, but she began to shake again, more violently this time.

He glanced around the room. He needed something more to warm her. He pulled his own duvet over her, and laid his hand on her cheek. Her skin was frigid. And still she trembled.

"S—still c—cold," she stuttered.

Gavin stood perfectly still for several seconds. She was covered with two heavy covers, a fire was blazing in the fireplace, and the room was growing much warmer than her own. Still, her face was flushed and her skin was cold. Would his own body heat offer some warmth? He groaned. He would have to get in bed and hold her until she stopped shaking.

Ignoring the sudden pounding of his heart, he lifted the covers. Against his better judgment, he crawled under the duvets and drew her into his arms.

His body reacted immediately.

"Bloody hell," he muttered. He forced himself to think about Merry's condition. Gradually, he realized how very chilled she was. The cold of her skin seeped through the cotton shirt he'd provided. He wondered if it was possible for her to be colder now than she was when he had carried her into the house.

He attempted to lace his fingers with hers and she gasped out loud. Lifting her icy hands, he rested them on his shirt. No, that wasn't going to help. He pulled at the buttons of his own shirt, and pressed her hands to his naked chest.

He groaned as her frigid flesh touched his warm skin. She moaned, as if in pain. She tried to pull her hands away, but he grasped her wrists and placed her hands under his arms.

She cried out.

"It's all right. We need to get you warm," he murmured.

She settled against him and it was his turn to moan. Slowly her hands began to warm. He reasoned that his skin was much warmer than her body. What he needed to do was strip off his clothes and the shirt she was wrapped in and press his body against hers.

He slipped from the covers and in seconds he was unclothed, naked as the day he was born. He scooted under the duvet and yanked his shirt away from her. Praying for self-control, he pulled her into his arms. The cold silk of her skin inflamed him more, and he cursed silently. He didn't need this.

She whimpered and snuggled next to him. He hoped she was uncomfortable enough with her cold body not to notice his reaction to her presence.

Slowly over the next hour, she grew less tense, and Gavin realized she had warmed up considerably. He knew he should crawl out of the bed but the temptation to hold her was so great he couldn't move. He rolled her over so that her bottom was pressed into his groin. He wrapped his hands around her rib cage, beneath the swell of her breasts.

Forcing himself to relax, he began to count to one hundred. By the time he reached the sixties, the activities of the day caught up with him and he drifted off to sleep.

Sometime during the night, Gavin stirred. Only half awake, he became aware of the warm, supple flesh resting against his arm. He lifted his hand. Soft, so soft, he thought, as his fingers closed around a perfect breast. He flicked his thumb over the nipple, and snuggled closer to the woman in his arms.

She mewled and he turned her toward him, stroking her from waist to hip and back. Slender, perfectly formed, he thought as he teased the tender flesh under her breast. He gathered her closer and ran his hands over her back, cupping her firm buttocks.

Hot, so hot, he thought as he pulled her closer still. She came willingly, although Gavin sensed she, too, was not yet fully awake. When she awoke, she would stop him. She had to stop him, for he had not the strength to stop himself.

He tilted her head so that he could reach her lips and then he gently pressed his mouth to hers. She moaned and he took instant advantage, parting her lips with his tongue. A taste, he wanted a taste.

Fully awake, but too involved in giving and getting pleasure, he murmured her name as he stroked her bottom lip. He thrust deep then withdrew, mimicking the other action his body desired. Not yet, he told himself, let the pleasure build, let her wake up and order him from the bed.

Suddenly, she was kissing him back, and this time

the sounds came from his throat. He sighed with satisfaction, still she said nothing, did nothing, and any thought of stopping deserted him.

He tasted her mouth, stroked her lips with his tongue, and allowed her the same privilege as she returned his attentions. When he switched his kisses to the tip of her nose, her eyelids, even the shell of her ear, she moaned a complaint. Raining tiny kisses, he worked his way down the column of her neck, pausing to nip at the pulse point throbbing at the base. He heard her sigh and he smiled. His ministrations pleased her and that increased his own pleasure.

His hands found their way to her breasts, and he cupped one then the other, smoothing his fingers over the flesh before he lowered his head to take one small nub into his mouth. He played his tongue over it, feeling it swell.

She arched against him and he drew the nipple further into his mouth, brushing it with his tongue. She twisted beneath him and he chuckled. She wanted the same interest applied to the other. He was quick to give the other breast the same treatment while his thumb flicked the damp nipple he'd just left.

She groaned and he nuzzled the soft skin under each breast then trailed his fingers over her stomach to the curls that guarded her woman's place. She tensed and Gavin quickly turned his wandering fingers to her legs. He smoothed the skin, teasing that place behind her knee before he skimmed the inner flesh of her thighs.

She moaned, and he rolled over her, holding himself above her as he claimed her mouth once more. While he kissed her, he slipped one knee between her legs, then the other, parting her for his ultimate invasion. Slowly, he lowered himself until her body touched his, from chest to groin. He reached between them and touched the small kernel that had her quivering in his arms. He fondled and teased her until she writhed beneath him. Her fingers clutched at his shoulders and he groaned. His vaunted control was slipping fast. He would have to make her his soon.

Merry awoke to pleasure. Kisses were heating the blood in her veins, and rational thought was out of the question. She delighted in the sensations streaking through her as desire curled around her. She had to participate in the feelings running riot through her. She had to return his kisses, do to him what he was doing to her.

Without warning, his mouth left hers, and he touched the tip of her nose, her eyelids, her ear, the column of her neck. She wanted to shout that he should kiss her mouth, do what he had done before but his head moved lower and lower. He touched her breasts.

Scorching heat traveled from the tip of her breasts to her woman's place and back. She reached for more of the intense tingling effect, arching against the hot mouth giving her such exquisite joy. Could she bear more? She didn't think so.

Once again his mouth deserted that part of her body. His head paused between her breasts, while his hands moved over her, toward the apex of her thighs. She tensed. For one instant a thought tried to surface, but before she could drag it into consciousness, his warm fingers trailed over her legs, her knees, behind her knees.

His lips found hers and once again all thought

dissolved into perfect pleasure. His tongue moved into the cavern of her mouth, and withdrew, inviting her to taste of him. She accepted his invitation.

She became so absorbed in returning his kisses that when his warm body touched hers it seemed natural, right, the way it should be, and she relaxed against him. She dragged weak arms up over his shoulders and kneaded the muscles that tensed and relaxed against her palms. With one hand she dug her fingers into the silk of his hair, enjoying the texture slipping through her hand.

"Now." He sighed into her mouth, and she felt his hand move over the mound between her legs. His fingers claimed a part of her that had never been touched before. Wild, unbelievable sensations raced through her and she dug her nails into his back.

A new kind of building tension had her arching against his hand, an entreaty for more, when suddenly his hand was gone and his manhood pressed against her. He drew back and thrust forward.

A sharp burning shocked her and she cried out. He stilled, and she attempted to fight her way out of the sensual fog that floated around her. But as his lips devoured hers, the hurt faded, and more pleasure enveloped her, blocking out most of the discomfort.

"I didn't think," he said against her mouth, but Merry couldn't put the thoughts together enough to figure out what he meant. He began to move against her and there was no time for anything as the building spiral of pleasure began again. Something was happening to her, and it was glorious.

He seemed to know what was going on in her, for he murmured, "Let it happen, Merry, let go."

She did. Her own body pulsed with a different kind of heat, an escalating thrill, pleasure beyond anything she had ever known. She cried out her satisfaction. When the rhythmic pulsing slowed, she sighed and sank into the mattress. Above her Gavin moved again and shouted her name. Instinctively she knew he had shared the same glorious sensations. He collapsed against her, breathing heavily. After a time, he rolled over, taking her with him.

"I don't believe it," he muttered. She wondered what he didn't believe, but she was tired to the point of exhaustion, and couldn't concern herself. Sleep called her and she snuggled into his warm body, all thought banished.

Gavin pulled her close and for a few moments he fought the tendrils of sleep. But he was too sated to fight for long and sleep overtook him.

Gavin jerked awake as a trace of light brightened the horizon. He stared at the woman in his bed. He groaned, remembering immediately what had happened, and the consequences. He grimaced. Well, he supposed it was time he married.

He rolled away from temptation and stood. He glanced down at her. She was curled into a ball. Another thought intruded and he remembered that she had been claimed by his brother. He staggered against the pain. His brother would never forgive him for this. But if Merry was interested only in money, she should be pleased.

He snorted. Of course, since the money was his much more than Kenneth's, she ought to be as pleased with his proposal as with his brother's. Well, no matter. First Kenneth had to sail, and after that, Gavin would approach Merry and offer marriage.

He left the room, taking some clothing with him.

He ambled to the room Merry had originally occupied, washed, and dressed. He made his way back
to his own room, tapped on the door, and stuck his
head around the jamb.

She was still asleep. He tiptoed into the room,
lifted his duvet away, and pulled her into his arms.
She snuggled next to him and he fought a spreading
smile. He carried her back to her own bedroom and
laid her on her bed. She rolled over and curled into
another ball as she slept on. Next, he gathered the
clothes he had ripped from her the night before,
folded them, and piled them on the chair. He
glanced at her one last time, regret pouring through
him. He didn't want to leave her, but they both
needed some distance. Besides, he had things he
had to do.

Merry stretched under the warm covers and
fought to awake. Emotions flooded her and she tried
to place the events of the previous night in some
order. She remembered being cold, cold enough to
imagine death. Gavin had carried her into the house,
but from where?

Escape! She had tried to escape. She'd managed
to get to the stables, mount the small mare, and ride
out into the storm. When a clap of thunder shook
the earth, the horse reared as if the devil himself
stood before them. Without a saddle, Merry slid off,
then watched as the horse raced away.

Gavin had found her moments later and brought
her back. Memories of a cold so intense her teeth
hurt when just the thought flooded her. She remembered rain soaking into her cloak, wetting her dress,
her shift, her feet, until she never thought she would

be warm again. He had carried her into the house and sat her in front of the fire. Merry started. When had he become Gavin?

From that point on, things were hazy. She struggled with strange images, trying to determine what was truth and what was dream. Oh, God forbid, could it all be true? She opened her eyes wide and stared straight ahead. The pleasure, the touching. Had she allowed . . .

Oh, dear Lord, she had. Here, in this room? Or in another room? She shook her head, trying to place the events.

What seemed so clear was the profound pleasure. That she remembered. He had given her more satisfaction than she could ever have imagined. And she had slept in his arms, in a different bed, in a different room. So what was she doing in her own bed?

He had undoubtedly carried her here after they had . . . She didn't want to complete that thought. Aching in places she wasn't about to question, she clambered out of bed, startled at her nudity. Shaking her head, she gingerly washed herself and retrieved dry clothes from the armoire. In a few moments, she was dressed and she sat at the dressing table, staring into the small mirror.

She was ruined. Merry groaned. Her father was a gentleman, and he would demand satisfaction. But she couldn't allow that. She didn't want her father battling his lordship over the issue of her honor. That had to be the ultimate disgrace. She groaned again, the sound reminding her of sounds from the night before, and she wondered how on earth she'd face Lord Dunleigh after what had taken place. She was certain now that what had seemed like a dream was real.

Tears burned at the back of her eyes, but she willed them away. After all, she was already on the shelf. At least she had enjoyed one night of lovemaking. She knew what pleasure was involved. Many spinsters, she imagined, didn't have that.

Steeling herself for the meeting to come, she left her room and made her way down the stairs. The house was silent as a tomb and she wondered where everyone had gone. The dining room had one setting laid in her usual place, but there was nothing at the head of the table.

"Coward," she snarled. He didn't have the courage to face her this morning. She filled her plate from the sideboard and ate her breakfast. The two women he'd employed from the village were missing today, and she wondered if he had sent them away. Well, it didn't matter, for she intended to spend all of this day in her own chamber. She would read.

After she ate, she made her way to the library, selected two more tomes, and slipped back to her room. She spent a good part of the morning reading. At least she tried. Images from the previous night flashed through her mind with every turn of the page.

"This is ridiculous," she muttered, feeling the heat in her face. "Concentrate on the book," she commanded. But it did little good. She read for only minutes before something from their intimate encounter—the kisses, the touches, even the sounds, teased her into another moment of captivating memories. She slammed the book shut in desperation and fled back down to the main floor. It was nearly lunchtime and she intended to use that as an excuse if she ran into the master of the estate.

He wasn't around.

Growing angry, Merry traipsed into the kitchen and found Cook and Mrs. Perry in whispered conversation.

"Mrs. Perry," Merry said, a little too loudly, "when did you return?"

Their guilty glances told her more than she wanted to know. They'd been talking about her, about her and Baron Dunleigh, Merry decided.

"I returned this morning," Mrs. Perry answered.

"I'm glad you are back!" Merry exclaimed.

"Are you all right, child? Have your bruises and those cuts and scrapes healed?"

Merry smiled. "All gone." She lifted the sleeve of her borrowed gown to display an arm no longer green, purple, and yellow.

"Good," Mrs. Perry announced, looking more than a little uncomfortable with the situation.

"Where is his lordship?" Merry asked, her voice steady and calm although her insides churned.

"He had business in the village," Cook supplied.

Merry wanted to ask, *What business? None of yours,* she told herself. Well, his lordship had spared her the embarrassment of facing him at the moment. She thanked the women.

"I'll be in the library, reading," she said and retreated to the library. Maybe in a room meant for reading she *could* concentrate.

Mrs. Perry called her for lunch and again she ate by herself. The hour was close to two in the afternoon when Dunleigh returned. He joined her in the library. Merry fought the fluttering in her chest. Some part of her was delighted that he was back, even though she battled an intense wave of embarrassment.

"We need to talk," he began. Merry stared into his somber face. She knew she wasn't going to like what he wanted to discuss. She needed to make her demands first.

"Lord Dunleigh, I insist you take me home. Immediately!" She dropped her book and stood, jamming her clenched fists on her hips.

"After last night, I give you leave to use my given name. Please, call me Gavin." From the look on his face, Merry decided he was as uncomfortable with his reference to last night as she was. She felt the heat flooding her face and inwardly groaned. She didn't want to talk about the night before.

"My lord"—she began.

"Gavin, please."

She sighed. "Gavin"—she paused, the name unfamiliar on her tongue—"I don't want to talk. I want to go home, now." She glared at him. He was going to take her home now, today, or she was going to start screaming.

"Merry, I'm not going to take you home until Wednesday." The look on his face told her he would brook no interference with his plans.

Merry gritted her teeth. This was Monday. That meant she would not get home for another two days. That was *not* acceptable. She whirled around and started for the door. "I'm going home today."

He grabbed her arm. "No! I said I would take you home in two days' time, after Kenneth sails. Think about him. He's going to be more than hurt when he finds out."

Merry froze. He still thought she and Kenneth . . .

"I told you, Kenneth was interested in my sister,

not me. Why won't you believe me?" She hated the pleading she heard in her voice.

Gavin looked a little unsettled. Could she finally be getting through to him?

"Please, I must go home. I suspect Charlotte and Aunt Sophia returned days ago. Kenneth has probably contacted my sister and alternative plans have already been made. They could be speaking their vows even now, at this very moment." This time she heard the panic in her voice.

She glanced at him but he looked like his resolve had only strengthened.

"The only person getting married anytime soon will be you. After last night we have no choice. We'll be wed as soon as I speak with your father."

Seven

"No!" Merry shouted. "No, we will not wed."

"Yes." His voice was rough.

"I have no intention of marrying anyone," she stated, her head in a whirl. "I don't care what the circumstances. I decided long ago that I would marry *only* for love. You don't love me. I—" She paused. She tried to tell him she didn't love him, but the words refused to pass her lips.

She dashed from the room, sick at heart. He still thought she wanted to wed his brother and he gave no thought at all to her feelings.

But what did she feel? His words had hurt. He offered her his name only because he had taken her virginity. She knew that and so did he. She wasn't going to let a night in his arms force her into marriage. After all, she had given up finding a husband a long time ago.

She sank onto her bed and stared at nothing. She liked him, didn't she? Yes, she did like him. In fact, he stirred something in her that she hadn't bothered to name. She enjoyed being in his company and they seemed to have a lot in common. She remembered the chess competitions and their discussions. Her enforced stay at Dunleigh Manor had been more than pleasant. But she wasn't going to marry a man who didn't love her! Nor did she intend to examine her feelings for him too closely.

Gavin stood in the library and watched helplessly as Merry rushed from the room. The pain that lanced his heart made little sense. But then none of his feelings for her made any sense. He enjoyed her company, he liked her immensely, and last night had been the most amazing union he'd ever experienced with any woman.

However, by the same token, no woman had ever disturbed him as Merry had, nor had he ever given any thought to wedding a woman he'd taken to his bed. So, what was there about Merry that had him seeking a special license to wed her as soon as he had her father's permission?

He didn't want to name what he felt. All he knew for certain was that he was a gentleman, he had bedded a virgin, and therefore they must be married as soon as possible. What if he had gotten her with child?

The thought of Merry swelling with his babe pleased him more than he wanted to admit. No matter what she said, they *would* have to wed as soon as possible.

It was not a bothersome thought. They had much in common, and he would always have a great chess partner. He chuckled. She certainly liked to win. She'd be horrified if she realized he'd let her gain the upper hand a number of times. He rubbed his chin before he ran one hand through his hair. On occasion though, she'd won fair and square.

He thought about how comfortable he felt in her

company. The hours they'd spent together in the library had been a delight. However, she stirred something in him he wasn't going to name.

He spun on his heel and left the library. He had work to do if he was going to take Merry home, speak with her father, and plan a wedding trip.

"Mrs. Perry, coffee," he called as he made his way to the study.

The rest of the afternoon dragged by and Merry kept to her room. Her feelings for Gavin were uppermost in her mind. As the dinner hour approached, she finally admitted that somehow, despite the fact that he held her captive, she had fallen in love with him.

Her heart in her throat, she donned another borrowed dress and started down the stairs. Mrs. Perry's tearful voice drew her to a halt on a stair tread.

"I thought she was better, your lordship."

"It's all right, Mrs. Perry." Merry heard the patience in his voice. "You'll have to leave immediately. Your sister needs you. I understand that. I'll have the carriage brought round."

Merry tensed as she realized that Mrs. Perry was leaving the house once more. Merry would be all alone with Gavin except for Cook, who'd offered no protection the night before. She trembled as she realized she would be at his mercy if he decided to come to her. A tiny voice in her head laughed with glee. *Don't lie to yourself, Merry, you would enjoy his lovemaking again, now wouldn't you?*

Merry turned and tiptoed back to her room. She'd

stay away from him. She wouldn't bother with dinner.

It was nearly ten that night when he knocked on her door.

"Good night," she called out, certain he intended to lock her in again. Instead, he opened her door. With her heartbeat increasing by the second, she stood and gasped, "What are you doing in here?"

"We need to finish our conversation." In the shadows, Merry couldn't see enough of his expression to decide whether he was angry or just insistent.

"We have nothing more to say to each other," she murmured, praying he'd leave. If he stayed he would be too much of a temptation.

"You need to give serious thought to my proposal. I might have gotten you with child last night." He stepped closer to her and Merry backed up.

"Not without love," she said.

"Love has little to do with begetting children," he scolded.

"I know that," she snapped. "I meant I won't marry without love. And *you* don't love me. You still think I intended to wed your brother."

Gavin stepped closer and Merry backed up again, this time her legs hitting the sideboard of the bed.

"But I could learn to love you," he whispered and reached out to touch her cheek.

Merry stiffened. His honor meant a great deal to him and somehow she knew he would say anything if he could get her to change her mind.

"No! I know you are only saying that because you think it's what I want to hear." She turned away, not willing to let him see the tears gathering in her eyes. "Just go," she murmured.

Gavin caressed her arm and she found herself being coaxed to turn. She inhaled as his lips brushed her mouth and she found herself leaning into him. All the emotions of the day spilled through her and she clung to him. How she wanted this! Dreams of last night and his kisses would trouble her for the rest of her life. With greater willpower than she thought she had, she pulled out of his arms.

"Lust changes nothing. I will not marry you." She pushed him away. He turned and walked to the door. All of Merry wanted to cry out to him to stay, to take her in his arms and to love her like he had the previous night. But it could not be, and she was a fool to even allow such thoughts. She listened as he closed and locked the door.

She prepared for bed, but hour after hour passed. Gavin's kisses, his loving, the pleasure she had experienced with him teased her until finally she hugged the pillow and cried herself to sleep.

Morning came and she dragged herself out of bed. What sleep she'd had did little to erase the images of Gavin making love to her. She wanted to go home. One more day and then she'd start trying to forget Gavin Sinclair.

Gavin waited for her at the breakfast table. Somehow, he had to convince her that marriage was the only acceptable solution for the situation in which they found themselves. Earlier that morning he'd received word that Kenneth's ship had sailed, so he intended to take Merry home this afternoon, but he wanted her agreement to wed before they left the manor.

He'd nearly finished his meal when she arrived, her shoulders squared, her eyes shadowed with purple smudges. She looked as if sleep had eluded her. What would she think if she knew he'd been unable to sleep as well?

"My brother's ship sailed last night," he began. "As soon as you agree to my plans for our wedding, I'll take you home." He watched carefully as she forced herself into a more rigid posture. Bloody hell, the chit was stubborn.

"Merry?" he questioned.

"There will be no marriage." She glared at him, then picked up a plate from the sideboard. "I'm hungry this morning. You needn't stay to entertain me. And I would like to leave for home within the hour."

Gavin sighed. She wasn't going to agree. Perhaps her father could make her see some sense. "I'll get the carriage ready. You'll have to tell me where your home is."

An hour later he handed her into the carriage.

"Why is the horse tied in the back?" she asked.

"I destroyed your horse. This animal will replace him."

His grim expression as he climbed in after her told Merry any argument she made would fall on deaf ears. She gritted her teeth. She would say nothing. He must have made the same resolution, for the only thing he said to her was, "It will take several hours to reach your home. We will stop to have lunch en route."

Merry blinked. She had no idea they were so far away from her home. She leaned back against the cushions and closed her eyes. Surely he wouldn't pursue the matter of a union between them with her father. Not when he knew she wanted nothing of the kind.

They stopped at a small inn for lunch and were on their way again in a little over an hour. Merry began to recognize the houses they passed and before long they pulled up before the cottage she called home.

She sighed as Gavin handed her from the conveyance and she swallowed her trepidation. Perhaps her father hadn't returned. Perhaps Aunt Sophia and Charlotte had stayed on at their party. She stepped forward and opened the door, Gavin directly behind her.

As soon as she crossed the threshold, Charlotte ran to meet her. "Oh, Merry, where have you been? We've been so worried."

Merry stepped into the parlor and took in the scene before her. A young man with a startling resemblance to Gavin sat beside Aunt Sophia, and her beloved father paced the carpet in front of the fireplace.

Chaos reigned for a moment as everyone started talking at once. Merry heard Gavin above the noise as he shouted, "What are you doing here?" Just then her father's deep voice rang out, cutting through the cacophony.

"Silence!"

He stopped in front of Merry. "Well, my girl"— he gazed at her beneath his bushy graying eyebrows and ran one hand through his disheveled hair—"you have some explaining to do. I get called away from France because no one knew where you were. Then I arrived at the cottage to find that my second daughter has been married to a fortune hunter for over a week. I can't even have the thing annulled. Now, would you like to tell me what has been going on around here?"

Gavin stepped forward. "Second daughter? Married? Kenneth, are you married to this young lady?" He pointed to Charlotte, his expression shocked.

Kenneth, seated beside Sophia, stood. "Gavin, may I introduce my wife, Charlotte Sinclair, and her aunt, Lady Sophia Palmer."

Her father turned toward Gavin. "You know this young man?"

"He's my brother," Gavin admitted. He glanced at Merry and then back toward Kenneth. Merry wanted to shout, *I told you so.*

"Sir," Gavin continued, "what did you mean by fortune hunter? Kenneth has a substantial income of his own."

Her father cleared his throat. "That has yet to be determined. And my second daughter has property which makes her quite a catch. Now, who, sir, are you?"

Merry watched as Gavin straightened and bowed slightly before the older man.

"Gavin Sinclair, Baron Dunleigh, sir, and this is my brother, Kenneth, who was supposed to have sailed last night for the Islands." Gavin glowered at Kenneth. "We'll discuss that later."

Kenneth had the audacity to grin. "I had no intention of going to the Islands. I got married instead."

Gavin turned back to her father. "And you, sir?"

"Herman Ward, father of the woman at your side and the young lady married to your brother." He extended his hand and Gavin solemnly shook it.

Gavin turned to his brother and glared at him once more. Merry had tried to tell Gavin that this was what she had tried to prevent. She gave Charlotte a look of disgust.

"When did you wed?" she asked.

Charlotte stepped back and laid her hand on Kenneth's arm, then smiled up at him, her eyes shining with happiness. "We married a week ago Monday. Aunt Sophia stood for us."

"Sophia, how could you?" Herman asked.

Sophia laughed and stood. "Young love. You know I believe in it. Now that Merry has returned, I must be on my way. I'm back to London. I've been away too long." With a swirl of silk, she flounced away.

Merry watched her aunt depart and turned back to her father, but Gavin already had him engaged in conversation. Merry had a very good idea what the subject of their discourse was and she had every intention of disrupting their discussion.

"Before you agree to anything the baron has to say, Father, I want you to know I refused his lordship's proposal."

Charlotte gasped and Kenneth chuckled.

"Don't say a word," Merry snapped. She turned on her heel and started toward the stairs. "The carriage ride was very tiring. I beg to be excused."

She made her way up the stairs, ignoring Gavin, who called after her. She lay on her bed, even though she still heard the voices below. She didn't care. She wasn't going to wed a man who saw her as a duty and nothing more. He didn't love her, probably would never love her, despite what he said. And if her father pressured her, she would remind him that he had promised her a say in her future.

Charlotte called good-bye and she heard the front door close. Two down, one to go. She wondered if Gavin would wait until she finally made her way down the stairs. She closed her eyes and prayed for sleep.

Eventually, she heard the front door open and close once more and then a carriage depart. She sighed with relief. Gavin had left; she could face her father alone.

She rested for a few more minutes before she decided to leave her room. She straightened her dress, freshened up, and descended the stairs. Her father sat in his favorite chair, his pipe in his hand, a curl of smoke circling his head.

"Ah, Merry, glad to have you join me. Are you rested now and do you want to tell me what all this is about? I've only gotten bits and pieces. There are things I don't understand. Start at the beginning so I can put it all together."

Merry sighed and sank down on a stool at his feet. She took a deep breath and explained how she found the note, the wild ride into the night, and her accident with Blackie.

"You could have been killed," her father said and patted her.

"I know," she whispered. "I did get quite a bump." She rubbed the spot on her head. "That was how I ended up at Dunleigh Manor."

"Tell me about the baron," her father ordered.

Merry hesitated. She wondered what Gavin had told her father. "He feels he's compromised my good name. That's why the offer of marriage."

He looked at her, his eyes sad. "I understand he has compromised you."

Merry swallowed the lump in her throat. "It

doesn't make any difference, not to me. He doesn't love me. I—it was a misunderstanding. Papa, you always said love was the most important ingredient in a marriage. You've told me over and over how much you loved my mother. I want a marriage like yours."

"But, daughter, love can grow." He rubbed her shoulder and she relaxed against his knees, just as she had when she was much younger.

"I married Sara to give you a mother, and I learned to love her." He paused and patted her head once more. "Oh, maybe not the same way as your mother, but Sara and I had a good marriage. Both you and Charlotte were happy, weren't you?"

She nodded, the lump in her throat growing.

"However, I did give you the choice of a husband, so if this Baron Dunleigh won't suit then the matter is closed. Of course, he doesn't strike me as a man to give up so easily." Herman chuckled, tapped his pipe on the tray beside the chair, and stood.

"It's late. I think we both need a good night's sleep. We'll see what tomorrow brings, shall we?"

Despite her lack of sleep the night before, Merry couldn't seem to relax. She twisted and turned. Gavin's face flashed before her eyes through most of the night. How could she forget him if he wouldn't leave her thoughts? She groaned, pounded her pillow, and tried to count the stars she could see from her bedroom window.

With the dawn, Merry dragged herself from bed and after a wash she dressed in her own clothes and made her way down the stairs. Bessy was busy in the kitchen, fixing breakfast.

"Oh, miss," she declared, "it's that glad I am to

have you back. Your papa was so furious that you were gone and her sister had gotten herself a husband, that he sent me home."

"Yesterday?" Merry asked.

Bessy nodded. "He came home yesterday morning. Said he had traveled all night. He was that upset that you were missing and then when he found out Charlotte had a husband, he got his ire up."

She glanced at Merry before she continued with her chores. Merry sighed. It seemed strange without Charlotte in the house. She donned an apron and started slicing bread for their meal.

A sharp knock on the door startled her and she glanced at Bessy. "Better see who that is. Papa needs his rest."

Bessy nodded and disappeared, only to return a moment later, breathless. "Oh, miss. The most handsome man wants to see you. I showed him into the parlor. Should I set a place for him?"

Merry had never seen Bessy so flustered. And she had a very good idea who had arrived so early in the morning. She untied her apron, informing the maid, "He'll be leaving in a few minutes. No need to set a place."

Bessy gasped as Merry strode from the kitchen. She had guessed correctly, for Gavin waited in the parlor.

"Good morning, Merry," he said.

"Not particularly," Merry replied. If he had the cheek to arrive before a decent hour, she saw no need to be polite. He must have read her thoughts, for he grinned at her.

"I came to ask when you want the ceremony to

take place and would you like for it to be in your church or mine?"

"I have no intention of going through any ceremony with you, my lord. I suggest you quit your suit and leave me alone." She wanted to scream that he didn't love her, but she had a feeling he would spout a false pledge in an attempt to get her to consent to wed him.

She spun on her heel and trudged back to the kitchen. "Bessy, show Baron Dunleigh to the door."

Bessy looked stunned, but for once the girl did exactly as she was told, and without comment.

However, Gavin arrived early the next day and the next. Merry sent him on his way each time, praying that soon he would realize she wasn't going to accept him. On the fourth morning, her father greeted their guest and Merry had to sit through breakfast with her father and Gavin discussing politics. Then the two men retired to her father's study. Gavin left an hour later.

Sunday morning arrived but Gavin did not appear. Merry wiped at blurry eyes, telling herself that was what she wanted after all. The man had finally gotten the message that she had no intention of marrying him, for a union without love was impossible for her.

She and her father went to church and came home to a quiet house. Charlotte and her new husband had mentioned they might visit, but they didn't arrive.

And there was no Gavin Sinclair. Merry refused to think about how much that stung.

She fixed her father something to eat and after the meal, Merry picked up a book and tried to read. It was useless. All she could think about was that

Gavin had finally acceded to her demand not to bother her again. And that thought hurt so badly she excused herself, donned her cloak, and went for a brisk walk.

When she returned, a young boy from the village waited on the doorstep. He held a large bundle in his arms.

"Mistress Ward, these is for you."

He thrust the bundle at her and dashed away. She didn't get a chance to ask him who had sent the bundle. Once inside the house, she pulled the oilcloth away from the contents and stared at a dozen deep red roses. However, there was nothing to identify the sender.

Less than an hour later, a knock on the door of the cottage indicated another visitor. Merry rushed forward, but once again another boy from the village handed her another cloth-wrapped bundle. This one contained a dozen white roses.

Merry sighed. Roses at the end of February? Who on earth was sending her such an extravagant gift? Again, there was no card to tell her who had sent the roses.

She arranged the flowers in a vase and stepped back. The flowers were beautiful but she couldn't help but wonder who had sent them two weeks after Valentine's Day.

Another hour passed and again there was a knock at their door. Merry rushed to answer it, wondering as she did who would greet her this time.

She looked up into the solemn face of Gavin Sinclair, then she noticed the familiar bundle he held in his arms. Without a word he handed her the cloth package.

"Come in," she invited, taking the package from him.

He stepped over the threshold and stood for a moment looking at her before he said, "Open it."

Merry glanced at the package in her arms. It was exactly like the two other bundles of roses that had arrived that day. She released the wrapping and gasped. Another bouquet of deep red and pure white roses lay against the cloth. This time, however, they were twined with green ivy.

Red and white roses and ivy. Marriage! She looked into his eyes. Stunned, she clasped the roses close to her bodice. "Where? Why?"

"I ordered them from many places. Of course, now that Valentine's Day is past they were a little hard to find." His face remained solemn. "Why? Because I wanted you to know how much I love you."

"You love me?"

He nodded.

"You didn't say," Merry whispered.

"Would you have believed me?" he asked quietly.

"Probably not." She shook her head. He looked annoyed for an instant, then his demeanor changed.

"And do you believe me now?" he asked, his expression anxious.

She glanced at the roses and at Gavin and she could see his love for her shining in his dark blue eyes. She laid the bundle aside and stepped into his waiting arms. His lips brushed her forehead. She smiled up at him.

"I love you, too, you know," she murmured.

"Your father thought you might." He grinned.

"I do," she said.

"So, you'll marry me?" His anxious expression was back.

She nodded, knowing he could see the love in her own eyes.

She gazed at Gavin and then at the roses. Any man who would go to the trouble of finding all these flowers and arranging to have them delivered as he had must love deeply. She smiled. The month of February and Valentine's Day would always be special. Cupid, indeed, had brought her true love.

BE MINE

Deborah Matthews

One

"My family is demented." Simon, Earl of Valentine huffed and strode across the room. He turned to his cousin. "Not one tight screw in the bunch. How would *you* like to be known as Lord Valentine the rest of your life? The king cursed the eldest sons of this family."

Matthew grinned. "Legend is the king was in love with the first lord's wife. Hence the name. Val, are you upset because Mama is here?"

He snorted and paced back across the room. "Of course not. I love your mother. If only she had a different name or a different life's objective."

Ennui painted Matthew's countenance and he slouched against the settee. "She loves her name."

"Yes, I know, and she takes it very seriously. Aunt Cupid is as queer as Dick's hatband." Val grabbed the poker and stabbed at the fire. Logs crackled and snapped.

Matthew studied him. "Now, Val, Mama likes to play matchmaker, but she isn't addled."

Val closed his eyes. "Just assure me she has no plans for me."

"You can never tell who Mama's next attempt is," Matthew said.

He opened his eyes and glared. Pointing the poker at Matthew, Val said, "Victim is more like it."

Matthew shrugged. "A Miss Lucinda is the intended bride."

"Lucinda who?"

"I don't know. I haven't met her or her parents."

"Matthew, please make certain I'm not the object of Aunt's design."

"All of Mama's plans have worked," he offered, but Matthew's words did not reassure Val.

"I think they marry just to get rid of Aunt Cupid. You must admit her schemes tend to go cockeyed." Val gave the fire another jostle with the poker.

Matthew grinned again. "Yes, but she is so serious. She thinks it her life's work. She believes there is a purpose to her name."

Val shoved the poker back into the stand. "Her mother was addled also. Everyone knows Cupid was male. What damns this family to be dominated by Cupid and love and such nonsense?"

"What do you expect with a title of Valentine?"

Val nodded and shook his finger at Matthew. "My point. It is the king's fault for naming the earldom Valentine. So feminine and dainty."

"Now, Val, no one thinks you dainty." Amusement flickered across Matthew's face.

Val's eyes narrowed. "You are laughing at me?"

"No, coz." Matthew laid his hand on his leg and straightened his face.

"You were laughing," Val accused and ran one hand through his hair. "Devil it, why could the king not give the first earl a strong name?"

Matthew's gaze followed Val back and forth as he

continued to pace. "You know, Val, it isn't the name so much as the man who holds the title. Everyone thinks you strong and masculine."

"And the reason for the stupid rhymes?" Val slammed his hand against the mantel.

"So, that is what has your dander up. You heard the children in the village singing that silly song."

Matthew's teasing tone irritated Val and accentuated his annoyance. His cousin did not understand his exasperation. He was not stuck with a namby-pamby moniker. Sometimes he wished he had not been the eldest son and inherited the Valentine title. "Yes, I heard the ditty about the Earl of Valentine."

Since inheriting the title, no one called him Simon any longer. Not even his relations. He even thought of himself as Val. Sometimes he felt like a mere shadow existing, not really living.

"Written years before you inherited the title. You have to be mature and ignore the childish nonsense," Matthew said with quiet emphasis.

Val reached into his watch pocket, but drew back empty fingers. "Damnation. I have lost the Valentine watch."

"Someone will find it," Matthew assured him. "It is quite distinct."

Val grimaced. "Yes, with cherubs, hearts, and flowers engraved all over. Were it not a family heirloom, I would have pitched it into the lake long ago."

"Good evening." The soft voice floated across the air.

Val quit pacing and forced a smile. "Aunt Cupid. Did you have a nice journey?"

The mulberry ostrich plume above her silver hair quivered as Cupid nodded. "Quite." She rushed across the Aubusson carpet. Her mulberry gown whispered around her slippers.

Indeed, his aunt resembled pictures of Cupid. Pudgy cheeks glowed with vitality and vivacity. Brown eyes twinkled with gaiety over her button nose. She only needed a bow and a quiver of arrows.

Val mentally shook his head. No, she would only hurt herself or someone else if armed.

She stood in front of Val and ordered, "Bend down."

Val complied and received a kiss on the cheek.

Cupid's gaze roamed the drawing room. "This is the loveliest room. The green and white are very restful. I'm glad no one has redecorated. Bless your mother's soul. May I hold a soirée in two weeks' time?"

The interior of his drawing room or a party was the last topic of conversation he desired. Val cleared his throat. "Yes. I don't mean to be inhospitable, Aunt, but why are you here? You could have held a soirée in your London town house."

"You look worried," she said. "But no need to fret. I'm going to help you." She patted his cheeks and her multitude of bracelets rattled.

Val closed his eyes as if in prayer. "Please don't, Aunt Cupid. I don't wish your assistance with a bride. Why do you not concentrate on your own son?"

Cupid giggled and sat beside Matthew on the settee. "He isn't yet ready for marriage."

Val opened his eyes. "Neither am I. I enjoy being a bachelor." Val sat in the chair across from his aunt and pleaded, "Please don't look for a bride for me. What of Benedict?"

She waved her hands in the air and her bracelets clanked again like a battalion of love armor. "Your younger brother has time. You are head of the family, so I must concentrate on you. I have no control. It is fate. Your time has come."

"Lucky me." Val groaned and turned to Matthew. "Help me," he implored.

Matthew shrugged. "Sorry, coz, if it is your time, then it is your time. Mama knows these things."

Val presented the first logical argument that came to mind. "But we are in the country. There are no eligible misses within twenty miles."

"You never know where you will find her," Cupid assured him, "And I'm already on the scent."

Val groaned. "Must you?"

She nodded.

Val gritted his teeth. He almost felt like a child throwing down a gauntlet to an adult. "You cannot make me marry."

Cupid sighed and glanced at her son. "He is going to be difficult."

"I'm afraid so, Mama." Matthew squeezed her hand. "Perhaps you should find someone else to matchmake."

Cupid shook her head. "No, it is Val's time."

Cupid showed no sign of relenting. Val struggled to keep the belligerence from his voice. His aunt might vex him, but he held no wish to hurt her. "Who says it has to be my time?"

She gestured toward the ceiling. "Fate. Destiny. Many call it different names."

"What if my destiny is to die unmarried? Perhaps it is Benedict's destiny to inherit the earldom and sire heirs." Val grinned, proud of his logic.

Cupid shook her head. "Benedict's destiny lies

elsewhere. Your son and son's son and so forth will continue to inherit the title. *Amor vincit omnia.*"

Val's grin vanished. "Love does *not* conquer all." He rolled his eyes and hurdled from the chair. He paced to the window and stared out the faint green glass. If the countryside were not in the grasp of a wintry chill, he would open the window and escape.

Bloody hell! He should have stayed elsewhere. He only recently straightened out the estates from his father's mismanagement. A bride was the last thing he wanted.

Fate had foreseen her vocation and named her Cupid. At least so his aunt was convinced. Usually her schemes went awry and it was only by the grace of God no one had yet been harmed.

Val had seen her bumbling ways many times. He was convinced that she really was not awkward, but merely paid no attention due to her hurry and great enthusiasm. A better, more loving heart would not be found anywhere, but she would strain an angel's soul. And he certainly was no angel.

Now she was persuaded to set her matchmaking eyes upon him. There seemed to be no words to discourage her.

Val strode to the cellarette and poured himself a brandy. He downed the amber liquid in one gulp and poured another. Grasping the snifter, he stalked across the room and dropped onto the chair. "I shall make you a wager, Matthew."

Boredom disappeared from Matthew's face and he straightened. Utter disbelief painted his brow. "You don't gamble."

Val nodded and hid his grin. He would make Matthew his ally with the one item he loved and could not afford. "This is a friendly wager between cousins. You have admired my new hunter."

"He is a fine bit of horseflesh." Awe filled Matthew's voice.

Val swirled the brandy snifter. "If I don't become betrothed while you are here, he is yours."

Matthew's eyes widened. "And if you do?"

"You shall give me Uncle Henry's diamond stickpin."

Matthew's fingers touched the stickpin in the folds of his cravat. "I like uncle's stickpin. He had no other relations to bequeath it to."

Val nodded. "And I like my hunter, but I'm willing to take the risk. How much of a gamble is it since I don't wish to marry?"

Matthew grinned. "Very well, coz. It is a wager."

Cupid crossed her arms over her chest and frowned. "That isn't fair, Val. You have just bought Matthew's assistance."

A slow grin tugged at the corners of Val's mouth. "It is to his benefit to make sure I remain unattached."

Cupid glanced from Matthew to Val, her frown deepening. "I'm disappointed in you. You have no confidence in my skills."

Val kissed her hand. "Aunt Cupid, the fact is I don't wish to wed. It doesn't mean I put no credence in your calling."

She stood and raised her chin. "I shall succeed anyway." Cupid flounced from the room without glancing back.

Dismay covered Matthew's face and he shook his head. "I'm destined to lose."

* * *

The carriage turned through the arch of a four-towered gatehouse into the courtyard of Valentine Hall. Balls of yew lined the drive. Grace Templeton inhaled a deep breath. The Valentine estate was an impressive sight.

"Lord Valentine must be very rich."

Grace gritted her teeth at her mother's greedy words. She glanced at her sister's pale face. "But what sort of man is he?"

Ida Templeton waved away Grace's words. "It doesn't signify. Your sister will be wealthy when she becomes Lady Valentine."

"What if he is an ogre?" Lucinda whispered. "What if he hits people?"

Lucinda's face was pale as bed linen. Grace grasped for words to ease her mind. "I'm certain he is a kind gentleman."

The majestic hall dominated the landscape. The red brick house had been built during the time of Queen Elizabeth by a previous Valentine earl. She wondered if the hall had been filled with love and laughter. How it would feel to be so loved by a man? Well, one thing was certain. She would never know that kind of love. She was too old for a gentleman's attention.

Flanked by octagonal bays, the mullioned windows stared down at her like vacant eyes. The coach halted and the front door opened. A footman descended the stairs to open the coach door and let down the steps.

Lucinda grasped Grace's hand. "Please don't leave my side."

"Hush, Lucinda," Ida hissed. "Your sister is only here because I could not leave her alone. *You* are the diamond of the first water. One look at you and the earl will fall instantly in love."

Ida clamored down the steps.

Grace squeezed Lucinda's hand. "I will not leave you alone with his lordship."

A small smile trembled on Lucinda's mouth. "You are the best sister, Grace. You aren't even upset that Mama seeks to marry me first and you are the older."

"Who would wish to marry me? I'm old, fat, and ugly."

"Don't say such," Lucinda cried. "You are only six-and-twenty and pretty."

"Come, Lucinda," her mother hissed. "Don't tarry."

Grace followed Lucinda from the coach, her small terrier clutched in her arms. The dog's gaze caught sight of a hare disappearing into the bushes and wriggled loose.

"Lachlan, come back here!" Grace called to no avail. She sighed and watched the small body disappear behind the copse.

"Go after him. You should have left the stupid mutt at home," Ida hissed.

Grace turned to her sister. "I shall return immediately."

Grace dashed between the shrubs. "Come back, Lachlan." Only silence met her ears. "Lachlan, cease being naughty and return to me."

"Is this your dog?" a deep voice asked.

Grace gasped and twirled around. A man grasped her terrier between large hands. Lachlan's dark muzzle snarled at his captor. His short legs tried to find purchase on the man's arms.

Dirt covered the man's worn clothes. Her gaze

seemed to travel forever up his long form to meet his eyes. "Yes."

"He was trampling my flower bed," the churl groused.

Gardening tools and mounds of dirt surrounded the man. She grabbed Lachlan from his grasp and hugged him to her chest. "I apologize. Isn't it too cold to plant now?"

The man's dark eyes flared, then he turned back to his work. "Some bulbs require cold before they bloom in the spring. Though I'm a bit late planting."

Grace sat on the bench a few feet away. "His lordship doesn't mind your late planting."

His dark head snapped up and he looked at her through narrowed eyes. "Mind?"

Grace's gaze searched the area. Certain they were alone, she lowered her voice. "One hears tales the earl has an awful temper. He doesn't mix in society."

"Indeed?" Sarcasm seemed to etch his voice.

She pushed her curiosity aside, then nodded and swallowed. She would find out soon enough what sort of man Lord Valentine was. "Not that I expect you to say. It would not behoove the gardener to make comments about Lord Valentine."

Humor flashed across the gardener's face. "True."

Not certain why he was amused, Grace filled the silence with words. "I apologize for not introducing myself. I'm Grace Templeton."

He stared at her a moment. "A pleasure to meet you, Miss Templeton." He glanced down at his dirt-covered hands, then dropped them to his side.

He did not give a name. Perhaps he thought it

above his station as a gardener. "Have you been at Valentine Hall long?"

"My entire life," he said.

"Your parents worked here also?"

The gardener picked up his trowel and shoved it into the hard ground. "Yes." Deft hands moved dirt aside. He set a bulb in the hole and covered it.

"Your job must be very rewarding," Grace said.

His hands stilled and he looked up. "In what way?"

She smiled and ignored the brisk wind biting at her nose. "You plant corms and seeds. They grow and produce beautiful flowers and delicious vegetables. To know that what you do manifests such—"

A stick snapped in the winter air.

The gardener looked up. "What is it, Downey?"

The old man duffed his hat and gray hair trembled in the breeze. " 'xcuse me—"

He cut him off. "Just say what you came to say."

"Mrs. Lynford sent word for ye to be returning to the hall."

"Thank you. I shall return momentarily."

The servant nodded and retreated.

Why would Cupid summon the gardener when visitors had just arrived? Grace tilted her head to the side and studied this man of the earth.

He appeared to be thirty or so. Very handsome with a square jaw. Magnetic eyes snapped at her. "Is something amiss, Miss Templeton?"

Heat flushed Grace's face and she cleared her throat. "No. I suppose I should go inside and greet my hostess." She stood, but did not walk away. "When I become bored, may I come out and enjoy your garden?"

"It is cold for walks in the garden."

Grace licked her bottom lip. "I don't mind the cold as much as I dislike idle gossip and chitchat. No one will note my absence."

Dark eyes stared at her, then he graced her with a beautiful smile. "Miss Templeton, anyone with sense would take note of you."

Confused by his statement, Grace opened her mouth to ask what he meant, but he held up his hand. "Go, now."

He sounded quite dictatorial. Perhaps because he was head gardener. Grace closed her mouth and walked away as fast as her legs would allow. She was shocked they did not collapse beneath her. What an enigmatic man.

Grace returned to find her mother and sister standing on the steps. "What took you so long?" Ida demanded. "We have been waiting."

"I'm sorry, Mama. I expected you to go inside. I spoke to the gardener."

"Gardener?" Reproach filled her mother's voice. "What would Cupid and Lord Valentine think of you conversing with their gardener? My hoyden of a daughter traipsing around the lawn talking to *servants.*"

Grace shrugged. "That I was polite?"

Ida hissed, "You are impossible. Can you not behave with propriety for once in your life?"

Heat burned Grace's cheeks, but she gave an honest answer. "It would seem not."

Ida glared, then turned. Grace followed her mother up the stairs where a black-clad butler waited. "Good day, madam. May I help you?"

Ida Templeton drew herself up. "I'm Mrs. Templeton. I and my daughters are invited houseguests."

The butler showed not a flicker of emotion

though he acted as if they were not expected. "Follow me to the drawing room and I shall inform Lord Valentine of your arrival."

They entered beneath a coat of arms. Black and white tiles checkered the entry floor. Magnificent paintings graced the walls. The Templeton art collection had been sold long ago. Grace's gaze darted around trying to absorb everything.

The Valentine drawing room was an elegant chamber. A sense of being out of place assailed Grace. Green and white striped silk covered the walls between dark green woodwork. Grace perched on the green silk settee and placed Lachlan beside her.

Lucinda settled beside her and whispered, " 'Tis beautiful."

Ida settled on the chair across from them. "Don't act so awed," she hissed. "We don't wish them to think us provincials."

The door flew open and a man stalked in. *Him!* Lachlan growled. Grace placed her hand on the dog's back before he could launch toward the man.

Dirt now gone, he was dressed as any stylish gentleman. A handsome man. Much more so than he had been in work clothes. Chiseled cheekbones and a square jaw intensified his features. Hair and eyes were as black as coal. He must be over six feet of muscle and brawn. The man wore the clothes, not the other way round as so many London dandies.

Short-cropped hair stood on end as if he continually ran his hand through it. The mussed hair made him appear as if he had just arisen from his bed. Zounds! Where had that thought come from?

His cold black gaze rested on Grace, then swung to Ida. "Madam, why have you invaded my home?"

The demand so flustered Ida that she forgot to stand and curtsy. "L—Lord Valentine, w—we were invited."

"Mrs. Templeton, I don't know you. Why would I invite you into my home?" A muscle flicked in his jaw.

"My lord." Her own anger flared and Grace hopped to her feet. She forced herself not to flinch under his withering stare. "My mother has faults, but she is not a liar. Mrs. Cupid Lynford issued the invitation." Grace glanced at her mother. "We should leave, Mama. Doubtless, we aren't wanted in this churl's home."

His expression changed from anger to dismay. Lord Valentine sucked in a deep breath. "Aunt Cupid invited you?"

Grace flashed him a look of disdain. "You are hard of hearing as well?"

He remained motionless for a moment, then his brows drew together in an agonized expression. "No. Just disbelieving that Aunt Cupid would invite guests and not inform me."

Grace opened her mouth to speak, but he held up his hand. "I know. You don't lie."

"Ida," the soft voice called from the door. Cupid rushed in and halted beside the earl. "I'm so glad you have arrived."

"We are leaving, Mrs. Lynford," Grace said.

"Leaving?" Cupid's troubled eyes turned to Lord Valentine and she tapped his arm with her folded fan. "You said I could have a party."

The muscle continued to tick in his jaw. "Yes, but I was unaware you invited houseguests. I apologize for the misunderstanding, Mrs. Templeton. You and your daughters are welcome to stay." He turned to the door, then halted. He pivoted and his hands clasped the doorjamb. Grace was surprised the frame did not crack beneath his grasp. "Aunt Cupid, have you invited anyone else?"

"No, dear. I thought the other guests for the Valentine festivity would be local."

"Valentine as in the family title?" Desperation laced his voice

Cupid smiled. "No, dear. We must celebrate the holiday of love. Where best to do so than at Valentine Hall with Cupid as hostess?"

"With games?" he whispered and hope disappeared from his eyes.

Cupid clapped her hands. "Of course. You shall be betrothed by the Valentine soirée."

Lord Valentine's face paled beneath his bronzed skin. "Aunt Cupid, I have informed you I don't intend to marry."

Cupid waved her hand in dismissal and bracelets rattled through the room. "Pish-posh. Fate is at hand."

He opened his mouth to speak, then snapped it closed. The earl merely turned and stomped from the room.

Cupid settled on the chair beside Ida. "I apologize for Val's behavior."

Grace felt sorry for the gentleman. Apparently, he held no interest in his aunt's machinations to wed him.

"Grace?" Lucinda whispered. "He *is* an ogre." Nervous fingers fiddled with the pleat of her gown.

Grace sat and patted Lucinda's hand. "He was merely taken aback by our unexpected arrival. Though, you shouldn't hope to marry him."

Lucinda shook her head. "I have no such desire. He is much too fearsome."

"Mama, perhaps we should depart. Your purpose here is at an end," Grace said.

If Lord Valentine held no wish to marry, why stay? Underneath the logic, Grace knew something else disturbed her. Not just having thought the earl was the gardener. Her unique reaction to this man was to be avoided.

"Don't be silly, Grace," Ida said. "A man never knows what he wants until a lady shows him. He hardly paid attention to Lucinda. Once he gets a good look at her beauty, he will be smitten."

"Very true, Ida." Cupid smiled at Lucinda. "What else could a man want in a wife besides beauty? Lucinda is beautiful."

Grace bit her tongue to halt her outrage. A man should want more. He should want intelligence and love. Beauty should be the last attribute needed for a good wife, but no one else seemed to think that.

"Stop your fretting, Grace," Ida ordered. "Lucinda shall bring Lord Valentine around."

Lucinda's blue eyes filled with fear and worry. Grace merely squeezed Lucinda's hand and said not a word. She could counsel her sister when they were alone.

"The next fortnight will give Val and Lucinda time to become acquainted," Cupid said. "By the time they dance at my Valentine soirée, they will be betrothed."

"Do you think to compromise Lucinda and force Lord Valentine to marry her?" Grace asked.

"Gracious, no." Cupid fanned her flushed face.

Determination lit Ida's eyes and Grace was sorry she had given her grasping mother ideas. She would stop at nothing to see Lucinda wed to Lord Valentine. At times, Grace wished she belonged to another family. Oh, she loved her mother, but she was much too materialistic. Determined to marry her youngest daughter to a wealthy peer.

Ida Templeton never gave any thought to Lucinda's sensibilities. A harsh husband would overburden her and Lucinda would never learn to speak up for herself.

Grace never had that problem, but it was not considered a desirable trait in a woman. The only burden she felt was the awful secret.

"Ah, here comes the tea," Cupid exclaimed.

A maid set the tea tray in front of Cupid and departed. Cupid dispensed tea to everyone and leaned back. " 'Tis good to know my Val will no longer be alone."

"I thought he had a younger brother," Grace said, then sipped her tea.

Cupid nodded. "He and Benedict have different interests. Benedict prefers London and Val elects to stay in the country. That is why I had to bring a suitable young lady to him."

"Do you mind if I stroll in the garden?" Grace asked.

"Of course not, dear," Cupid said. "It is rather cold."

"I shall retrieve my coat and will be fine for a time." Grace sat her teacup on the table.

Lucinda said, "I shall join Grace."

"No, Lucinda," Ida said. "We have things to discuss with Cupid."

Disappointment covered Lucinda's brow. Grace said, "We shall walk together later, sister."

Lucinda nodded. Grace squeezed her sister's hand

in a silent display of support and escaped, Lachlan keeping pace with her strides.

Val chucked a pebble down the path. Why did his aunt have to bedevil him? He preferred a simple life with no fuss or quibble. If he desired female companionship, he visited a widow that lived near one of his other estates.

In the company of other ladies, he felt like a hulking beast unfit for genteel company. He reached into his watch pocket. Damn! If the Valentine watch had not belonged to previous earls, he would not care if he ever saw it again. It was much too dainty.

Gravel crunched, bringing feet toward his den. Could he find no solitude anywhere? Perhaps the person would not notice him sitting on a bench sheltered between the yews.

"My lord!" Surprise threaded her voice.

Manners called Val to his feet. He bowed. "Miss Templeton."

"I didn't expect anyone else to be in the garden in the cold." She pulled her cloak closer around her.

Lachlan snarled. She whispered, "Hush."

"I have never been like others. Do you wish to sit?" Only good manners made him offer. He preferred to be alone.

Miss Templeton nodded and perched on one end of the bench. Lachlan lay at her feet, his gaze intent upon Val. Val settled beside her.

"I apologize for our unexpected arrival."

She sounded quite sincere. As if she wished to be here as little as he.

Val dragged his hand through his hair. "Don't agitate yourself. My ire has nothing to do with your family. I'm accustomed to Aunt Cupid's intrigues. She means well. I apologize for not introducing myself in the garden."

Truth be told, he had enjoyed her thinking him someone other than Lord Valentine. He had merely thought she was paying a short visit on Aunt Cupid. Not staying as a houseguest.

"Accepted. I suppose my mother does also. One may wish for relations to be different, but can't do much about changing them."

Val nodded. "So true."

Misgivings shadowed the green eyes that glanced at him. Shadows of copper and russet gleamed in her fiery hair.

An image reappeared in his mind when Grace Templeton had faced him in the garden and drawing room. Of feminine curves that would fill his hands. All of a sudden, his clothes were too constricting and sweat popped out on his forehead.

Val inhaled a deep breath. Bloody hell!

"Are you ill?"

The soft voice broke through his haze and he stood. Lachlan growled, but he ignored the dog. "No, Miss Templeton. Excuse me, but I must return to my ledgers."

Val stalked away, but was very aware of the intense green gaze that burned into his back.

Cupid glanced at Matthew. "The first meeting did not go well. Val hardly looked at Lucinda, much less admired her."

Apparently, Mama was annoyed. She seemed set upon her plans to wed Val to Lucinda, even against Val's protests. Matthew admitted he did not understand Val's reluctance. Every peer thought of marrying and producing an heir, but for some unfathomable reason, Val did not.

Why? The question intrigued Matthew. From all his observances, Val's father had not treated his mother with contempt. It had been a typical marriage each having their own interests and spending little time together. The previous earl had attempted to maintain his estates in good order, but seemed not to have the aptitude his son did.

He and Val were close, yet they never discussed anything of an intimate nature. So he never knew Val's deepest thoughts and regrets or even wants. Surely, even Val wished for his life to be different in some way. Since inheriting the title, Val had lost all his joy and spontaneity. He was growing into an old man before his time.

Matthew smiled. "Perhaps you will fare better at dinner. Is Miss Lucinda that beautiful?"

Cupid nodded. "Her hair is as pale as moonlight and her eyes blue as the sea." She glanced at her son. "It is really too bad of you to have made that wager."

Matthew patted her hand. "I'm truly sorry, Mama. I'm unable to afford horseflesh such as Val and you know how I love horses."

"Even as a child you were horse-crazed. I blame it on your father." Cupid shook her head.

Matthew grinned. "You make it sound like an odious trait."

Her brown eyes reproached him as only a mother could. "When you go against your mother's wishes, it is."

"What of the older Miss Templeton?"

"You are changing the subject," Cupid charged.

Matthew shrugged and grinned.

Cupid sighed. "The sisters are altogether different. She isn't the beauty Lucinda is, but pleasant enough with red hair and green eyes. She doesn't hesitate to speak her mind while Lucinda is meek."

"Do you really think a meek bride is right for Val?"

Cupid nodded. "You don't understand these things. A man wishes for a beautiful wife he may mold."

Matthew frowned. "I'm a man, Mama."

She smiled. "I know, dear, but you haven't given any thought to marriage."

"Apparently, neither has Val."

"That doesn't signify. Fate is at hand for Val." Cupid smiled and tweaked his cheek as if he were still a small boy.

He wondered just what Val would think of the beautiful Lucinda. Perhaps she would turn his mind to marriage, but he would do whatever he could to keep them apart.

Guilt twinged through Matthew. Perhaps Val really did need someone. Oh well, Val was old enough to decide for himself whether he wished to marry or not.

Matthew stood and held out his hand. "Shall we go down to the drawing room? I fancy a look at the Miss Templetons."

TWO

"Dinner is served, my lord," the butler intoned from the drawing room doorway.

Val sat his sherry glass on a table and stood.

"Val, be a dear and escort Lucinda into dinner. No need to stand on ceremony. Ida and I will follow you young people."

Val gritted his teeth. Aunt Cupid was in full matchmaking mode. No telling what she had planned.

Matthew said, "Should you not escort the elder Miss Templeton, coz?"

"I believe you are correct, Matthew." Val held out his arm to Grace Templeton. "Shall we go into dinner, Miss Templeton?"

She laid her hand on his arm, though worry etched her brow. She probably would be scolded later, Val thought. Yet she did not hesitate to tweak her mother's nose. "Thank you, my lord." Even through glove and coat sleeve, her hand seemed to burn into his skin.

Cupid cursed under her breath and Val bit back a smile.

"Miss Lucinda?" Matthew held out his arm.

Val led the group into the dining room and pulled out the chair next to his.

"That isn't where Grace's place card is," Cupid said.

Val's gaze searched the table. "I don't see place cards, Aunt."

Cupid scurried to the table. Hands on her hips, she huffed, "I specifically set names to the seats."

Matthew shrugged. "It doesn't matter. We are an odd number of ladies and gentlemen." He pulled out a chair for Lucinda.

Lucinda's eyes moved from Val to Cupid to Matthew.

"Mr. Lynford is correct," Grace said and sat in the chair Val held. His fingers lightly grazed her back, then he quickly stepped to his chair beside her at the head of the table.

Lucinda followed her sister's lead and sat. Matthew moved to the chair between Lucinda and Val. He looked across at Grace and smiled.

Not wishing to give his aunt a moment to rectify their places, Val smiled and gestured to the two footmen holding chairs. "Aunt Cupid, do you and Mrs. Templeton intend to dine with us or shall you stand there frowning all evening?"

Cupid shook her head and muttered, "Might as well not cause a farce"—she frowned at Val and Matthew—"this time." Both ladies reluctantly sat and the soup was served.

Grace's hair was rich and gossamer beneath the candlelight. Silk roses entwined through her coif. Her face was carved with a delicate beauty. Yet a strength permeated her being.

Sheer white lace layered over mull for her gown. A band of pink silk roses studded the hemline. Usually, he did not notice a lady's clothes, but a man could not help but notice Grace Templeton.

Her neckline was cut daringly low. Soft shadows frolicked around the high-perched breasts. Smooth breasts that would taste sweet and pleasing and hips that a man could hold on to. Val cursed himself for recognizing her womanly curves.

"Perhaps we could go shooting tomorrow, Val." Matthew rubbed his hands together. "We could provide birds for the dinner table."

His name drew him out of his reverie. He smiled at Matthew. "Of course."

"The flowers are beautiful." Grace gestured to the epergne spilling forth pink and white roses. "You must have a conservatory?"

"Yes. I have enlarged the conservatory many times."

Grace glanced around the table, then settled her green gaze on Val. "What else do you grow?"

"Dahlias, violets, and lilies as well as fruit. One never knows from month to month what new plant will arrive from some foreign land." Val smiled. "I'm quite proud of my oranges and have been experimenting growing strawberries."

"It would be exciting to travel the world," Grace said.

"Have you traveled much?" Val consumed a spoonful of soup.

Grace shook her head. "Papa said I should have no interest in other places."

Cupid clucked her tongue. "That is unfortunate. I enjoyed Greece the most of my sojourns."

"The home of your ancestors," Lucinda said.

Cupid turned quizzical eyes to her.

Pink flushed the younger Templeton's cheeks. "Greek mythology. Cupid."

"Actually, Eros was the Greek god of love. Cupid was Roman mythology," Cupid explained.

Lucinda smiled. "I beg your pardon. My lessons are long forgotten."

Cupid waved her hand, forgetting the soup spoon she held. Soup sprinkled the table. Sighing, she laid her spoon down and dabbed at the lace with her serviette. "No need to apologize. Not everyone is interested in mythology."

Matthew sipped his wine. "Mama, do you have anything planned for your visitors tomorrow?"

"Oh, yes." Cupid's cheeks glowed. "A visit to a castle ruin, then a game to see who shares their picnic luncheon with whom."

Val groaned. "It is too cold to picnic, Aunt Cupid."

Her smile broadened. "Of course, it is. That is why the couples will eat in the conservatory and the garden folly."

Val's brow arched. "With chaperones, of course."

Cupid shook her head and glanced at Mrs. Templeton. "We are in the country Val and Matthew are honorable men. We can dispense with chaperones."

Val said, "But, Aunt—"

Cupid laid her spoon down and turned her gaze to Val. "Do you plan to ravish a young lady?"

Heat infused Val's cheeks. "Of course not," he barked.

Cupid nodded. "Then Grace and Lucinda will be safe."

Matthew grinned. "But what of me, Mama? You didn't ask if I plan to 'ravish a young lady'?"

Cupid rolled her eyes. "I know my own son. You would never take advantage of a woman."

Lucinda stared at her soup bowl, a faint blush on her cheeks.

Matthew cleared his throat. "Miss Lucinda, do you like to ride?"

Lucinda shook her head and glanced up. "Horses frighten me. They are so very large." Her whispery voice trembled.

"You only need instruction," Matthew said. " 'Tis no need to be frightened of a gentle beast."

"Val can teach you," Cupid offered.

Val cleared his throat. "I'm afraid I will not have time, Aunt. I can't neglect *all* my responsibilities."

"I will be delighted to be the instructor," Matthew said, then glanced at Val. "I'm a better rider than he anyway."

Val snorted. "Since when? As I remember, the last foxhunt you fell on your"—Val cleared his throat—"head."

Lucinda gasped and jerked her head up. "You fell from a large beast?"

Val regretted his words. He did not consider they would frighten the younger Miss Templeton.

Matthew frowned at Val. "Indeed, but I was uninjured."

"We have missed your presence in London, Lord Valentine. Do you not intend to go to Town for the Season?" Mrs. Templeton asked between sips of soup.

"No, madam. I'm too busy with estate affairs to squander my time with such frivolities. I only make time this fortnight to please Aunt Cupid."

Cupid smiled across the table and sat her glass down atop her plate edge. The crystal tilted and fell.

A footman rushed over to clean the spill and Cupid ignored the entire incident. "Val is good to me. My two nephews and Matthew are my only remaining family."

Val raised his wineglass to salute Cupid. "I try, Aunt."

Even when she sent his world spiraling. Control was the one detail Val prized most. Perhaps because he had lacked control when his father lived. But when Aunt Cupid was present, his control vanished and there was nothing to be done. He could not throw her out of his home. Though he was tempted at times.

Like now. If not for his guests, he would have eaten alone, then read until bedtime. Or perhaps visited the squire and talked of farming.

Unlike so many, he enjoyed the country. He was not content to leave the management of his estates to stewards and land agents. He actually enjoyed life here much more than the society of London.

Val glanced at Lucinda. Pale hair gleamed in the candlelight. Why had Aunt Cupid chosen her? She did not look hardy enough to live in the country. More a delicate orchid that must be cultivated in a conservatory away from life's harshness.

Yet Grace was like the valiant snowdrop. Pushing upward through snow and paying no heed to the winter chill. Surviving over all odds. Val chastised himself. He was getting downright maudlin.

"Val?"

His name penetrated his haze and he looked at Matthew. "Yes?"

Matthew shook his head. "Where the devil were you? Mentally balancing your ledgers or shearing your sheep?"

Irritation flashed through Val at being caught woolgathering. "Neither," he answered and said no more.

Matthew frowned. "We shall speak of it later."

"I think not."

Matthew rolled his eyes and glanced at Lucinda. "When they were passing out frankness, Val received a double dose."

Lucinda giggled.

"Lucinda!" Mrs. Templeton admonished. "Apologize to Lord Valentine."

Lucinda's smile died and she stared at the table. "I beg your pardon, my lord. I wasn't laughing at you."

Val smiled to put her at ease. "No need to apologize. I didn't think you were."

So Mrs. Templeton was a harridan who kept her daughters in line. Val glanced at Grace. Was she so malleable for her mother? He doubted it.

The remainder of dinner flowed without further conundrums. With the conclusion of the fruit and biscuits, Cupid stood. "Shall we leave the gentlemen, ladies?" She cocked an eyebrow at Val and Matthew. "Don't tarry too long in your male bastion," she ordered and led the ladies from the room.

Once the door closed behind the ladies, the butler poured them a glass of port. "Thank you, Giles. That will be all." Giles bowed and departed.

Matthew sipped his port, then said, "What do you think of the Templetons?"

Val pushed back from the table, stretched his legs out straight, and crossed his ankles. "The mother is a shrew who tries to control everyone."

"Do you not think Miss Lucinda is beautiful? Moonlight is her hair and the ocean is her eyes."

Val rolled his eyes. "You sound like a poet. I suppose she is beautiful in a classical sense, but too much of a mouse. Now the elder Miss Templeton would be a challenge to the right man."

Matthew's brows rose and a flash of humor crossed his face. "Indeed? Are you the right man? Need I protect you from her also?"

"Are you baiting me?" Val growled.

Matthew shook his head. "Of course not, coz. You sound quite taken with the chit."

"No. My only plan is to keep Aunt Cupid's scheme at bay."

"Are you certain, Val?"

Val twirled his glass between his fingers and gazed into the dark liquid. "Very certain."

Matthew propped one elbow on the table and studied Val. "Mama will be disappointed. You will be her first failure."

"I'm sorry, but I don't intend to marry to please Aunt Cupid. No matter how much I love her. Anyway, when she chose a bride for Thorndyke, did he not marry the girl's mother instead?"

Matthew nodded. "By the wedding she had forgotten that pesky little detail."

Val sighed and downed the remainder of his port. "I suppose we should join the ladies."

"Yes. I have already upset Mama enough by disposing of her place cards."

Val chuckled. "Well done. I never dreamed she would set name cards at the dinner table."

"Mama will do whatever she deems necessary to throw you and Miss Lucinda together." His voice was apologetic.

"Then I'm happy to have you on my side, Matthew. Let us see what trap Aunt has for me in the drawing room."

Matthew laughed. "I'm right behind you."

"You must mind your tongue."

Grace winced at her mother's harsh tone and the look on Cupid's face. Apparently, Cupid did not know her mother well.

Lucinda stared at her clasped hands in her lap. "Yes, Mama."

"Lord Valentine wasn't offended," Grace said.

Grace worried about Lucinda. Her cheeks were as pale as new fallen snow.

The secret buried in her heart ate away at her. If only they would return home, no one would have to know the truth. The truth that so embarrassed Grace. But there was nothing to be done about it. She felt as helpless as a newborn kitten.

"Lucinda is doing fine," Cupid said. "Men always think they don't wish to marry until a reason is served. Val will see Lucinda as an excellent wife. They will have beautiful babies."

Pain knifed through Grace. She was not sure why. After all, she hardly knew Lord Valentine. Why should she care whom he made beautiful babies with? A baby with thick black hair and laughing black eyes stared at her from her mind. Grace shook her head to dislodge the image.

Her concern was Lucinda. She needed a more gentle husband. Someone who would not trod on her delicate feelings.

"How are you enjoying your visit, Grace?" Cupid asked.

"Very well, thank you. The landscape is beautiful."

Cupid nodded. "Val is very proud of his estate."

Lucinda's lips protruded. "I haven't seen anything outside these four walls."

"And well, you should be satisfied. You can't set Lord Valentine's matrimonial eye if you are roaming about outside," Ida chastised.

Grace gritted her teeth. Would her mother never slacken her reins? No, she was intent upon Lucinda marrying a wealthy peer.

"Grace, move away from Lucinda's side. Leave room on the settee for Lord Valentine," Ida commanded.

Grace glanced at her mother. Her face was set in immovable lines and her eyes were as hard as marble. Grace vowed to stay where she was.

The drawing room door opened and the gentlemen strolled in. Val's black evening clothes suited him. Only his white shirt and cravat broke the solid black. Grace chastised herself. She should not call him Val even to herself, but some unknown emotion about him caused a want of intimacy.

Grace's fingers itched to brush his cheek with her fingers. Black already shadowed his jaw.

Ida signaled with her head to Grace to move away. Grace raised her chin and surveyed Lord Valentine. "Did you gentlemen enjoy your port and cigars? One always wonders what gentlemen do that the ladies must leave them alone."

Ida gasped. "Grace!"

The earl chuckled and settled onto the chair next to Grace. One leg stuck straight out. He was much too close. Bay rum infiltrated her senses.

"Matthew and I don't indulge in cigars and one

glass of port is our limit. The remainder is merely talk."

Grace almost breathed a sigh of relief. Well, at least he was not a drunkard. "Talk of what?"

Lord Valentine shrugged. "Nothing very edifying, Miss Templeton. Shooting and horses and such."

"You must forgive Grace, my lord. She can be unmindful of her tongue at times." Ida frowned at Grace.

"No need to apologize, Mrs. Templeton. 'Tis a pleasure to find a young lady who can speak of something other than fashion and the social whirl."

Heat flushed Grace's cheeks. "Much to Mama's chagrin, I don't know those subjects well." A small smile touched his lips and Grace found it impossible not to return the disarming smile.

"Lucinda has no such thoughts also. She is a scholar."

Four sets of eyes turned to Ida.

One dark brow rose a fraction. "Indeed?" Lord Valentine turned to Lucinda. "What scholarly avenues do you study?"

Lucinda's wide eyes pleaded with Grace.

Mr. Lynford cleared his throat. "I daresay Miss Lucinda is bright enough to do anything she wishes. Not everyone feels compelled to demonstrate their intellect."

Lucinda bestowed him with a bright smile. "Thank you, Mr. Lynford."

"I can't wait until tomorrow," Cupid said. "My little game shall be interesting."

Grace grimaced. One thing of which she was certain. Somehow the game would be rigged to put Lucinda with Lord Valentine. Whatever would she and Mr. Lynford talk of?

Three

The next day dawned clear. They had just returned from a sojourn to a castle ruin where Matthew had managed to escort Miss Lucinda.

Val stared at the two wicker baskets. Yellow ribbon and flowers decorated one, white ribbon and flowers the other.

Val hated games. They were as dull and useless as the Prince Regent.

"Lucinda shall choose first," Cupid said.

"Shouldn't Miss Templeton go first since she is the eldest?" Matthew asked.

"I'm certain she doesn't mind," Cupid said.

Ida glared at Grace. She inhaled a deep breath and said, "Of course not, Lucinda. Please proceed."

Val guessed the agreement was against her better judgment. Could it be a coincidence that the white ribbon and flowers matched Miss Lucinda's gown? Val thought not.

Matthew leaned forward and lowered his voice so only Lucinda heard his words. Pink flushed her cheeks.

Cupid shook her finger at him. "Leave her alone, Matthew."

"Yes, Mama." Matthew's words were agreeable, but amusement flashed in his eyes.

Lucinda inhaled a deep breath and picked up the basket decorated in yellow.

"You should choose the other," Ida suggested and winked at Lucinda.

"I like this one." Lucinda's soft voice was barely audible and she stared at the floor.

"Well, the other is mine then." Grace picked up the white-decorated basket.

Cupid frowned at the four young people, then sighed in resignation. "If Matthew and Val look in their pockets, they will find a bit of ribbon to match the baskets."

Both plunged their hands into their pockets. Matthew drew his out and smiled. "Well, look at that. Yellow."

"And mine is white," Val said and tried not to laugh at Aunt Cupid's expression of pique.

"Miss Templeton and I shall go to the conservatory."

Matthew nodded. "And to the garden folly for Miss Lucinda and I." He grinned at Cupid. "This is indeed a splendid game, Mama. Don't know why we have not played it before."

Val appropriated the basket from Grace's grasp and held out his arm. "May I escort you to the conservatory, Miss Templeton?"

Tension knotted Grace's stomach, but she forced a smile and laid her hand on his arm. An arm that was as firm as stone.

She tried to force a casualness to her voice she was far from feeling. "Thank you, Lord Valentine." Black eyes shimmered down at her. What was hidden behind those obsidian orbs? She felt awkward and clumsy.

Why did this man's proximity generate an uneasiness? Uncertainties she had never experienced surged in every fiber of her being.

A terrifying awareness washed over her. Egad, what was this strange attraction to Lord Valentine?

Val held the conservatory door open. Grace dropped back to reality. She had not even been aware of their advance.

Light streamed through the glass roof and walls bathing the plants. Hot air drenched with humidity and the aroma of humus hit Grace full in the face. She inhaled deeply.

"Would you like to eat elsewhere?" Val asked.

Grace shook her head. "I find the conservatory pleasant."

"A lot of ladies don't like the heat and smell."

His expression was strained tight. He did not like Cupid's game or having to eat luncheon with her. Perhaps she should put both of them out of their misery.

"I suppose I have always been different. Much to my mother's chagrin."

The earl smiled. "You shouldn't vex yourself. I find different is usually an improvement."

Grace inhaled a deep breath. "I will not be offended if you return to your study. I'm accustomed to being alone."

A hand to her arm halted her. She turned and met his dark gaze. His face softened. The words seemed to be dragged from deep within. "It has been many years since I picnicked in the conservatory and I admit I'm out of practice, but I look forward to our luncheon."

Grace smiled and nodded. "Very well. I—" She inhaled a deep breath. "Cupid forced you into this. I did not want you to feel you must carry through."

He shrugged and said, "I must eat."

His pragmatic words irritated Grace, even though she herself was not here of her own accord. She followed him through a jungle of plants and flowers. Many of the exotics Grace had never seen.

A round woven willow table perched in the middle of the conservatory on a square made of blue ceramic tiles. Water splashed nearby. A lion perched on a pedestal spouted water into a pool.

"Do you eat alfresco here often?"

"Not any longer. Mama always enjoyed eating here." Wistfulness filled his voice.

"I miss Papa also. Mama was a little different when he lived." Humiliation heated her face. Her mother's peccadillos were embarrassing to contemplate. She could only hope Lord Valentine never discovered them.

Dark brows shot up in surprise. "Also?"

Grace nodded. "When you spoke of your mother, your voice filled with sadness and longing."

Val shrugged. "It is difficult having only my brother, aunt, and cousin remaining. Then, Aunt Cupid worries that the Valentine line will cease."

"Men wed young ladies barely out of the schoolroom. There is plenty of time for you to marry and produce an heir."

His lips twisted into a cynical smile. "Not according to Aunt Cupid."

Grace rambled down a row of orange trees growing from boxes. "You have some lovely plants."

Val followed her. "Thank you."

Grace rested an orange in her hand. "How do they taste?"

Val tugged one of the fruits loose. "Like an orange. You've never eaten one?"

Heat flushed her cheeks again. "No."

Pulling a knife from his pocket, he sliced the orange. He held out a half to her.

Juice dripped over his fingers. An urge to lick his fingers clean assailed Grace. She would start with the little finger and work her way over to the thumb. Something clenched in the pit of her stomach. From where had that image come? His steady gaze bore into her in silent expectation.

Another image came to mind. Of being crushed within his embrace and his warm lips kissing her. Excitement jangled down the length of her nerves.

Grace chastised herself. She was growing demented. Imagining such improper things. She accepted the orange half and sniffed. The aroma was pleasant. She touched the tip of her tongue to the fruit's meat and smiled. " 'Tis good."

Grace bit into the orange. Juice dribbled down her chin and she laughed for the joy of it.

Val quickly ate his half unmindful of the dripping juice.

Val pitched the rind into a pot and strode away. Grace finished eating her orange and threw her peeling in the same pot. He dipped his handkerchief in the pool and washed his mouth and hands. Then returned to her side.

Grace held her hand out, but Val shook his head. "Allow me."

His black gaze burned into her as he gently washed her fingers, chin, and mouth. Then a finger caressed her bottom lip. "I wager your lips taste as sweet as strawberries," he whispered in a husky voice.

"You do?" Her voice quivered.

Val nodded. "I know it is imprudent of me, but I have to know." He lowered his head until his lips touched hers. Her hands clutched his shoulders to steady herself in the unfamiliar maelstrom and she drank in the sweetness of his kiss.

Grace felt like magic had transformed her into a marble statue. Unable to move. Unable to breathe. Unable to think.

The caress of his lips set her body aflame. An unfamiliar emotion flowed from her lips to the tips of her toes.

A realization dawned in her sluggish mind as her body burned. This was passion. This was what the poets spoke of.

Raising his mouth from hers, he gazed into her eyes. "Bloody hell!"

The words were like a plunge into frigid water. Her face grew hot with humiliation. Knowing he had not enjoyed the kiss drove a knife through her heart. "A man intent on remaining unwed should not kiss proper young ladies." Good Lord, she sounded like some prim vicar's wife.

Concern etched his brow. "I apologize for my lapse in propriety. You have my personal vow it will never happen again."

Grace nodded, afraid if she spoke her voice would break. His vow saddened her, but it was for the best.

His black gaze was an enigma. "Shall we eat our luncheon?" Val clasped her hand and led her to the table.

Grace fluttered her fingers over the white ribbon. "You were meant to luncheon with Lucinda."

"Mmmm hmmm."

Grace opened the basket and placed the wine-glasses on the table. She started to pull out the various dishes. "Would you have kissed her?" Instantly, she wanted to take the words back.

Placing his fingers under her chin, Val forced her to meet his gaze. "I don't go about kissing ladies willy-nilly, Grace."

Heat flushed her cheeks. "I apologize, my lord. It was a silly question."

"Grace, please call me Simon."

"S—Simon?"

He nodded. "No one has called me by my Christian name in many years. Not since my mother's death."

"Very well, my—" Grace inhaled deeply. "Simon." She placed the last of the food on the table, then handed Simon a plate and serviette.

"Now, what has Cook sent us for luncheon? I'm famished." Simon poured wine into the glasses.

The picnic consisted of mutton, meat pies, apricot fritters, fresh bread, and cheese. Neither said a word as they filled their plates, then sat facing each other.

Simon bit into a pie. Grace watched as his jaws worked up and down. She mentally shook herself and took a bite of mutton.

"How long has your family known Aunt Cupid?"

Grace swallowed and answered, "About four months. Mama met her at a musicale in London. They started talking and decided you and Lucinda should marry."

"Why Lucinda?"

Grace shrugged. "It is apparent she will have less

trouble finding a husband. She is young and beautiful."

For a moment, he studied her. The dark gaze intent on her caused a shiver to bolt down her spine. Then, he softly said, "I disagree. *You* are quite pretty."

She experienced a gamut of perplexing emotions, not quite certain how to take his declaration. The words were something she had not expected from the churlish earl. "You jest, Simon."

"Not at all. Anyway, some men want more in a wife than beauty."

"Such as?" she asked in a choked voice. She was a fool for continuing the conversation, but something held her.

Simon shrugged. "Intelligence. Loyalty. Love."

Grace regarded him with somber curiosity. "Can't a man fall in love with a number of women? Men in London seem to love more than one."

Simon's long fingers wrapped around the stem of his wineglass and he stared into the wine a moment. Then said, "Lust, not love. There is a difference."

Warmth heated her face once again. She had never blushed so much. "Were your parents happy in their marriage?" she asked and nibbled a bit of cheese.

"Papa wasn't a villain by any means, but he didn't love Mama. He couldn't give her what she desired and caused her much unhappiness. Yours?"

"Papa traveled a lot. Sometimes—"

"Yes?"

Grace inhaled a deep breath. "Sometimes I thought he traveled to be away from Mama. They argued a lot when he was home. Then, after a few days, he would pack up and leave again. I often wished to go with him, but he said I must stay and take care of Lucinda."

"That was unfair of him to expect you to care for her."

Grace shrugged. "I did not mind."

"How old were you when he died?"

"Ten." Unease grasped Grace. They were skirting too close to subjects better left alone. She would be mortified if Simon discovered her secret. "You are quite indulgent of Cupid."

Simon glanced at her over his wineglass, as if trying to determine why she had changed the subject. He nodded. "She means well. Aunt Cupid has a kind heart."

"Yes. That is unusual for members of the *ton*."

"Do you enjoy London?" Simon popped a wedge of bread into his mouth and chewed.

Grace smiled and forced her attention away from his mouth. "No, but Mama and Lucinda do. I shall be glad of the day when I'm of an age to stay alone."

"You prefer the country to London?"

Grace nodded. " 'Tis unusual, I know, but I feel like a duck among peacocks in Town."

Simon opened his mouth to speak and Grace held up her hand to halt his words. "I don't seek a compliment to contradict me."

Simon smiled. "I would not offer a compliment simply to soothe your feathers, but the truth is you are quite lovely."

Grace shook her head. "I'm too old and curvy. Men prefer delicate beauty and fragility."

"Not all men."

Heat flushed Grace's cheeks. "The fashion in London is blond hair and blue eyes."

Simon reached across and fingered a loose tendril of her hair. "And some men are witless."

Her heart thundered against her chest. She wrenched her gaze away from his and stood. Her serviette fell to the floor unheeded. She had to remove herself from his closeness. Simon wove a spell that must be broken.

Her back burned from his staring gaze as she walked away. Grace fingered a waxy leaf. "The jasmine will be quite wonderful when it blooms."

Simon inhaled a deep breath and stood behind her. Heat emanated from his closeness. "Mama loved jasmine. Those did not arrive before she died. They have never bloomed."

She turned to face him and stepped back. He was much too close. "But there are buds."

Simon combed his fingers through his hair. "They fall before blooming. No one knows why. I used to talk to the bush as if I talked to Mama."

His sadness squeezed Grace's heart with regret. Apparently, he still missed his mother very much. She regretted that she could not console him, that she did not feel the same about her own mother. "Perhaps we should go back," Grace suggested.

"You haven't finished eating." Simon fingered his watch pocket and frowned.

"I find my appetite has disappeared."

"I apologize for discomfiting you," Simon said. " 'Tis reprehensible of me."

Regret clouded his eyes. Grace smiled. "Not at all. Truth be known, I enjoy your companionship."

Simon returned her smile. "I'm glad. I wouldn't wish you to think me a churl."

"I would never think such," politeness made her reply.

Looking uncomfortable, Simon abruptly changed the subject. "I wonder what Aunt Cupid has in store for us tonight. It is about time for her to change tactics."

" 'Change tactics'?"

Simon nodded. "Matthew and I have outwitted her three times now. She will think to change her battle plan. Her next stratagem will be the opposite of what she wants."

" 'Opposite'?" Lord, why must she repeat his words?

"She will think we will change her intention once again and when we do, we will end up the way she wishes."

A frown creased Grace's brow. "I don't understand."

"Her next plan will be staged to put you and me together, but when Matthew and I change it to outwit her, then I will actually end up with Lucinda."

"How do you know this?"

"Knowing Aunt Cupid my entire life. One has to be quick to outwit her."

"Will she attempt to compromise Lucinda? All it would take is one compromising situation." Grace knew her mother would stop at nothing, but she did not know Cupid well enough to know how far she would go.

"Aunt Cupid is not devious. Then again, I'm not one to be forced into something I don't want, especially marriage."

"Yes, you made your position quite clear upon our arrival."

Hoods dropped over Simon's eyes, veiling his thoughts. Grace wondered what lay behind his enigmatic gaze. And what would he really think if he knew the secret behind their visit?

"Matthew is wonderful!" Lucinda sighed and stared at nothing, a dreamy expression on her face.

"Matthew? When did you stop calling him Mr. Lynford?" Guilt washed over Grace. She could not believe she had called his lordship Simon. Now she reproached Lucinda for the same transgression.

Pink flushed Lucinda's cheeks. "He requested I call him Matthew during luncheon. To think he goes to so much trouble to be with me. He quite outwitted our mamas."

"Lucinda," Grace said in a gentle tone, "their design is simply to keep Lord Valentine and you apart. They wish to thwart the matrimonial plans of Cupid and Mama."

"Matthew quite enjoys my company," Lucinda insisted.

"Of course he does." Every man gained pleasure just looking at angelic Lucinda. "But that doesn't mean he wishes for more than an innocent association while we are here. I don't wish to see you hurt."

Lucinda squeezed Grace's hand. "Don't fret over me so, Grace. I'm a woman."

Grace bit back a smile. "A naive young lady, who has no experience with gentlemen. Anyway, Mama will never allow you to marry Mr. Lynford."

"Matthew is all that is kind and good. Anyone should be pleased to form a connection with him."

"Lucinda, you know what Mama wants for you. A title and money. That means Lord Valentine."

Lucinda's lips protruded in a pout. "I can't like Lord Valentine. He is much too somber."

"You haven't given yourself time to know him. Lord Valentine's company is quite enjoyable."

Lucinda's brows rose. "Then, you may make Mama happy and marry him."

Heat flushed Grace's face and she shook her head. "He has made it quite clear that he has no wish to marry."

"Perhaps he will change his mind."

Grace shook her head again. "He is too adamant."

"Matthew isn't titled, but perhaps he has a fortune." Hope filled her eyes.

"I would not count on that, Lucinda. I—I heard rumors about Mr. Lynford while we were in London."

Lucinda's head tilted to one side and her blue eyes stared at Grace. "What sort of rumors?"

Grace hated to hurt Lucinda, but she needed to understand the truth. Understand that one did not always get what one wanted from life. "He is a libertine. He has loved and abandoned many women. He even—" Grace dropped her voice. "He even takes married ladies to his bed."

Blood drained from Lucinda's face, but she tilted her chin up. " 'Tis the way of society. No one marries for love."

Grace clasped Lucinda's hand between hers. "Maybe so, but you are delicate. You could never withstand such a marriage, especially if you loved the gentleman. It would tear your soul apart."

"I'm not a piece of china that will shatter at the slightest provocation. You have always treated me so, but I'm hardier." Lucinda shrugged. "Perhaps not as strong as you, but I'm not the weak flower you think."

Grace sighed. "I'm sorry I treat you as fragile. My intent has always been to protect you from hurt."

A strength she had never noticed before filled Lucinda's face. "I know, Grace, and I love you, but it is time for me to stand upon my own. I have always wished to be like you."

Grace forced the words out over her bewilderment. "Like me? But you are so beautiful."

"And so are you. You possess such mettle. Nothing or no one ever bows you." Lucinda smiled tentatively.

"It's not considered a good trait in a female. Mama doesn't approve." Grace rose and paced to the window.

"I think it quite admirable. I have always been envious of your fortitude. What did you and Lord Valentine speak of?"

Heat flushed Grace's cheeks. "Nothing of consequence." No, he had just kissed her once and she had wanted more. A thought flittered through her mind and she turned. "Did Mr. Lynford kiss you?"

"Of course not," Lucinda huffed. "He is too much a gentleman."

Well, so much for Lucinda considering Simon a gentleman. He had kissed her quite soundly. Even though he had acted like he did not enjoy the kiss and did not say he enjoyed her companionship. Perhaps he was a rake who kissed every woman. And she had wished him to kiss her again.

Grace sighed. She really must not be alone with Simon again. Some intuition screamed that her heart was not safe and it would mortify her for Simon to know the truth.

Not that Simon was in any danger of losing his heart. He had made his feelings on marriage quite clear. Only a fool would lose her heart to such a man.

"What is wrong, Grace?" A gleam of suspicion shimmered in Lucinda's eyes.

"Naught. I'm merely contemplating what we should do. Cupid may have another scheme for tonight."

" 'Tis not our worry. Matthew will make certain he is my escort."

"Yes, he will assist his cousin in any way, but Cupid may outwit them."

Lucinda frowned. "I don't care what you say. Matthew wishes to be with me. He doesn't do this merely for his cousin."

The door bounced open. Ida glared at Grace, then walked in and shut the door. "It is about time you returned. And what do you think you were about, Grace?"

Grace's head snapped up. Her mother could not know about the kiss. "I beg your pardon?"

"Going off with Lord Valentine. He is meant for your sister." Grace had known her mother would be displeased, but she had never seen her quite this angry.

"It would hardly have been polite to refuse to go with him. Cupid arranged the picnics for our enjoyment." Well maybe that was not totally accurate. Her plan had been to get Simon and Lucinda together.

Ida's nostrils flared with fury. "Lucinda was to go with his lordship."

Grace raised her chin and met her mother's angry gaze. "I know. What would you have me do? Make a scene? Perhaps Lord Valentine doesn't like dramas played out in his home. I would have given him a disgust of us."

"That is true, Mama. Don't berate her," Lucinda said.

Surprise filled Grace. Lucinda had never spoken to their mother so. Thankfully, she seemed not to notice.

Ida shook her finger at Grace. "Very well, but don't let it happen again or you shall face the consequences." Ida tromped out of the chamber.

"Don't let Mama upset you, Grace. You could not stop the way things evolved." Lucinda clasped Grace's hand between hers. "I quite enjoyed the way everything turned out."

Unfortunately, she had also enjoyed the outcome. Grace blew out a large breath. Apparently, it was hopeless to keep Lucinda from hurt. Now, just how did she protect herself? She had never expected affection to come so quickly.

Four

"Come back, Lachlan," Grace called and hurried after the terrier. His nose seemed to have picked up a scent and was intent to track. The light layer of snow that had fallen during the night did not deter Lachlan's merry chase the slightest.

Behind the yew Lachlan's excited barking commenced. Grace broke through the bushes and Lachlan ran to greet her, then back to his quarry. "Sit, Lachlan."

The dog crouched at her feet, his tail wagged furiously, and he waited to be commended for his game. "Good morning, Simon."

Simon rose to his feet. He brushed at the dirt staining his knees, but did not manage to wipe them clean. He flashed her a devastating grin. "Good day, Grace. You look beautiful this morning."

Heat flushed her cheeks. "Thank you. Cupid is searching for you for breakfast."

"I wanted to finish planting my bulbs. I shall join you there in half an hour."

Grace nodded.

"Will Lachlan be joining us?"

Grace laughed. "No. I shall leave him in my bedchamber to nap."

Apparently bored with their talk and disappointed from a lack of attention, Lachlan bounded over to Simon and grabbed a boot tassel.

"No, Lachlan," Grace shouted.

Simon frowned down at the terrier. "Leave my boots be, dog."

Grace hurried over and stooped down, well aware of Simon's presence hovering over her. She tried to pry the dog's mouth open to no avail. Lachlan growled and shook his head as if to tame the tassel clutched in his jaws. Two more shakes of his head and the prey was free. Lachlan turned and ran further into the garden.

Grace stood. "I'm sorry, Simon. Lachlan is usually better mannered."

Simon shrugged. "I shall forgive Lachlan on one condition."

"What?" Grace whispered.

"After breakfast, meet me in the garden folly."

Her heart thundered in her chest. "Very well, Simon. I would have met you there anyway," she confessed, unable to halt the words.

He drew one finger down her cheek. "I'm glad."

Grace stared into his obsidian eyes and shivered at the fires burning there.

He clasped her hand. Time seemed to slow as he brought her hand to his lips and kissed her bare palm. Grace shivered. "I shall see you soon in the dining room."

Grace nodded. "Until then." She turned and followed Lachlan's escape. Her fingers curled around her palm, still tingling from Simon's lips.

Excitement bounded through Grace. The anticipation was almost unbearable. Would Simon kiss her once again? She knew she would be powerless to resist him. If she were honest with herself, she would admit she hoped for a kiss. He had left her lips burning to feel his again.

Lachlan lay on a snowless patch of grass, the tassel between his paws. His face looked like he was grinning. Grace grabbed the tassel in one hand, then picked the dog up. "Bad boy," she scolded and hugged him to her chest. She knew that was not the proper way to scold him, but she could not be too angry. He had given Simon an excuse to ask her to the folly.

Grace sighed. First, Cupid was a matchmaker. Now, Lachlan was getting into the act. Well, just as long as he did not get Lucinda and Simon together.

"We shall have another game after breakfast."

At Cupid's announcement, four sets of eyes looked up from their plates. Matthew cleared his throat. "Mama, Miss Lucinda wishes to ice-skate. I have agreed to escort her to the lake."

Cupid nodded. "And so she shall, but a lottery will choose her partner." Cupid turned to Grace. "And what do you wish to do, my dear?"

Grace forced herself not to glance at Simon. "I thought to visit the garden folly."

Cupid nodded. "Very good. Only no one knows with whom."

Ida smiled. " 'Tis wonderful to have such an ingenious hostess. In my day young ladies wouldn't have been allowed to wander about unescorted with a gentleman."

"It still isn't proper," Grace murmured, now with a stronger sense of why. She had experimented with a kiss or two, but none had ever excited her like Simon's.

Cupid waved her hands and her bracelets jangled. "Now, now, we are in the country. No one will object. My boys are too gallant to do something they shouldn't."

"Perhaps the ladies prefer to choose their own escorts, Aunt," Simon offered.

Cupid grinned. "Yes, but it is nearing St. Valentine's and we must have fun and games."

"Indeed?" Simon's brow quirked. "And why is that?"

Cupid frowned. "Because this is my house party and I decree it. Will you deny an old woman a little pleasure?"

"You are never old unless it behooves you in some way," Simon protested, then sighed and looked at Matthew. "I suppose we must indulge her."

Cupid smiled and nodded. "You are good to me, Val."

Matthew laid his serviette on the table. "So, Mama, how will you conduct this lottery?"

"I haven't yet decided."

"May I suggest—"

"No, you may not," she interrupted Matthew, then smiled at him. "I don't wish any assistance from you so you may know how to rig my game."

Matthew pounded his fist on his chest. "You wound me, Mama. I would never do such a thing."

Cupid snorted. "Only if you have the opportunity."

"I have an idea," Ida said.

Cupid held up her hand. "Don't say it in front of them, Ida. These two scamps must have no clue." Cupid looked around the table. "If everyone is through, adjourn to the drawing room. Ida and I will be along in a moment."

Once in the drawing room, Matthew turned to Simon. "What shall we do?"

Simon settled on a settee and crossed one ankle over his knee. Confidence radiated from him. "There is no need. This time Aunt Cupid will be prepared for our shenanigans. So, she will fix the lottery the opposite of what she wants. We need do nothing." His fingers probed his watch pocket and he sighed.

Matthew smiled. "You are correct, Val. Mama will think to outwit us this time."

Lucinda frowned. "Are you certain, my lord?" Pink flushed her cheeks. "Not that I don't wish to spend time with you."

Simon smiled. "Don't vex yourself, Miss Lucinda. I don't take offense."

The door opened and Cupid bounced in, followed by Ida. "We are now ready. This will be simple by drawing lots." She held a glass bowl out to Matthew. "Choose a name, if you please."

Matthew pursed his lips and studied the two slips of paper. Then he drew one out and opened it. He looked at Grace. "Miss Templeton."

Cupid nodded. "Then, Val will skate with Lucinda."

Simon smoothed his coat sleeve and stood. "I haven't drawn a lot."

Cupid wrapped the bowl between her chest and arms. "There is no need with only four."

"But I would like to see that this was a fair lottery," Simon argued.

Cupid raised her chin. "You accuse me of cheating?" Indignation filled her voice.

"If it behooved you, yes."

Cupid grabbed the paper still sitting in the bowl, then pitched it into the fire. She placed the bowl on the mantel. The glass wobbled. She pushed it further back before it could fall. "I'm greatly offended, Val. Your mother would be ashamed of you."

Simon rolled his eyes. "This was rigged."

"It was not." Cupid clapped her hands together and the jangle of her bracelets echoed in the silent room. "Very good, children. Now, off to the lake and the folly."

A look of extreme smugness filled Ida's face. Grace glanced at Simon and Matthew. "Do nothing, indeed!" She looped her arm through Lucinda's. "Let us go retrieve our cloaks and bonnets, sister. Maybe these two *intelligent* gentlemen can figure out their mistake."

Once on the stairs, Lucinda whispered, "I don't wish to spend time with Lord Valentine. I can claim an illness."

"That wouldn't be well done. Cupid has been all that is good and kind. 'Tis only a few hours. His lordship is an interesting companion."

Lucinda sighed. "If you say so, but I wished to skate with Matthew."

Grace tried to find words to reassure her sister. "Life hands everyone disappointments. You must bear this one for a short time. Then, we shall meet back here for chocolate. And Mama will be happy that you spent time with his lordship, but you mustn't tell him anything about us." Surely Lucinda would not reveal the Templeton secret.

Disappointment welled within Grace. She bit back the sigh that rose to her lips and wished that accepting this was easier. She had been looking forward to meeting Simon in the folly. Perhaps even exchanging a few kisses.

Oh, well, this was for the best. She must not begin to enjoy Simon's kisses too much or she would be sorely disappointed when they departed.

"Do you promise not to kiss Matthew?"

Lucinda's question jerked Grace from her thoughts. "Really, Lucinda! I don't intend to kiss anyone." Her eyes narrowed. "Has Mr. Lynford kissed you?"

Lucinda shook her head. "I had hoped he might this afternoon. He looks as if he would be quite good at it."

"You mustn't allow him any liberties, Lucinda. A kiss can be quite damaging to one's reputation. You mustn't kiss a man until you are betrothed."

Lucinda nodded, but Grace felt like the vilest hypocrite. She should practice what she preached, but she had enjoyed Simon's kisses and soon there would be no more. At least when she left Valentine Hall she would have a few warm memories to enjoy in her spinsterhood.

The February wind nipped at Val's nose as he tied the last skate onto his boot. Miss Lucinda was already careening around the frozen lake, a rapturous smile on her face. She had declined his assistance in tying on her skates. Quiet surrounded him. Only the sound of skates swishing on ice could be heard.

He cursed his own arrogance again. Aunt Cupid had outwitted them. Instead of being with Grace in the folly and stealing a few kisses, he was consigned to spend time with a witless child.

Val stepped onto the ice. Ankles wobbled a moment, then he steadied himself. It had been years since he had skated, but the knowledge returned quickly. He glided to Lucinda's side. "I see you enjoy skating."

"Yes. I like the freedom." Lucinda glanced at him. "Papa would take Grace and me skating when he was home."

"I miss my parents very much also."

"You do?" Surprise colored her voice.

"Yes. I'm not the emotionless man some believe." That admission dredged up from deep inside him. He was not certain why he had shared it with Lucinda.

"I never thought that. Grace wouldn't have enjoyed your company if that were so."

Something knotted in his stomach, acute but unknown. Why did even talking of Grace cause unwelcome reactions? "She told you that?"

"She was trying to reassure me about this afternoon."

"Did Miss Templeton tell you anything else?"

"No, but I know she enjoyed the conservatory. She is the one who grows vegetables at home." Pride was strong in her voice.

"Do you have a large home and staff?" Val winced to himself. Why was he so curious? Grace Templeton's life was none of his concern.

"Only one maid of all work and Grace and I share the same bedchamber." She glanced at Val and pursed her lips. "Please don't tell Mama I said such."

"Of course not, but why?" Val silently cursed his curiosity again.

"Mama likes people to think we are very well off, but Grace says we shouldn't put on airs."

"Your secret is safe with me. Does Miss Templeton have any admirers?" Val asked. Uneasiness welled in him. He really should leave talk of Grace alone.

"There is one neighbor who wishes to marry Grace, but she has refused him twice." Lucinda shoved her hands deeper into her muff.

Trees glided by as their skates carried them around the ice once again. The day was beautiful, but Val hardly noticed. Did she refuse because her heart was unclaimed? He must ask. "And why is that?"

"She doesn't love him, which Mama thinks is a paltry reason. Grace also says he only wishes a wife to look after his six children."

Well, Lucinda was certainly a font of information. "Mrs. Templeton doesn't try to force Grace to accept?"

Blue eyes studied the panorama before them. Then Lucinda said, "Yes, but Grace can be quite stubborn when she has a mind to."

Val's stomach clenched into a tight ball. "Is this neighbor wealthy?"

"No, but Mama says Grace will never receive another offer. His wife died about a year ago."

"A year? And he already looks for another wife?" Lucinda nodded. "Why do you find that disturbing?"

"If I lost a wife I loved, I don't believe I would ever recover. I certainly wouldn't wish to marry within a year."

" 'Tis what Grace says."

The wind whipped around them, ruffling hair and coats. "Does she dislike children?"

"Oh, no, but those six are quite unruly. They need discipline."

Val was uncertain why he wished to know so much about Grace, but the need lay within him. Too heavy and solid to ignore.

Lucinda glanced at Val from underneath her lashes. "Are you and your cousin very close?"

"Yes. When Cupid's husband died, they moved in with us for a time."

"Were they left without a home?"

Val wondered why Lucinda was curious about Matthew. Did she ask for herself or Grace? But she had answered his questions, so he would return the favor. "No, she thought Matthew needed the male influence of my own father."

"Matthew is an only child?"

"Yes. Did you enjoy your picnic with him yesterday?"

Pink flushed Lucinda's cheeks. Val was not certain if it was the skating or the talk of Matthew.

"Yes. He is quite charming," Lucinda gushed.

"Indeed, a lot of ladies seem to think so."

"They do?" Her voice rose a fraction.

Sorry he had blurted out such a statement, Val tried to rectify his slip. "All of Aunt Cupid's friends find him charming."

She glanced at Val from the corner of her eyes. "Does Cupid do a lot of matchmaking?"

"She thinks it her life's calling. I just wish the calling were elsewhere this time," Val said.

"She means well."

"Yes, but still it is irritating to have my own aunt throw young chits in my face. I mean no offense, Miss Lucinda."

"None taken. 'Tis apparent you and I would not suit," she whispered.

"Indeed?"

Lucinda squeezed her muff into her waist. "You seem to like living here in the country."

Val nodded.

"I on the other hand, wish to live in London." Lucinda held up a second finger. "You are interested in farming and intelligent pursuits. I prefer dancing and gossip. If only Mama's idea of a husband for me suited my own."

He should not get involved in the Templetons' affairs, but that knowledge could not halt him. "Stand up to your mother," Val suggested against his better judgment.

"I try, but I have never been as brave as Grace."

Val looked at Lucinda a moment. The wind whipped at her bonnet, but it sat securely atop her blond hair. This was not the silly empty-headed chit he had presumed. Or the fragile young lady he had expected.

Gray clouds broke for a moment. Weak sunlight glared off the frozen lake, transforming the ice into a mirror.

Val regretted he had missed time with Grace. He was ashamed to admit that he had planned the rendezvous so he could kiss her again. It had been eons since he had enjoyed kissing a woman and Grace seemed to fit him well.

Val bit back the groan that rose to his lips. Guilt soared like an enormous bird. He was a knave. His intentions were quite reprehensible. No matter her age, she was quite the innocent and he had planned to take advantage of her and steal a few kisses with no intention to marry.

He vowed he would not be alone with Grace again. Their fortnight visit would soon end and life could return to normal.

But just what were Grace and Matthew doing at the folly? Matthew was quite a rogue with women. No, he could trust his cousin. He would not kiss an innocent miss.

Then again, *he* had never stolen kisses. Was it the moon? Or had Aunt Cupid discovered a love dust that cast a spell? He smiled to himself. Cupid would be thrilled with such a potion.

Hearts, birds, and flowers decorated the stone façade. Cherubs that looked too chubby for their wings to support soared. Grace traced one gloved finger over a heart. Ghosts seemed to linger over the structure.

" 'Tis named the Temple of Saint Valentine," Matthew said as he watched Grace examine the folly.

"When was it built?"

"Eighteenth century. Legend says if a man kisses a woman here he will be bound to her forever," Matthew said.

"A nice fable." Gnarled oak trees towered over the folly, bare limbs swaying in the breeze.

"You don't believe in myths?"

Grace shook her head. "Silly superstition."

Matthew held the door open. "Shall we go inside and I will start a fire?"

Grace climbed the four steps. Her gaze took in every detail of the folly as Matthew lit the already laid fire.

Small, but comfortable. Latticework benches graced two sides. Tall plants secluded one corner.

Grace peeked behind the green curtain and discovered a chaise longue piled high with pillows. A ceiling window poised above the chaise. At night one could lie on the chaise and gaze at the star-filled sky. The fragrance of the fire filled the chamber.

Taking a deep, unsteady breath, Grace turned and walked back to the fireplace. Matthew lounged casually against the white mantel. Silver veins shot through the marble like broken rivers. "What do you think of the Valentine folly?"

"Very nice." Grace rubbed her gloved hands together and held them out to the crackling fire. "Do you and his lordship come here often?"

"Not since Val's mother passed away. She loved coming here. During the summer, she would make the entire family trek out here for luncheon. The doors make for a nice flowing current."

Another door sat across from the one they had entered. Stained glass windows graced both. They were also decorated with cherubs, hearts, and flowers.

"Miss Templeton, may we speak bluntly?"

"Of course, Mr. Lynford," Grace said, though his question brought unease. Bluntness usually meant unwelcome truths revealed.

Matthew stared into the fire, then glanced at Grace. "I hate to disenchant you, but Mrs. Templeton will be disappointed. Val doesn't intend to marry."

Grace looked down at her hands clasped in front of herself. "Lord Valentine hasn't hidden his expectation of remaining unmarried."

" 'Tis not anything against your family. He has no hesitation about letting his brother's sons carry on the title."

"And if he has no sons, you and your sons will inherit."

Matthew's eyes widened in surprise. "I have no desire to inherit the earldom. I have a prosperous estate and I enjoy London society. That is all I wish for out of life."

Grace smiled. "I thought every man wished to be a peer."

He shook his head and smiled. "Since inheriting the title, Val has lost all his spontaneity. He trudges along thinking only of his sheep, his tenants, and his plants."

"But that is good. He doesn't shirk his responsibilities. People depend upon him," Grace said.

Matthew nodded. "Yet, why shouldn't he have a bit of fun now and then?"

"I find it hard to believe he has none. Surely, there are local assemblies." Grace felt as if a hundred butterflies flittered around her stomach.

"Val never attends. The only time he leaves here is to visit another estate or farmers." Matthew tilted his head and frowned. "I think that is why Mama decided to find him a bride. She doesn't wish him to be lonely."

"Some people enjoy being alone."

Matthew nodded again. "But lonely and alone aren't the same. One can be surrounded by people and still feel lonely."

Yes, like she felt so many times. Even in the crowded ballrooms and drawing rooms of London, she felt isolated. Sometimes she thought the loneliness might burst her heart.

" 'Tis too bad Mama chose the wrong sort of woman for Val for he really does need someone."

Grace's breath caught in her throat. "Wrong sort?"

"He and Miss Lucinda don't share the same interests."

Grace forced a casualness to her voice. "Mr. Lynford, are you recommending Val to me?"

Astonishment etched his brow. "Good God, no!"

Her face grew hot with humiliation. Of course not! How stupid of her to think such a thing.

"I merely wish you to understand why Val will not marry your sister," Matthew said.

Grace nodded. "You need not fret, Mr. Lynford. Even if Mama doesn't, Lucinda and I understand. Lucinda has no wish to marry his lordship anyway."

"But Val is a great catch. Every mama's prize." Matthew sounded quite shocked.

Grace smiled. "Not every young lady wishes to marry a man simply for title and wealth."

"Any number of young ladies would be thrilled to marry Val," Matthew said, unable to conceal his offense.

Mirth rippled through Grace. "Not Lucinda. She is quite a romantic."

"And are you a romantic, Miss Templeton?"

Grace shook her head. "I'm too old. Romance has passed me by."

"Nonsense."

"Thank you, Mr. Lynford, but I'm at my last prayers."

Matthew frowned. "You should think better of yourself."

"That can be difficult when you have only met with disparaging remarks."

Blond brows arched just like Simon's. "Miss Lucinda?"

"No. Mama never has a kind word to say to me. As a matter of fact, she was quite upset with me after the picnic." Grace examined the tiled floor to avoid looking at Matthew.

"Why?"

"Apparently, she thought I should have done something so Lucinda would have been with his lordship."

"Don't pay her heed, Miss Templeton. When Val and I set our minds to something, it is difficult to naysay us. Shall we return to the hall?"

Grace nodded. "Thank you for showing me the folly."

He performed a courtly bow and smiled. "It was my pleasure, Miss Templeton."

Grace took his arm and followed him back to Valentine Hall. She wondered if Simon and Lucinda were back yet? And just how much had they enjoyed each other's company?

Five

Val sipped his chocolate and scrutinized Grace. Pink flushed her cheeks. She sat beside Lucinda on the settee talking too softly for him to hear.

"What are you frowning at?"

Matthew's question jerked him from his preoccupation. "Naught. Did you enjoy the folly?"

Matthew grinned. "Yes. Miss Templeton is an amusing companion."

"Indeed? Just what did she do to amuse you?" Val's teeth clenched.

Matthew frowned. "What the devil is wrong with you? You are like a bear with a sore paw."

"Don't be ridiculous, Matthew," he insisted with rising impatience. He wanted to hide his annoyance from his cousin, yet for some mysterious reason he seemed unable to.

Matthew rolled his eyes. "Of course, coz." Sarcasm laced his voice.

"What do you think the ladies are whispering about?"

Matthew shrugged. "Perhaps Miss Templeton is telling Miss Lucinda how much I impressed her."

Val clenched his mouth tighter, determined not to

answer Matthew with a scathing retort. What the devil had they done in the folly?

Lucinda stood and strolled across the room. "May I pour you gentlemen more chocolate?"

Matthew beamed a smile. "Yes, thank you, Miss Lucinda."

"No, thank you," Val mumbled and crossed to the settee. He sat beside Grace and stretched his arm along the settee back.

"Did you enjoy skating?" Grace asked.

"Not particularly. Did you enjoy the folly?"

"It was quite interesting, though I wish your invitation had prevailed." Pink painted her cheeks again.

Val ran his fingertips across her bare neck. She quivered. "As do I."

Ida and Cupid entered and frowned at the foursome. Apparently, they did not like the way they had divided up. In his aunt's world, men and women should be divided two by two. Sort of like the ark, Val mused, but he was not with the woman she seemed to think suited him. After all, to his dismay the entire reasoning for her games and the Valentine soirée was to match him with Lucinda.

"Val?"

"Yes, Aunt Cupid?" Now what did she have planned? He merely wished to sit by the fire. It was merely his age and nothing to do with Grace by his side, he told himself.

Cupid gestured to a window. "There is plenty of daylight remaining. You should take Lucinda to view Hadrian's Wall."

"Who is Harridan?" Lucinda asked.

"Hadrian," Grace repeated. "A Roman emperor

who built a masonry wall across the boundary of England and Scotland with forts and garrisons."

Val turned to Grace. "Would you like to take an excursion to the wall, Miss Templeton?"

Grace smiled and excitement filled her voice. "Yes."

"Val, what of Lucinda?" Cupid asked.

Val cleared his throat. "Of course, Miss Lucinda and Matthew are welcome to join us."

"Thank you, my lord, but I believe I shall stay by the fire. Skating quite exhausted me," Lucinda said.

"I shall keep Miss Lucinda company," Matthew said.

Cupid said, "I need you to perform an errand."

Matthew frowned. "Very well, Mama, if it is necessary."

Ida glared at Lucinda. "You shall go with his lordship."

"But, Mama—"

"Don't argue," she snapped. "Go retrieve your cloak and bonnet this moment."

Lucinda nodded and rose. "Come along, Grace."

"Grace will stay here with Cupid and me," Ida stated.

"I need her to assist me to get ready, Mama."

"Very well." Ida turned to Grace. "Help your sister, then return to the drawing room."

"Yes, Mama." Grace looked at Val. "Thank you for the invitation, my lord. I'm sorry I can't accept."

Misery replaced the pleasure on her face. Disappointment twinged through Val. Apparently, fate had decided to spare him Grace's company.

Val reached out as if to grab her arm, but

dropped his hand back to his side. Best not to intrude between mother and daughter. It was none of his concern. "I shall meet Miss Lucinda in the foyer in half an hour."

Lucinda cried, "I must have at least an hour."

Val gritted his teeth to halt his retort. He hated peevish young misses who took forever, but he could do nothing but be polite. "Very well. *One* hour." Val leapt up and fled the room.

Damnation! The last thing he wanted was to spend the remaining afternoon with Lucinda. Well, there was nothing to be done. At least, he would not be tempted to kiss the annoying Lucinda. This bright idea to keep him away from Lucinda was not turning out very well.

Simon paced the tiled floor and slapped his gloves into his hand. His greatcoat billowed behind him like a sail. Apparently, he was impatient. Grace knew Mama would be angry, but Lucinda had talked her into this madness. She inhaled a deep breath, raised her chin, and descended the stairs.

Simon spun around and his mouth dipped into a deeper frown. "Where is Miss Lucinda?"

Grace smiled, betraying nothing of her annoyance. "She is much too tired for an excursion. Knowing I wish to go, she thought not to spoil the trip for me."

His left brow rose a fraction. "And what of Mrs. Templeton's instructions?"

Grace dropped her gaze to adjust her glove. "I suppose she shall be disappointed."

"Disappointed? I would venture outright angry," Simon suggested.

Grace raised her eyes to meet his. "I'm accustomed to her contempt, my lord."

"Very well, Grace, if you are willing to subject yourself to your mother's anger, I shall not deny you a jaunt to Hadrian's Wall." Simon buttoned his greatcoat and tapped his hat into place. Then he pointed to Lachlan. "But *he* isn't going."

A low growl emanated from the small dog. "Of course not." Grace leaned down and rubbed Lachlan's ear. "Be a good boy while I'm gone."

Giles opened the door. "Any instructions, my lord?"

Simon glanced at Grace, then said, "If no inquiries are made, I see no need to inform anyone of Miss Templeton's whereabouts. However, we don't wish anyone to worry over her absence."

The butler bowed. "Very good, my lord. Have a nice excursion, Miss Templeton."

"Thank you, Giles." Grace walked out of Valentine Hall in a daze, aware only of Simon's presence.

He assisted her into the carriage, then climbed in behind her. Grace busied herself arranging one of the lap rugs over her legs. Simon's mere presence across from her was daunting enough without looking into enigmatic black fire.

The coach jerked into motion and Grace clutched her reticule to her chest. "Is anything left of the garrison?"

Simon replied, "The remains of a circular chamber. No one knows its purpose."

Grace turned her gaze to the passing scenery. The last of the snow dusted a few places here and there. Tree branches, devoid of leaves, looked like skeletal fingers reaching, reaching but never quite touching the sky.

"Is anything amiss?" Simon asked.

"No," Grace answered. "I'm merely enjoying the scenery. Northumbria is beautiful."

" 'Tis more so in the spring. Daffodils and blue-bells dot the slopes." Love of the land imbued his voice.

"Do you pick the flowers?" Heat burned her cheeks. What a provincial question to ask an earl.

The light in his eyes died. "Not since Mama's death."

"I'm sorry."

Simon shrugged. "One must accustom one's self to disappointments and deaths. 'Tis what makes up life."

A realization dawned on Grace. Mr. Lynford was correct. Simon was lonely. Though he had a brother, aunt, and cousin, he still felt very much alone since his parents' deaths. Why was he so adamant against a wife? She would be a companion to him. Of course, she told herself, his affairs were none of her concern. If he wanted to live alone, that was his choice.

"Do your aunt and cousin visit you often?" Now, where did that come from?

Simon grimaced. "This particular visit is one too many."

"Yes, my lord, you have made that quite clear," Grace snapped and turned back to the window.

Must he constantly remind her they were un-wanted. If only she could escape this place, but Mama would never leave before the Valentine eve-ning soirée. She still maintained visions of Lucinda and Simon.

"I beg your pardon, Grace. I don't mean to be inhospitable."

Grace nodded.

"If I could just make Aunt Cupid listen to me. She will not credit my decision to remain unmarried." Desperation filled his voice.

"At least her interference comes from a loving heart." Grace could feel Simon's gaze upon her.

"As opposed to your mother's?"

Dread burned in Grace. How much did he know?

"Very few actually marry for love. Your mother's wish to marry her daughters well is nothing to be ashamed of."

"Daughter," Grace mumbled.

"I beg your pardon?"

Grace blew out a deep breath and finally met Simon's gaze. "Daughter. Mama has accepted no one will ever marry *me* other than our neighbor, whom I've refused. Lucinda is her last hope. After all, Lucinda is beautiful enough that any man would want her."

A dark brow raised in contradiction and Grace corrected her statement. "Well, almost any man."

"And why has Mrs. Templeton given up on your forming a good marriage?"

"I'm too old, too plain, too curvy."

"You shouldn't listen to your mother," Simon grumbled, his eyes hooded like a hawk's and his face as emotionless as a smooth lake.

"Why?" Grace stared down at her clasped hands, uncertain why she asked. After all, Simon was a man above her station. Many times she had lain awake at night and wondered about the perplexing population called men.

Simon swung across the carriage, and before Grace knew what had happened, he was squeezed into the seat beside her. He clasped her hand between his.

"Do you enjoy torturing me?" he growled.

Grace tried to give his shoulders more space, but it was impossible side by side. "N—no. I'm not certain what you mean."

Simon wrapped one arm around her waist. "I mean to kiss you."

She leaned further back. "Y—you said you would never kiss me again."

"Then I lied." His voice was hard and his eyes glinted with something Grace could not identify.

"I shall slap you," she warned.

Simon smiled and his strong white teeth reminded her of a wolf. "A small price for a kiss from your sweet lips."

Lips came down on hers, punishing and angry. Not certain why he was piqued with her, Grace restrained her impulse to kiss him back and remained as still as a statue.

Simon lifted his mouth and stared into her eyes. "Damnation," he mumbled, then kissed her again, but this time gentle lips covered hers.

Grace wrapped her arms around his neck and kissed him back. Flames leapt through her blood once again. She tried to throttle the dizziness, but Simon left her giddy and reckless.

Simon drew away and stroked her cheek with his thumb. "It is beyond comprehension."

"What?" Even to her own ears her voice wobbled.

"How you make me forget myself. I'm not in the habit of kissing proper young ladies."

"So, you kiss improper ladies?" she retorted.

Simon replied in a husky voice, " 'Tis not a proper question for a lady to ask."

"I have been feeling most improper the past few days." Egad, if he only knew what she thought about in the deep of night.

"Grace—" Simon moved to sit across from her again. He stretched out his legs as best he could. One hand rested on his knee and he opened and closed it. Clench and unclench.

"You don't have to say it again, Simon."

Dark brows arched. "You possess the ability to read my mind?"

Grace smiled and nodded. "You said the same thing the last time you kissed me." She inhaled a deep breath and lowered her voice. "I don't wish to marry, Grace, and I shall never kiss you again."

Simon stared at her a moment, irritation arched across his brow. Then his deep, rich laughter filled the coach.

"Bloody hell! You mimic me well, Grace."

Heat filled her cheeks at her own audacity. "I'm glad you aren't angry."

"Never. I see I shall have to strive to vary my responses."

Grace tilted her head to one side and studied Simon. "One wonders if you break all your vows so readily."

Simon sobered. "No. It is the only vow I have ever broken."

Oh, if only being averse to marriage was a breakable vow for Simon. Grace pushed the silly wish away. He had been quite honest and honorable about his intentions.

"Is Mr. Lynford an honorable man?"

Simon appeared surprised at her question, but did not comment. "Matthew? Yes."

"Even in his dealings with young ladies?" she whispered.

"You need have no fear Matthew will take advantage of Lucinda. He isn't a seducer of innocents."

"Is he opposed to marriage?"

"He has no special affinities for or against marriage. Matthew enjoys himself too much with the ladies."

"But you just said—"

Simon held up his hand. "He doesn't seduce innocent young ladies. He enjoys himself with other"—Simon searched for a word—"sorts."

Heat flushed Grace's cheeks once again. "Oh!" Well, that was clear enough. The gossip was true. But why did he give Lucinda so much attention? Lucinda was accustomed to being the center of a gentleman's regard. Yet she could find no reason for Mr. Lynford to be so accommodating, besides his cousin's reluctance. Could there be another motive?

"I can hear the gears turning all the way across the coach, Grace. What are you thinking?"

"Nothing of import."

The coach slowed and turned. Grace braced her hands on the seat. "Are we close to the wall?"

Simon peered out the window. "Just a few more miles."

Silence descended, except for the jangle of the harnesses and the wheels on the road. Grace wondered if Mama knew of her open defiance yet. Severe payment would be extracted, but she would not worry about that now. She would enjoy her excursion with Simon.

"Why did you ask about Matthew?"

Simon's voice snapped her mind back to the present. A scowl darkened his brow.

Should she tell him of Lucinda's infatuation? No, best to keep her own counsel. "Concern about Lucinda."

"Matthew enchants women very easily. You spent time with him at the folly." Simon shrugged.

"He is quite charming," Grace agreed.

Simon demanded, "And did you kiss him?"

"You are the only gentleman at Valentine Hall I have kissed."

Simon scowled. "Just how many men have you kissed?"

Grace shrugged. "A few."

The coach drew to a halt. Grace peered out the window. "Ah, we must be at the wall." She folded the lap rug and set it aside.

A footman opened the door and let down the steps. " 'Adrian's Wall, milord."

Not waiting for Simon, Grace bounded out. She heard Simon muttering and following behind her.

Was he actually jealous? she asked herself. He acted quite like it. Grace hugged the notion to her heart.

Not much of the former fifteen-foot high wall remained, but it stretched as far as the eye could see in both directions. Grace stepped up onto the stones and walked a short distance to a circle.

"Blast it, woman, be careful!" Simon roared. "You'll fall and break your neck or twist your ankle."

"I'm quite capable of keeping my balance," Grace said. "It is only a few feet high."

Simon stalked over to stand behind her. "I wonder what it was," Grace said.

Sounds of marching boots and clanking swords almost seemed to hover over the ground. Grace rubbed her arms and tried to banish the ghostly sensation.

"You are cold," Simon said. "We should return to the carriage."

Grace shook her head. "Please allow me a few more minutes." For she knew she would never return to this place of ghostly armies once she departed Valentine Hall.

"What do you have to say for yourself?" The angry voice bounded off the walls.

Grace looked up from the cheval glass where she readied to step into her gown for dinner. "Lucinda was exhausted, Mama. She couldn't bear the trip."

Ida stalked across the room and stood beside the mirror. Anger mottled her face. Grace retreated three steps. "I'm sorry, Mama."

"You shall have no dinner. Were we elsewhere, I would punish you more severely."

"Yes, Mama."

"I will beat you if you mess up my plans." Ida marched from the room and slammed the door behind herself.

Grace gulped. Her mother had never hit her before, but she did not doubt her threat. She replaced her gown in the armoire and pulled on her dressing gown.

Well, she did not mind missing dinner. Mama always said she needed to lose a few pounds. She dropped onto a chair and picked up her book.

Not certain how long she had read, Grace was startled by a knock. "Enter."

A maid walked in carrying a silver tray. "Yer dinner, miss."

"But Mama said—"

"His lordship says I was to bring ye dinner and ye are to eat every bite."

Grace peered at the tray as the maid uncovered the dishes. " 'Tis too much, Alice."

"Nay, miss. His lordship says ye need nourishment after yer exhausting trip to the wall."

Grace picked up an orange and smiled.

"His lordship picked the oranges hisself, miss."

"Does my mother know he sent a tray?"

Alice shrugged. "His lordship isna accustomed to tell folks his business. Now, sit yerself down and eat."

"Can you pass a note to Lord Valentine without anyone knowing?" Heat burned Grace's cheeks.

Alice nodded. "I make sure he be the only one whats sees it, but hurry up afore yer food gets cold."

Grace sat at the escritoire and pulled out a piece of vellum. She chewed the pen tip for a moment. The people of London thought her an odd duck. Mama treated her with contempt. Outside of Lucinda, Simon was the only one to treat her with kindness. She dipped the quill in the ink and wrote.

The fire crackled and popped as Simon stared unseeing. Though he did not look at the vellum, he was aware of its presence on the table beside him. The words were burned into his heart. How many other women would have appreciated a dinner tray and a gift of oranges?

What made Grace so different? Never before had he wanted to kiss a young lady and keep right on kissing her. His every vow was met with defeat when he was alone with Grace.

"Your brandy, my lord."

Val accepted the snifter from his valet. "That will be all for the evening, Stedeman."

"Very good, sir."

Val sipped his brandy and waited until Stedeman had departed. He leaned back in his chair and stretched out his legs. He really should go to bed rather than sitting in his bedchamber in his dressing gown, contemplating his irksome houseguest.

Perhaps if he cataloged her attributes such as he did with his farm animals, the answer would reveal itself. After all, she was not a classical beauty.

Fiery red hair crowned her head. Eyes as green as jade and lips sweet as berries. Alabaster skin soft to his farm-rough hands. Ample breasts heavy over full hips.

The images his mind conjured generated reactions in his body his mind tried to deny. After all, it had been a time since he had been with a woman. That was all it was. Grace Templeton was nothing special.

Even as his mind said the words, he recognized the lie. There was no way to make himself believe the utterance. Since Grace's arrival at Valentine Hall, he felt more alive than he had in ages. When her lilting voice called him Simon, he experienced a lightness and happiness long gone from his life.

What would he do about Grace? Val dropped his head back and closed his eyes. Damnation!

Six

The last week had been a haze of stolen glances and contempt. And kisses. Simon seemed to kiss her whenever they were alone. He and Matthew had managed to outmaneuver Cupid on every intrigue. Grace had spent more time alone with Simon than she had ever spent with any man. Even her father.

After every kiss, every touch, Simon would curse, scowl, and vow never to be alone with her again. She was a fool. Common sense told her that. Heartbreak was the only outcome possible.

Grace squeezed the vellum in one hand and leaned against the folly door. Was she losing her mind? The late afternoon sun illuminated the stained-glass window and painted a rainbow across the floor.

"Grace?" Simon's deep voice boomed.

Her heart drummed against her chest and joy bubbled in her. She swallowed hard and only managed a feeble answer. "Yes."

Simon's note asking her to meet him in the garden folly had brought happiness as well as trepidation. He walked over to Grace and took her hands in his. "You are trembling."

Yes, she was amazed she could even walk. But

his invitation drew her like a moth to a flame. As if destiny were at hand and she was powerless to stop it. No matter how much leaving Simon would hurt.

"Are you frightened of me?" Pain knifed through his voice.

"No"—she hurried to allay his pain—"I—I'm just nervous. A gentleman has never asked me to meet him privately."

"I don't feel much of a gentleman presently, but I couldn't help myself, Grace. I had to see you alone. It has been murder spending time with you, yet unable to kiss you. May I kiss you again?" His warm breath fanned her cheek.

Grace inhaled a deep breath and her world spun on a tilted axis. The scent of bay rum infiltrated her senses. He was so very near. And she only wanted to be closer. "Yes."

Ebony flames engulfed his gaze. Large hands circled her waist and Simon smiled down at her. Anticipation almost overwhelmed her.

He brushed a gentle kiss across her forehead. "You are so sweet," he whispered. Then his lips touched hers like a whisper.

The entire world swirled around her. The vellum fluttered from her fingers and she clutched his shoulders, trying to find purchase in the maelstrom. The heady sensation must be like opium, she thought, or the sweet taste of strawberries and cream. Barely controlled power coiled in Simon. She sensed the restraint in his lips and hands.

Last night in the warmth of her bed she had admitted the truth to herself. She loved Simon. Passion had slumbered in her, but Simon had awakened a yearning.

Knowing Simon did not want to marry caused a fear, but she was willing to set it aside for a moment. She would never love another man and this was her opportunity to experience the sensation that only happened between a man and a woman.

Simon continued to linger, savoring her lips like a fine wine, and she reveled in his drugging kiss. All rational thought had soared from her at his first touch, but her mind became totally vacuous when his hand cupped her derriere and squeezed.

No man had ever touched her so intimately. She pressed closer, craving his warmth like a flower thirsts for rain. The shock of his manhood against her startled her for a moment, but she pressed even closer.

Simon lifted his head, leaving her mouth burning with fire. "Bloody hell, Grace! You should slap my face."

She shook her head. "I want—" She squeezed her eyes closed.

His thumb caressed her cheek. "Tell me what you want. I shall do my damnedest to deliver."

Grace took a deep breath and opened her eyes. She gazed into black depths. "I want you to make love to me." God, he would think her a cyprian, but she did not care. She wanted to take everything of his sweet memory with her.

"Do you know what you are asking? You will be compromised. By *me*." His voice was deep and dark as a river.

She forced the words out to set his mind at ease. "I don't expect you to marry me."

"How does a proper young lady come to such a decision? I only meant to kiss you."

She shrugged. "I can't explain it." The truth was

she would not. He would never know of her love. "Sometimes in the dark of the night one wishes for something to ease the pain of life."

"I know quite a bit about loneliness, but, Grace—"

She laid her fingers over his lips. "Please, Simon. Don't deny me this one thing. Make love to me and fulfill my wickedest desires."

He kissed her fingertips one by one. "I must be a madman to agree. This scheme has disaster written all over it."

"You don't find me attractive?" she whispered over her pounding heart.

"Good God, how can you think that? It has taken all of my self-control the last few days not to pounce on you and ravish you."

"Then, relinquish your self-control. Ravish me."

Simon's mouth curved into an unconscious smile. "May God, and you, forgive me, but I can't resist your entreaty."

Clasping her hands in his warm, strong ones, Simon led Grace around the curtain of plants. He stood at the foot of the chaise longue and peered down at her. "Are you certain?"

A smile trembled over her lips and she nodded. She had never been so certain of anything. Lucinda would be stunned and Mama mortified, but they would never know of her indiscretion. Happiness was difficult to find. She would hold the secret next to her heart to warm her on cold, lonely nights.

He relegated his coat, waistcoat, and cravat to a chair. Dark hair peeked from his shirt opening. Grace combed her fingers through the bristles and felt as if she petted a lion or some dangerous unknown creature.

His mouth covered hers again, more hungry and

demanding. His tongue thrust past her lips and played a dueling game with hers. Excitement rippled through her. The foreign sensation was erotic and seductive, just as he was.

Simon trailed his fingertips down her arm and savored her shivers. He did not recall ever desiring a woman as he did Grace. Like a tonic quickening through his veins. As if he were bewitched.

Pins rained to the floor as he slid his hand through her hair. Red fire spilled down her back and over her shoulders. "I like your hair loose," he whispered against her lips.

One hand moved gently down her back, unfastening her gown while the other fondled her breast. Her nipple erect to his touch. An exotic fruit he could not wait to sample.

He slid the gown over her head and tossed the wool onto the chair. Simon stared down at the beautiful vision before him. Full breasts brimmed over her stays and pink flushed her cheeks.

"You are beautiful," Simon whispered.

Grace shook her head in disagreement.

He cupped her cheek and raised her head to stare into her jade eyes. "You *are* beautiful. And enchanting. You quite take my breath away." He drew his knuckles over her cheek. "Your skin is creamy silk. As soft as a newborn lamb's. And pink brushes your cheeks like a sunset."

A shy smile softened her lips and Simon brushed his thumb across her bottom lip. "Your soft lips taste as sweet as honey and your eyes are the deepest jade."

She whispered, "You need not offer me so much flummery."

"I speak only the truth. I'm amazed some man hasn't snatched you up for his bride."

"I guess the gentlemen of London are more discerning."

"More like witless." Gently, he eased her down on the chaise sliding one knee between her legs. Her neck looked a delectable treat. He nibbled her ivory skin, as soft and sweet as her lips.

Grace tilted her head to allow Simon better advantage. His mouth was warm and moist on her neck and she was feeling the same in other portions of her body. The pit of her stomach clenched at the touch of his hand on her breast while his other hand unknotted the strings of her stays. The thought flittered through her mind that he seemed to know much about undressing a lady, but all thought disappeared when he twirled her nipple between his thumb and forefinger.

An urge to touch him welled up in her. She tugged his shirt from his breeches and fluttered her fingers across his chest. Simon sucked in a deep breath and shivered.

Simon yanked his shirt off and threw it to the floor. Then he slipped off her corset and shift. His hair-roughened chest covered hers and Grace gasped.

He whispered in her ear, "I enjoy the feel of you against me."

The provocative words made Grace tremble. "I quite like it, too." Grace ran her hands up his biceps, the muscles hard beneath her fingertips. Today of all days she did not wish to be timid. She wanted Simon to enjoy their interlude. Perhaps he would even think of her now and again.

She moved her fingers to the falls of his trousers, but he caught her hands. "Not quite yet, love."

"I—I have seen Polyphemus before."

His dark brows rose. "Polyphemus?"

Grace nodded. "That is what Papa called"—she took a deep breath—"called it. He was a Cyclops in Homer's *Odyssey* distinguished by one eye." She tilted her head. "I never quite understood the name."

Simon appeared as if he struggled not to laugh. "You will soon learn why. And where did you see Polyphemus?"

"When I was a young girl, some of the village boys would strip their clothes to swim."

"Well, my dear, you will see something different from your childhood memories."

"How much can it change?"

"A good bit. Now, if it meets with your approval, I would like to return to ravishing your alluring body."

Grace nodded and moved her hand to one garter. His hand caught hers. "Please leave your stockings on." His fingers stroked the bare skin above one garter. "I find it very erotic."

"Very well. You may return to ravishing me now."

A sensuous light glowed from his dark eyes. "Thank you, Miss Templeton."

His tongue laved one nipple while his hand stroked the other, causing a stirring in the pit of her stomach. The fabric of his breeches scraped the inside of her thighs.

Grace stroked one rounded buttock and Simon jerked against her. She smiled and did it again. He growled but did not take his mouth from her breast. She could feel his manhood straining to be free.

His knee pressed against her most intimate center, awakening her to a deeper desire. No longer able to think coherently or speak, a jetty of desire swirled around her. Hands and lips continued their hungry search of her body even as his knee kneaded and stroked.

Her nails dug into his shoulders and her body arched. Sensation burst through her. Nothing had ever felt like this. She had certainly not expected the feeling to be so acute as to cut through her very being. Smoldering flames blazed his black gaze. Knowing that Simon found her desirable provoked an intensity and enthusiasm.

Simon lurched off the chaise. Cool air brushed Grace's body and she reached toward him. He removed his boots and breeches.

Grace gasped as she stared at Simon in all his nude glory. He grinned and came back down on top of her. She gasped as his body covered hers. Flesh against flesh, man against woman. The engorged manhood now pressed into her hip. "Are you still certain, Grace?"

She swallowed and nodded. Bracing up her courage, Grace brushed her thumb over the vermilion tip. Soft as velvet. Simon twitched and groaned. The reaction emboldened her and Grace wrapped her hand around the rigid length. The male strength of him heightened her desire and a tremor rolled through her.

The cool hand against his hot extremity pushed Simon toward the edge. He gritted his teeth and tried to hold back. He wanted Grace to enjoy the moment, but his self-control was fading fast as she ran her hand up and down.

He snagged her wrist. "Leave Polyphemus be, Grace, or I shall lose all my self-control."

Grace giggled and brushed her hands across his buttocks. "Then what shall I play with?"

"I shall give you something to play with," he growled and moved between her legs. Did he know what he was doing? Hell, did she? "Last opportunity to change your mind, Grace."

She shook her head. "Please don't stop."

"Very well." He plunged inside her tight passage. She gasped a silent gasp and her eyes opened wide. It was the most difficult thing he had ever done, but he stilled and stared into jade. "Grace?"

"Y—yes?"

Simon squeezed his eyes tight, attempting to maintain control. Grace was divine ecstasy. "The pain will go away soon."

"I didn't know it would hurt." Her voice was low and breathy. "Is your pain gone?"

His eyes jerked open. "Mine?"

She nodded.

" 'Tis not pain I feel."

"Oh."

"Does it feel better?"

She nodded and smiled. She had never expected to feel so full and tight. Or the pain of her shattered maidenhead.

Simon began to stroke slowly in and out, urgency filling his eyes. Passion once again coiled in her stomach like a clockwork wound too tight.

Pleasure exploded and Grace dug her nails into Simon's shoulders again. He lurched into her one last time and groaned her name. He collapsed on top of her and nuzzled her neck a moment.

She snuggled against him and savored his presence. This had been so different from what she had expected. She lightly caressed his back. "I love you."

Grace wanted to bite her tongue off. Now, why the devil did those words slip out? But Simon did not move or stir. Thank God he must have fallen asleep. He would never know of her declaration. Grace closed her own eyes and enjoyed the feel of Simon against her.

Simon lay half on top of her, breathing deeply. Grace stared at the darkening sky. She must have dozed. A sliver of moon shone amongst the twinkling stars.

Perhaps she should slip away while he slept. Still moist from their lovemaking, Grace squirmed from beneath Simon.

A hand snagged her wrist. Simon looked at her from half closed eyes. "Where are you going, love?"

"B—back to the hall. 'Twould be havoc if we are seen together." She glanced down. "Especially disheveled."

One side of his mouth lifted in a grin. "I can get you back without being seen. Something might happen to you alone."

Suddenly embarrassed staring at his nakedness, Grace turned her back to Simon to dress. It was ridiculous being flustered now after having met his lovemaking with such reckless abandon.

"Is something wrong?" Simon asked.

"N—no. I—I don't wish to be seen."

She heard no noise, but two hands touched her shoulders and squeezed. Grace hugged her corset to her chest, feeling quite undressed only in her shift.

"I shall take care of you, Grace. No one shall ever know."

She nodded, unable to speak. How would she ever look Simon in the eye across the dinner table? Would anyone discern of their afternoon activity?

She jumped at the sound of his voice, his breath hot on her ear. "Slip your corset on and I shall tie it."

Hurrying to finish dressing, she pushed everything else from her mind. She would worry about matters later.

Her corset firmly in place, Grace pulled her gown over her head and Simon secured the fastenings. He brushed his hands down her arms, then pulled her back to his chest and rested his chin on her head. "You are ready to return."

"N—not quite. My hair."

"Running your fingers through it will be enough."

"You should get dressed," she murmured.

Simon chuckled. "Does my nakedness embarrass you?"

Grace nodded.

"It didn't seem to moments ago."

Grace inhaled a deep breath and turned to face him, intent on keeping her gaze locked on his, but her eyes did not cooperate. Scratches marred his broad shoulders. Black hair sprinkled his chest, which narrowed to chiseled hips above sturdy legs. His manhood stood at attention. Heat flushed her cheeks and she finally met his gaze.

He grinned at her. "Do you approve, madam?"

"Yes." Then she stepped forward. She wrapped her arms around him and kissed his cheek. "Thank you, Simon."

His cocky grin disappeared and he caressed her cheek. "For what, my dear?"

"For giving me memories that I shall hold dear during my spinsterhood."

Some emotion filled his eyes, but Grace did not wait. She snatched up the fallen note and rushed out of the folly intent on escaping him. She could only hope he had not heard her declaration of love. To be saved that indignity. And he would never know her darkest secret.

The next morning Grace entered the conservatory and listened. She could not wait to see Simon again. Over last night's dinner table, she had been unable to meet his gaze, but no one seemed to guess about their rendezvous. She would savor every minute remaining of their visit. Then be content alone the rest of her life.

Simon's deep voice sounded a few rows over. A smile covered her face. She felt like a hunter who had just sighted her quarry.

Who was he talking with? She halted one row over and listened. It was Matthew, but his words sent a chill down her spine.

"Well, St. Valentine's is almost upon us and I seem to have won our wager. You are still unbetrothed. Still free of the parson's mousetrap." Matthew laughed.

"Matthew—"

"You aren't about to renege on our wager?"

"No. The hunter is yours."

Matthew chuckled. "And I get to keep my diamond stickpin. What is wrong, coz? You look quite put out. You shouldn't wager if you don't like paying up."

" 'Tis not that. I feel badly that we used Grace and Lucinda in our wager."

"Ah, they will never know. 'Tis not as if we ruined the ladies."

The words were like a splash of cold water. Tears welled in Grace's eyes. Oh, she was quite ruined, but she could have withstood that. Somehow a wager made her love seem sordid.

What if she were with child? Too late to worry about that. She rubbed her hand over her stomach. She had allowed love to blind her. Now the price might be high, but she would pay it. And if there was a child, she would raise him or her with all the love the father did not want. She tiptoed toward the door.

Pain gripped Grace in its unclenching grasp and icy fingers spread through her stomach. The harsh reality of life had risen up and chomped her.

Shock yielded to anger. She had known Simon did not wish to be married, but it all had been a wager. She and Lucinda had been a sport to these two men. For a horse and a stickpin. The beautiful memory she had hoped to take with her was now soiled.

Nails bit into her palms. She leaned against the wall and squeezed her eyes shut. She was furious with herself. For allowing herself to be vulnerable to Simon and fall in love. Pressing her hand to her face, she commanded herself not to cry.

Grace withdrew from the conservatory and made her way upstairs. To a duty she hated. She tapped on the door.

"Come in," Lucinda called.

Grace entered the bedchamber and leaned against the closed door. Lucinda was radiant in a pink gown.

"I wanted to make sure my gown fit for the Valentine soirée tomorrow night," she breathlessly intoned and twirled in a circle. "Do you think Matthew will like it?"

"You are very beautiful. Lucinda, sit down." Grace dropped onto the bed and patted the space beside her.

The smile died from Lucinda's face and she sat. "What is wrong? You have the same look on your face when you told me Papa died."

Grace inhaled a deep breath. "Nothing quite so terrible as that. I overheard a conversation between Matthew and Simon."

"Grace! You shouldn't eavesdrop," Lucinda scolded.

"Purely by accident. I wish I hadn't heard the words, but I can't ignore them."

Lucinda's head tilted to one side. "What?"

"We were a wager to them." Grace clasped Lucinda's hand between hers. "By keeping you and Simon apart, Matthew has won Simon's hunter."

"But Matthew loves me." A tremor ran through Lucinda's words.

"Men don't make the women they love into a game. We depart the day after Valentine's. We must hold our heads up high and not let on that they have hurt us."

"Us?"

Tears shimmered in Grace's eyes. "I fear I love Simon. 'Twas foolish, I know, but I couldn't help myself. He kissed me several times," she blurted.

Astonishment touched Lucinda's pale face, but her

eyes were gentle and understanding. "We will stay in our chambers until tomorrow night and we will not dance once with them at the soirée."

"Then we shall depart the next day and never see them again." Grace sobbed as pain gnawed at her heart and torment filled her breast.

Lucinda wrapped her arms around Grace. "Please don't cry. It breaks my heart to see you so. You have always been so strong."

"I have never fallen in love and allowed a gentleman liberties."

The hand soothing Grace's back stilled. "Just what did you grant Lord Valentine?"

Mortification flowed through Grace. "I prefer not to speak of the familiarities I permitted. I made the wrong decision."

Lucinda's eyes narrowed. "Just how far did his coach travel?"

Grace shrugged and wiped the tears from her face. " 'Tis not important. I shall retire to my chamber now." She stood and squeezed Lucinda's hand once more. "I wish I could say all will be well, but one can't expect life to turn out the way one wishes. Nor the way Mama desires."

"Mama will be angry that her plan failed."

"So be it. Mama isn't accustomed to getting her way in everything." Grace inhaled a deep breath. "It pains me to say such a thing about our own mother—"

"Yes?"

"You had better keep your door locked. Mama may be trying to figure out how to compromise you into a wedding."

Lucinda's eyes rounded. "Do you think she would really attempt such a dastardly thing?"

Grace nodded. "I think Mama will do anything to get her way."

"Then, you should keep your door locked also."

"Me? 'Tis you she thinks to marry to Simon."

"But I have seen the way he looks at you when he thinks no one is looking. I don't believe he would allow Mama to force him into a marriage with me."

"You imagine things, Lucinda. He looks at me no special way."

Lucinda snorted. "To be the elder you can sometimes be quite naive."

"You shouldn't snort. You aren't a horse," Grace chastised.

Lucinda rolled her eyes. "And you are changing the subject. I really believe Simon and Matthew are intrinsically decent men. I can't imagine them playing fast and loose with us."

"Now, who is naive?" Her chest ached where her heart lay smashed in a hundred fragments. For twenty-six years Grace had enshrouded her heart in cotton wool. Finally, she had unwrapped it, only to have it shattered to smithereens.

Perhaps later she would be able to enjoy the memories as her life stretched before her. However, now she just wished to push the hurt from her mind, but that was impossible.

Val paced across the Aubusson carpet and peered out the window. Winter twilight had settled on the countryside. "Have you seen the Miss Templetons today, Aunt?"

"Yes."

"Perhaps we should call the physician if they are both unwell."

Cupid shook her head over her needlework. "They just need rest from their megrims. Mayhap the trip here has been too much excitement. They plan to take a dinner tray in their chambers tonight so they will be rested for the Valentine soirée tomorrow night."

"Ouch!" Cupid yelped and sucked her finger.

Val stepped toward his aunt. "What is it?"

Cupid smiled a sheepish smile. "I'm fine. I merely stuck my needle in my finger."

Val took up pacing again. "I could call on the ladies and inquire after their well-being."

Cupid's needlework dropped to her lap and she peered at Val. "You know you can't visit their chambers. Has my plan worked anyway? Are you concerned with Lucinda's health?"

"I would be concerned with any visitor's illness, Aunt. You shouldn't hope your plan has worked." Beneath his breath, Val muttered, "As you wished anyway."

"Ida and I are keeping a close eye on the young ladies."

"Where is Mrs. Templeton?"

"Resting before dinner."

"The entire family is ailing?" Val asked.

"No, Ida is just resting. Ladies of a certain age can't do everything they once did."

"Then, why aren't you in bed?"

Cupid frowned. "Because I'm not yet of a certain age."

Val smiled and bowed. "I beg your pardon."

Matthew strode into the drawing room, still

dressed in riding clothes. His blond hair tossed in disarray. "Has Miss Lucinda made an appearance?"

"No," Val answered. "Both Miss Templetons are still holed up in their bedchambers."

"You should send for the physician, Val. They could be quite ill," Matthew said.

Cupid sighed and laid her needlework down. "They aren't ill. Just vexed with a megrim."

"Both of them?" Matthew demanded.

Cupid nodded.

Val's eyes narrowed. "That is quite odd that both are afflicted at the same time."

"And what do you know of young ladies' complaints?" Cupid asked, exasperation evident in her voice. "They will be fine by tomorrow night. You two act like worried husbands."

Val straightened up and looked down his nose. "Don't."

"I must agree with Val, Mama. Do you not expect a host to be concerned about his guests?"

Cupid nodded. "But this isn't mere concern." Cupid's eyes narrowed. "Val? Is there something you haven't told me?"

"No, Aunt, there is not. Don't get any wild starts in your beautiful head."

Cupid smiled and stood. "I shall go check on the young ladies again. I don't want the two of you to continue to fret."

Val watched Cupid leave, then turned to Matthew. "Have you tried to visit Lucinda?"

"I thought of it, but her mother patrolled the corridor. Why would both of them be unwell?"

"I don't know, Matthew, but to me this smacks of prevarication."

"But why?" Matthew demanded.

Val shrugged. "I haven't a clue, but I intend to visit Grace tonight."

Matthew's brows shot up. "In her bedchamber?" he whispered.

Val nodded.

"If you are caught, you will have compromised the young lady."

Val shrugged. "So be it." It was not as if he had not already compromised her.

Matthew's eyes narrowed. "Are you planning to wed Grace?"

"Of course not. I don't wish to marry," he lied, for he did not know what course Matthew would take to halt him and win his hunter. But one thing he knew without a doubt. His life would not be worth living without Grace by his side.

A growl interrupted Val's thoughts and he turned to see the small ball of fur standing in the drawing room. Snarling at him. "What have I ever done to you, Lachlan?"

Matthew chuckled. "Paid his mistress attention?"

"I have been awaiting this moment." Val strolled over to the table and raised a cover. He sat on the settee and placed a plate on the floor. "Here you go, boy. A nice beefsteak."

"Bribery?" Matthew asked.

"Well, there is an old saying about joining them if you can't beat them."

Lachlan took one small step toward Val and sniffed the air.

"Yes, boy, this beefsteak is all for you. Come on, now." Val wiggled the beef in the air.

Lachlan took two steps forward, lowered his head, and growled once. Then took two more steps.

"He is slowly making his way to you," Matthew whispered.

"Before the night is over, I intend to be Lachlan's best friend," Val murmured.

Matthew's brows rose. "Indeed? Is that to make points with his mistress?"

Heat flushed Val's cheeks. "Not at all. I just want to be liked by all animals."

"Of course," Matthew said, but he did not sound convinced.

Grace stared into the tester as she lay in the dark. Moonbeams spread across the floor in a river of light. Today had been difficult. She was not the sort of miss who lay abed.

Cupid had checked on her several times and told her wild tales of Simon being worried. Ha! She knew better.

Truth be known, her feelings were a smidgeon hurt. Simon had not even attempted to visit her. Propriety had never stopped him before.

Maybe he was relieved to be rid of her for a day. He had not had to play the tender gentleman. He could do whatever he wished with no thought to her. Why, she doubted she had even crossed his mind.

A scratching sounded at the door. Her breath stilled in her throat and her heart pounded against her chest. Grace slipped out of bed and tiptoed across the chamber. She opened the door a crack and peered out. The corridor was empty.

Then something pressed against her ankle. She looked down. "Lachlan! Where have you been?" Grace opened the door wider and the terrier scurried in and leaped onto her bed. His tail wagged in a fury. Something was clutched in his teeth.

"What do you have, boy?"

Lachlan dropped the object into her hands and Grace spread it out. "A man's glove?" She stared at the glove a moment, then realization dawned. Simon's glove!

There were only two gentlemen present and Simon's hand was larger than Matthew's. "How did you come by this?"

"He stole it from my chamber," the deep voice whispered across the room.

Grace jumped and turned. Dressed in a dark blue dressing gown, Simon stood at the door. Black bristles stubbled his cheeks.

"You must leave immediately." She felt so vulnerable dressed in nothing but her night rail. Thank goodness it was dark or the light would have revealed everything to Simon. Heat burned her cheeks. He had already seen everything and more.

"I shall, but I wanted to see you. I have been concerned."

"Cupid has checked on me several times today."

"And your mother?"

Grace shook her head. "Only Cupid."

"I wanted to send for the physician, but Cupid insisted he wasn't needed."

"She was correct. Just a megrim that will eventually go away."

"So, you still have your megrim?"

Grace rubbed her forehead and nodded. She forced the words out. "Thank you for your concern, Simon." Words that were not true.

Simon paced across the floor and wrapped his hands around the bed poster. Instead of growling in warning, Lachlan quivered from his head to the tip of his tail.

"He isn't barking," Grace murmured in amazement. "A few days ago you would have been terribly angry at him for taking your glove."

Simon rubbed Lachlan's head. "We have cried friends."

"Indeed?"

"Mmmm hmmm."

"Just how did you accomplish that?" Grace asked.

Simon chuckled. "A couple of beefsteaks and a few games of fetch."

Grace laughed. "The one thing Lachlan likes better than me is food and playing. You bribed him to be your friend!"

Simon shrugged. "I suppose." His dark gaze met hers, then dropped to the expanse of her bare neck. "I would do anything for you, dear heart."

Desire shivered up Grace's spine and the pulse at the base of her throat hammered. She wanted so desperately to be in his embrace. What had happened to the levelheaded young woman of this morning? The one who had decided their friendship was at an end because he had toyed with her. Now she fought the urge to fling herself into his arms and cover his face with kisses.

His large hand cupped her cheek. "I hope you feel better by tomorrow night. I can't wait to dance with you. To hold you in my arms once again."

Grace swallowed past the lump in her throat, but said nothing. She was afraid he would hear the tears in her voice. The tears she fought so hard to halt from falling.

"I can't think Aunt Cupid will play any fast

games, but I wish we could. If you didn't have a megrim, I don't know if I could leave you tonight."

Simon sighed and his lips touched her cheek like a whisper. "I have stayed too long. You need your rest. Plus Aunt Cupid and Mrs. Templeton would be ill-pleased to find me in your bedchamber after midnight."

Grace inhaled a deep breath. "Good night, Simon."

"Good night, my heart." He ran one finger down her jaw.

A scream of frustration rose up the back of her throat. She needed more time to ease the pain of his betrayal. If only his sweet words and kisses were true. Grace bit her lip until it throbbed with her pulse.

Simon turned back at the door and smiled. "Until tomorrow."

Grace nodded and he was gone. Anguish peaked to shatter the last shreds of her composure. She dropped onto the bed and buried her face in her pillow. The tears could no longer be held back and she wept. Lachlan burrowed next to her.

She was not certain how long she yielded to the tears. She sat up and dried her face. She had not cried since Papa had deserted her in death. Now another man she loved would not only leave, but had stained her sweet memory.

Lachlan stuck his wet nose in her hand. A small smile tugged at her lips. "Well, I still have you. You're one male who has not deserted me."

The terrier whined and wagged his tail. After Cupid's valentine soirée tomorrow night—Grace's breath caught in her throat. Midnight had come and gone. The party was actually tonight. And then life would return to normal.

They would return to their small house until Mama decided to go to London and search once again for a husband for Lucinda. At least Simon would never know the embarrassing truth.

Seven

Grace stared into the cheval glass. Dark encircled her eyes. Sleep had been absent last night.

A light tap sounded on the other side of the door. "Come."

A maid entered. "Yer breakfast tray, miss."

"Thank you, Alice."

"Ye want I pour yer chocolate?"

"I shall do so myself."

The maid curtsied and hurried out. Grace took one last look in the mirror and ambled over to the tray. Her hand halted in midair to the chocolate pot.

A bouquet of jasmine blooms lay across a letter. She picked both up, then sniffed the flowers. Sweet and pure.

She ran her thumb over the red wax seal. Her heart thundered against her chest. A dull ache of foreboding squeezed her.

Grace carefully opened the seal and unfolded the letter. Red and pink cherubs soared around the full page, marked Dobbs and Company. She inhaled a deep breath and read the poem proclaiming love.

Her hands trembled and she dropped onto a chair.

Though the valentine was unsigned, she knew Simon was the sender. Did he have no shame? Must he carry the game this far? She felt sick at heart being the object of his wager, but she would recover. But would Lucinda?

Closing her eyes, Grace leaned her head back and wished she were elsewhere. Tonight's valentine soirée was the last place she wished to be in the torment of Simon's presence. Would they believe the excuse of a megrim and forget her? Probably not.

Grace ran her finger over the jasmine petal. Soft as velvet. Like Simon's lips when he had kissed her. She had been so thrilled until she learned of his perfidy. Well, at least her secret would depart with her. Simon would never know her embarrassment.

Grace rose and marched to the fire. She drew back her hand to pitch the valentine into the flames, but hesitated. How could she destroy the declaration? Though it was false, she still loved Simon. She had never known this wretchedness of mind. Tears choked her throat and she walked away from the fireplace.

No, she could not burn the valentine, but make it a memento of her insipid sentimentality. After all, she would never love again.

Val surveyed himself in the cheval glass. His face looked pale and gaunt. He had lain awake most of the night, thinking of Grace. A knock sounded at the door and his valet moved to answer it. He could not hear the words, just merely muffled voices.

"Excuse me, my lord, but a *maid* insists upon seeing you personally." Stedeman's voice filled with outrage at her cheekiness.

He bit back a smile. "Very good, Stedeman. I shall see her."

Alice entered and curtsied. Staring at the floor, she said, "I beg yer pardon, yer lordship, but I must return this to ye." She held out her hand.

Val's breath caught in his throat as the candlelight flickered on a gold cherub. He took the pocket watch from her and ran his thumb over the engraving. "Thank you, Alice." He took a coin from his pocket and held it out.

Alice shook her head. "I didn't find it, sir. I'm only the messenger."

"Take the coin anyway."

Her fingers snatched the coin from his before he could change his mind. "Who found my watch?"

"Miss Templeton. In the garden. She spent a long time cleaning and polishing it, though the whole time she cursed ye."

"Cursed me? What in the devil for?"

Alice shrugged. "Something about a wager."

Fear clutched Val's heart. How did she know of the wager? Was that why she had sequestered herself in her bedchamber? That must be the reason.

"Thank you, Alice."

She curtsied and Stedeman herded her out. "Anything else, my lord?"

"No, Stedeman. I'm on my way downstairs to the soirée."

"Very good, sir." The valet bowed and let himself out.

Val slipped the watch into his pocket and brushed his hand over it. Everything was as it should be. Grace possessed his heart. He felt whole once again. Now he just had to explain the harebrained wager and claim her for his own. Forever.

* * *

Dancers swirled beneath flickering candlelight. An air of gaiety filled the chamber. Val's gaze searched the partygoers, but still he saw no sign of Grace.

"Where are Grace and Lucinda?"

Val turned and faced Matthew. "I have no idea. I shall send a maid up to inquire."

"Isn't necessary. I heard Mrs. Templeton send someone up. She is quite anxious. Time to snare you is running out."

Val frowned. "Does she know you have feelings for Lucinda?"

Surprise etched across Matthew's face. "What makes you think that?"

" 'Tis obvious." Val sighed. "I'm in love myself."

"With Lucinda?" Alarm colored Matthew's voice.

"Grace. I haven't seen her all day. As if she purposely avoids me."

"Ah, there they are." Matthew sighed. "Isn't Lucinda beautiful?"

"Not as beautiful as Grace." Several young men circled the two Templeton sisters.

"I better claim a dance before every buck in the room does so." Matthew marched toward them and Val followed him.

Desperation was strong in his soul. He must speak to Grace. Just the sound of her voice would brighten his evening.

Grace's throat constricted as she watched Simon march toward her, purpose etched on her brow. He looked neither to the right nor left as he pushed his way through the circle of gentlemen surrounding

Lucinda. Simon bowed. "Good evening, Miss Templeton."

She curtsied and looked away. "My lord." Heat flushed her cheeks. If she could only make it through the evening.

"Will you walk with me?" Simon asked.

She shook her head. "I must stay with my sister."

Simon clasped her arm and tugged her toward the French doors, leaving her no choice but to follow or be dragged. He halted only when he was away from the light filtering through the windows, then leaned against the balustrade.

"What is amiss?"

"Nothing of import." She hated her quivering voice.

Simon sighed. Grasping her chin, he forced her to look at him. "Tell me the truth."

Grace considered what to do. Escape into the garden? But he would only follow. Perhaps the truth was best. "I know of your wager with Matthew. This has been some sort of—of game to you." Tears welled in her eyes.

"Never a game. The wager was simply to keep me from marrying Lucinda. I can't bear to see you so distressed."

"You have caused my distress," she cried.

His thumb caressed her cheek. "And I'm sorry. Truly I am. I have nothing but admiration and respect for you. And love."

Grace gasped. "You speak the truth?"

"Yes." Simon dropped to one knee and pleaded, "Forgive me and marry me."

Her heart thundered in her ears. "Marry you?" Her voice was a soft whisper. "But you don't wish to marry."

"So I thought. I didn't wish to make a woman as miserable as my mother, but I find I can't live without you. Mama's jasmine bloomed. I think it is an indication of my right choice."

"You believe in such signs?"

Simon shrugged. "No, but there are things we don't understand."

"But—" She inhaled a deep breath. "I can't."

Anguish seared his countenance and he stood. "You despise me."

Her hand grasped his arm. "Not really. Even though I had never expected you to marry me, discovering the wager hurt, but I still love you."

"Then, why do you decline?"

"I—" She turned her face away. "There is something you don't know."

"In the folly you said you loved me and you have now declared it again."

Her head snapped around and she studied his face. "Then you did hear me?"

Simon nodded. "I returned the words in my head, but couldn't say them aloud. Now, I want the entire world to know I love you."

"I do love you, Simon."

"Whatever the problem doesn't matter. I want you to be my wife."

"My mother—" Grace squeezed her eyes tight. How could she tell him?

Simon brushed his knuckles down her cheek. "Don't fret, dear heart. I can bring her around to agreement."

Grace shook her head. "You don't understand. There has been a purpose besides a well-made marriage."

"Tell me, Grace, and I will make it right."

Perfect words, but she could not allow him to do so. " 'Tis not your problem."

Simon grabbed her by the shoulders and pulled her to him. He touched his forehead to hers and stared into her eyes. "I must insist."

She swallowed. "Mama is deep in debt. She expects her son-in-law to pay them off. 'Tis not right or fair, but that is Mama."

Simon chuckled. "Is that all? Money. If you love me, I shall agree to pay any debt she has."

Grace said, "But you don't know Mama. She is greedy and it will never end."

"Grace, do you love me?" His warm breath fanned her face.

"Yes."

"Do you wish to marry me?" His breath seemed to still as he awaited her answer. He did not have long to wait.

"Yes."

"Then we shall come to an understanding with your mother." His tongue traced the fullness of her bottom lip. "May I kiss you to seal our betrothal?"

The undeniable truth was that she loved Simon and would never be whole without him. His proposal was the culmination of her heart's wish. Could she forgive the wager? Grace searched her heart.

A smile tugged at her lips and happiness filled her. "Oh, yes."

He covered her lips with his. His hands squeezed her waist and crushed her against him. Her arms encircled his neck and she shivered against him.

A throat cleared and a voice shattered the passionate haze. "Excuse me, coz, but kissing a young lady so ardently isn't very proper."

Simon sighed and raised his head, but did not release his hold. He stroked her bottom lip with his thumb. "Remember where I was. I suppose we should go in and announce our engagement."

Matthew scurried over. "You are going to marry?"

Grace smiled. "Yes."

"My hardiest felicitations. I know you shall be very happy." Matthew clasped Simon's shoulder and grinned ear to ear. "Well, damnation!" Matthew murmured and his smile fell away.

"What the devil?" Simon demanded.

"I owe you a stickpin."

Simon shook his head. "Keep the stickpin and the hunter is yours as well."

"But—"

Simon interrupted. "If you hadn't helped me avoid Lucinda, I wouldn't have spent so much time with Grace and fallen in love."

Matthew grinned again. "I say, Val, that is generous."

Hands clapped and a giggle rose in the air. Simon turned. "You heard?"

Cupid hurried across the balcony. "I'm so pleased my plan worked. I knew you and Grace were perfect."

Grace and Simon exchanged glances. She considered reminding Cupid that she had chosen Lucinda for Simon. That it was Simon and Matthew's plan that had brought them together. She discarded the idea. After all, Cupid's plan had brought her to Valentine Hall.

She smiled and kissed her cheek. "Thank you, Cupid."

"Yes, thank you, Aunt. You truly deserve your name." Simon kissed Cupid's other cheek.

Simon had unlocked her heart and soul. He was hers. Now and forever. Her own true valentine.

If you enjoyed the stories in this anthology, be sure to look for *Irish Eyes,* available wherever books are sold in March 2002.

Is it the lilt to their speech? Their lover of laughter? Their famed tempers, as quick in passion as in anger? Whatever it is, when it comes to romance the Irish have an undeniable allure, and in these stories you're invited to feel the special magic of Irish eyes—and hearts—smiling . . .

"Finally and Forever" by Tina Donahue

When Captain Aidan O'Rourke stopped at a local inn for a mug of ale, he found spirited Briana Mac-Cullen—a lass with fire in her flashing green eyes. Helping her find a missing claddagh ring sounded like a simple task—until Aidan realized he had lost his heart to Briana.

"The Keepsake" by Jill Henry

Reduced circumstances may have forced Maeve O'Brien into service as a kitchen maid, but nothing could destroy her pride. And loving Connor Raeburn, the newly titled lord, would only ruin her reputation. To say good-bye, she gave him the one thing of value she owned, never expecting that he would give her unending love in return.

"For the Love of Aileen" by Elizabeth Keys

Only his father's deathbed wish could bring Rourke McAfferty back to Ireland, especially when he had spent the last six years working with an infamous pirate to flout the penal laws. But lovely Aileen Joyce soon provided a compelling reason to stay—forever, if he could spend it with her.

Stella Cameron

"A premier author of romantic suspense."

__The Best Revenge
  0-8217-5842-X $6.50US/$8.00CAN

__French Quarter
  0-8217-6251-6 $6.99US/$8.50CAN

__Key West
  0-8217-6595-7 $6.99US/$8.99CAN

__Pure Delights
  0-8217-4798-3 $5.99US/$6.99CAN

__Sheer Pleasures
  0-8217-5093-3 $5.99US/$6.99CAN

__True Bliss
  0-8217-5369-X $5.99US/$6.99CAN

Call toll free **1-888-345-BOOK** to order by phone, use this coupon to order by mail, or order online at **www.kensingtonbooks.com**.
Name_____
Address _____
City_____ State _____ Zip _____
Please send me the books I have checked above.
I am enclosing $_____
Plus postage and handling* $_____
Sales tax (in New York and Tennessee only) $_____
Total amount enclosed $_____
*Add $2.50 for the first book and $.50 for each additional book.
Send check or money order (no cash or CODs) to:
Kensington Publishing Corp., Dept. C.O., 850 Third Avenue, New York, NY 10022
Prices and numbers subject to change without notice. All orders subject to availability.
Visit our website at **www.kensingtonbooks.com**.

DO YOU HAVE THE
HOHL COLLECTION?